T0304857

# Death by Numbers

# DEATH BY NUMBERS

## Jo Cunningham

CONSTABLE

CONSTABLE

First published in Great Britain in 2024 by Constable

1 3 5 7 9 10 8 6 4 2

A CIP catalogue record for this book
is available from the British Library.

ISBN: 978-1-40871-934-3

Typeset in ITC Stone Serif by Hewer Text UK Ltd, Edinburgh
Printed and bound in Great Britain by Clays Ltd, Elcograf S.p.A.

Papers used by Constable are from well-managed
forests and other responsible sources.

Constable
An imprint of
Little, Brown Book Group
Carmelite House
50 Victoria Embankment
London EC4Y 0DZ

An Hachette UK Company
www.hachette.co.uk

www.littlebrown.co.uk

# 1

## *Life in Life Insurance*

The numbers were out. Numbers that predicted causes of death in seaside resorts. The usual suspects – cancer, stroke, heart attack – were accurate, so that was some consolation. But Una had underestimated the amount of accidents: misadventure with a shopping trolley, donkey stampede, and a hanging basket (begonias) that had ceased to hang.

She looked up at the LED lighting suspended directly above her head, glanced down at her screen and then back up again. Still there. The sixth floor of Katapult Insurance remained a low-risk work environment. It was her career that was precarious. Until 5.29 p.m., today had been within one standard deviation of an average Friday at the office, and then an email from Internal Audit had arrived. There was a tiny gap between the number of accidental deaths she'd predicted in her research and the actual number that had happened. This project was supposed to clinch her promotion to team leader. Getting the numbers right was usually the one thing she didn't worry about.

Una's colleagues were zipping up their backpacks and making their final Ctrl-Alt-Del of the week. She didn't want to spend the weekend brooding over the email and Ajay was still in his glass cubicle, one of four that formed the corners of the open-plan floor. She picked up her comfort biro and clicked it on and off as she walked over to him. Inside, he stood behind his standing desk, headset resting on his greying temples, looking at the screen as if it was an actual colleague. He spotted her and waved her in.

'Hi, Una, how's it going?' he said, swiping the headset mic away from his mouth.

'Fine,' she said, continuing to click the pen as she stood opposite him; it seemed wrong to sit in the chair facing his standing desk. 'Do you have a few minutes?'

He scanned her face as if he were proofreading a PowerPoint presentation for typos. 'Of course. I wanted to catch up with you on a few things anyway. Shoot.'

'It's about the seaside figures,' she said. 'I need to review the accidental causes of death. There's a tiny discrepancy with the rolling three-month projections based on the customer claims data. You know how Internal Audit can be. I'll work extra hours to get it sorted.'

Ajay tugged at his right ear lobe. 'Yes, I saw that mail. Now hear me out on this. My feeling is that we need a fresh pair of eyes on it. So, I've sent it over to Tim.'

Una gripped the biro at close to shatter pressure. This was a disaster. For fifteen years, since joining the graduate scheme together, she'd been in Tim's shadow. He was the only other internal candidate with the right level of experience for the team lead role. Ajay, their boss, was department head and would make the key decision.

'I think it would be better staying with its original owner,' said Una, mid click. 'Me.'

'Don't take this the wrong way,' said Ajay. 'Your stuff is always top notch – you're the departmental expert in spotting worst-case scenarios. But as I've mentioned to you before, you're sometimes reluctant to try newer methods, and stick to what you've done in the past. I don't want Internal Audit on my back.'

'But it was my research and I want to find out what's wrong with it.' Una's voice was getting high-pitched and a little whiny. Not a power move.

Ajay pushed his rimless glasses back up his nose. 'Okay, here's an idea. You can work on the research together, as a team. I'm keen for Tim to be more collaborative, and for you it would be a learning opportunity to see how he approaches things. The dream team!'

Una's biro-clicking had now reached a personal best. Everyone knew that Tim was terrible at working with other people. This wasn't the dream team, it was the nightmare pair.

'And one more thing,' said Ajay. 'I'm sure you're aware of the department's balanced scorecard and the importance of everyone respecting and engaging with the workstreams that make up that scorecard.'

What was the balanced scorecard? Fortunately, Una had learnt various styles of nod from an Active Listening webinar. She performed a 'please carry on' nod towards him.

'I noticed that you've not booked any holiday this year and you carried over fifteen days from last year.'

'I've had a lot of deadlines recently,' she said.

'I appreciate that, but we're only at 99.5 per cent for the department and we need to be 100 per cent to turn green.

You know that senior management review these figures closely, and your lack of holiday is affecting our scorecard health.'

Una frowned. 'But I like coming to work. I don't get why I'm being penalised for showing up.'

Ajay was silent. This meant she was in the wrong but he wasn't going to tell her.

The truth was, holidays were challenging now that most of her friends had kids. Last year, she'd gone on a group tour of 'Jewels of Italy', but the group hadn't appreciated her concerns about the rising water levels in Venice, and became actively hostile during that challenging trip to the Leaning Tower of Pisa.

'Okay, sure,' she said. 'I'll definitely take time off. Soon.'

'Thanks. So that's everything then. Have a great weekend.' Ajay picked up his headset. 'Got a call now, if you can close the door on your way out.'

Una walked out of the office, staring at the grey fire-retardant carpet. Was she losing her touch? Was assessing life expectancy a young person's game? Reviewing the disputed numbers would take hours of work. Time for coffee. As she walked towards the kitchenette, a sound emerged, the electric swish of Lycra thighs rubbing together in metronomic rhythm as their owner strode past her. Blazing into the middle of the floor in an orange one-piece cycling outfit was Neoliberal Tim.

'Guys. Heading off now,' he said, waggling a cycle helmet over his Lego-worthy signature haircut. 'Have a great week-end. Do you want to know what I'm doing tomorrow? I'm zorbing down Parliament Hill. For charity.'

4

His announcement barely caused a ripple among the operations team, and his brow furrowed as he strode towards the kitchenette. Una followed in his wake and found him fully focused, decanting juice from a coconut into a water bottle.

'Hey, Tim, cycling home?' She sluiced out her mug in the sink in a casual manner. 'By the way, just been in to see Ajay. How's it going with those seaside figures?'

'Interesting reading on the accidents,' he replied. 'There was the standard stuff – runaway lawnmowers, robot vacuums gone rogue – but then some new ones. Not seen a hanging basket before.'

'You know, Ajay said we should work on it as a team. So perhaps we can brainstorm together on Monday.' She shuddered inside. Brainstorming encouraged people to spout stupid ideas instead of filtering them out before they opened their mouths. But it would be an opportunity for her to see if Tim had uncovered anything useful.

He drew himself up to his full height. 'No thanks. I'm a Tim player, not a team player.'

Una bored into the mug with a scouring sponge and rotated it with force. 'Fine. Absolutely not a problem.'

'Look, Una, there's nothing significantly wrong with your original work. It's solid, competent analysis. But let's face it, you're not exactly known for being innovative or bold. Don't take it personally. I've simply been brought in to take things up a gear. I'll be happy to take you through my findings once I'm ready.'

She stabbed at the decaf espresso setting on the drinks machine with her index finger. A button she pressed every day in exactly the same way. Then she whacked the double shot option. There, that was innovative and bold.

'Fine. I've got my own approach that I'm working on anyway, something new.'

'Really? Sounds intriguing. Tell me more,' said Tim.

'It's still a work in progress.'

'No problemo, see you Monday. And cheer up, at least we're not in Pet Insurance.' He swigged from his bottle and then sprinted towards the lifts.

Una returned to her desk. She couldn't say any more to Tim about her new approach, because she didn't have one. She only had her tried and trusted methods, just as Ajay had said.

She started from scratch and reviewed all the factors she'd used to predict the causes of death from the client data: age, gender, marital status and income level. Then she went on to the health factors: smoking, alcohol consumption, diet and level of physical activity. After twenty minutes, she was so focused on her screen, the motion-sensitive lighting plunged her into darkness, and she had to stand up and wave to make the light above her come back on. She was startled by a figure nearby and turned to see herself reflected in the window. Her reflection looked more scared than she was.

Sitting hunched over her computer, alone in the office, with a coffee and a small packet of yoghurt-coated raisins from the vending machine to sustain her, Una wondered if she was doing enough to maximise her own life expectancy. She'd read an article that morning about how a good level of social connectedness could add 2.1 years to your life span. Most of the sixth floor had gone to Naomi's leaving drinks. The Dog and Bucket would be noisy, people spilling out onto the kerb, and she'd struggle to hear anyone speak. But perhaps she should have gone along anyway to say goodbye to Naomi instead of sitting here with only the hum of the air conditioning for company.

A small *meep* came from her phone, a text from an unknown number.

*Did you get this una ken got me a smart phone xx*

Her phone began to ring, a known number.

'Hi, Mum.'

Her mother would be perched on the fold-up chair in the hall, on the landline in her flat in Eastbourne where she'd lived ever since Una had gone to university.

'Did you get my text?' said Mum.

'Yes.'

'My first ever text! Ken got me a smartphone. An Apple one.'

'Did he now?' said Una. 'He seems to be splashing the cash a lot recently.'

Mum had been 'stepping out' for the last six months with this Ken, who lived nearby with a widescreen TV and a Ventolin inhaler. Ken was generous – she must check his credit history.

'I just wanted to see if you're free this weekend and whether you wanted to pop down. That would be good, as I've got some news to tell you.'

Una chewed on a raisin. She'd intended to log in at the weekend and work on getting the seaside figures back in line. She had nothing else arranged except for a spin class

7

and her monthly call with Amara on Sunday. She'd thought about going to see the photography exhibition at the Natural History Museum, but didn't want to walk round there on her own.

'I'll have to see. There's some urgent stuff at work that I need to look at over the weekend.'

'Think about it, we'd love to see you. You don't have to come to the bingo tomorrow if you don't want to, and we're going to visit your dad's grave, but I understand if you still don't feel—'

'Look, Mum, as I said, I've got a lot on at the moment.'

'That's okay, I know your job is important to you.'

Una's priority was to sort out the seaside numbers and clinch her promotion, but there were other numbers letting her down. Number of visits to Dad's grave – 0. Number of visits to Mum cancelled over the two years since Dad had died due to working weekends – 3. She was statistically underperforming as a daughter, and going to see Mum this weekend would help to combat that. Besides, given all these peculiar seaside accidents, she could carry out a quick risk assessment while she was there. If Eastbourne was a hotspot of danger, she could suggest to Mum that she move somewhere safer. Away from the dreadful Ken.

She sighed. 'You know what, I can do some work at yours. I'll get the train tomorrow morning.'

'Great! I'll be in all morning. Is there anything in particular you want to eat? I've got quite a few ready meals in the freezer.'

'Better get back to work now. Hang on, what's this news you mentioned?'

'I'll tell you when you're here. Nothing to worry about.'

A phrase that only made her feel the opposite of what was intended.

'Okay, bye, Mum.'

Una packed up her laptop and headed for the lift. On her way out, she passed Tim's desk. On top of a grubby copy of *The Fountainhead* perched the Perspex trophy that he'd won for being Young Actuary of the Year (London and SE) 2009. That was then. Now she, Una McMurray, twice shortlisted for Young Actuary of the Year (London and SE), would fix those numbers before Tim if it was the second-to-last thing she ever did.

# 2

## *The Gift for the Actuary
Who Has Everything*

It's no coincidence that the collective noun for seagulls is 'a shitstorm'. Una had given up a Saturday morning snooze to prepare for her trip to gull-infested Eastbourne. There'd been no recorded deaths from direct seagull attack, but she didn't want to be the first. Mirrored aviators protected her eyes – if a seagull attacked her, it would see one of its own reflected in the lenses and back off. In addition, she'd donned a waterproof jacket for protective cover from overhead strikes. And so it was with a confident stride that she made the twenty-minute walk from Eastbourne station to Mum's flat.

It was an unusually sunny January morning, but that was fine, she'd applied plenty of SPF 50. She passed the noisy but gull-free shopping centre and entered a maze of neat terraced houses and prim bed-and-breakfasts before arriving at Morningview Mansions, a small block of 1950s flats on one of the side streets that led to the waterfront. She buzzed and went up to Mum's flat: two bedrooms, two bathrooms (one en suite) and a lounge/dining area. Sea glimpse possible if you flattened yourself against the fridge.

'Look at you, you look well,' said Mum, pulling her into a hug. 'Put your bag over there and sit yourself down. You can take your sunglasses off in here, you know, there's no seagulls.'

Una sat in the cushion-dense armchair and Mum placed a scalding mug of tea in front of her on the glass (glass!) coffee table before placing her own mug on the arm of the sofa opposite.

'There you go. Nice cup of tea for you,' she said, her newly highlighted hair glinting in the sunlight. She was wearing a turquoise linen dress and a necklace of large orange beads that bobbed up and down with hope. Her appearance had changed over the past six months. It must be Ken's influence.

Una did a 'spot the difference' on the room.

'What's that?' she asked, pointing to the mantelpiece.

Mum beamed. 'It's an Amazon Echo. Ken got it for me as one of my Christmas presents. He's always spoiling me. That reminds me, I've got your present from him tucked away.'

She opened a teak-effect cupboard with a conspicuous but acceptable tilt – they'd had a tense afternoon last year putting it together, lacking Dad's spirit-level attention to detail for self-assembly furniture. Taking out a parcel, she placed it on Una's lap. Una carefully dismantled the wrapping paper to reveal a pair of mid-range binoculars.

'Thanks, Mum.'

'Don't thank me, thank Ken, it was all his idea. He'd been reading about urban birding on the internet and thought of you. I'll get her some binoculars, he said. And there you are.'

'But I've never expressed any interest in urban birding, or any other sort of birding.'

There was a scrabble of keys at the front door, and then a head appeared slowly around it.

'Hiya!' said Ken.

Ken's body appeared as well. It was dressed in Adidas trainers, jeans, a black leather jacket and, at the point where it joined his head, a stripy scarf.

'He had a makeover,' said Mum.

'Taken years off me,' said Ken. He windmilled towards Una for a hug, but she quickly folded her arms and he turned it into a hearty shoulder pat. 'How are you, Una love?'

'Fine,' she said, as Ken walked over to kiss Mum on the cheek. She avoided witnessing this exchange by focusing on Mum's mug of tea. Had it moved nearer the precipitous edge of the sofa arm using some ancient mysterious mechanics, like a moai approaching the coast of Easter Island?

'Hey, Una,' said Ken, splaying himself across the sofa. 'Let me show you our latest gadget. What's the weather like, Jeanette?'

'Jeanette?' said Una.

'That's the name we give to—'

A voice arose from the mantelpiece. 'The temperature is currently ten degrees Celsius and will fall to a low of six degrees this evening. Sunny spells are expected although becoming more overcast late afternoon.'

'It's amazing, does the telly listings too,' said Ken.

'I mean . . . you could just look out of the window to check on the weather,' said Una.

'Don't you have one of these?' said Ken. 'I thought your Generation Snowflake would be all over this. My Anton got me one. You'll meet him soon enough. And you know what, I think you'll get on with him like a house on fire.'

Based on this observation alone, Una was not looking forward to meeting Anton.

'I'm not Generation Snowflake,' she said. 'And no, I don't have one.'

A machine that could be hacked by malign powers capable of operating devices around her flat? What if she woke up to find herself being attacked by the hoover, with one of its more tortuous nozzle attachments sucking at her flesh? Or the kettle boiling with a level of water below its element? No, letting one of these modern monsters into her flat didn't bear thinking about. But it was worth noting down as a future project – a risk assessment of smart home appliances.

'Thank you, Jeanette.'

'No problem, Ken.'

Ken chuckled. 'She's got nice manners, has our Jeanette.'

'Well, I think it was a lovely present.' Mum reached over and squeezed Ken's hand.

Una watched their show of affection with a degree of detachment. Ken had breezed into Mum's world just as she'd started coming to terms with her new life without Dad. Why couldn't she have stayed living on her own, like Una? It was fine, 95 per cent of the time.

'Do you have something to say to Ken, Una?'

At any time, Mum could deploy a phrase that regressed Una back to childhood.

'Thanks for the binoculars, Ken.'

'You're very welcome. I love buying presents for people. You know what, I should take you out shopping,' said Ken, slamming down the mug that Mum had handed him. 'Get you some new clothes. With your colouring you can really carry off strong colours. Winter jewel, in my opinion.'

'I don't need any new clothes,' said Una, wondering how Ken was funding this thoughtful gift bonanza.

'It's just that you often wear the same sort of stuff,' he said. 'I worry you're stuck in a fashion rut. Don't take it personally, Una, that's just me. I speak as I find.'

'I like to wear the same sort of clothes every day. That way I don't need to waste time deciding what to wear.'

A tip she'd picked up in a Women in Statistics chatroom.

'Well, you'll need to get your glad rags on tonight. We're off to the social club, if you're up for it?' said Ken.

The local social club. A place of watercolour painting, bridge and Brazilian jujitsu that attracted a high percentage of elderly samples. It was the last place she wanted to go. Instead she'd stay in and continue reviewing the data. So far, everything she'd looked at only confirmed the original findings. There must be something she was missing, something subtle that was affecting the numbers.

'I think I'll skip tonight,' she said. 'I might have to log in for a bit. Got some urgent figures to look through.'

'No one ever got to the end of their life and looked back and wished they'd spent more time working,' said Ken, gulping his tea and smacking his lips.

This was something Una agreed with. She avoided any regrets by getting in earlier and leaving later than her colleagues. And what was the alternative to work? Sudoku? Badminton? Other people's company? Perhaps she should show her face a bit more at the Women in Statistics events.

'I'm sorry, it's a project that's really important for my career.'

'It's fine, Ken. She's very committed to her work,' said Mum. 'She's always been like that.'

Una's stomach tensed. She'd come down this weekend to make amends for focusing too much on work over the past two years, and here she was reverting to her normal behaviour.

'You know what, I will come tonight,' she said. 'I made quite a bit of progress on the train this morning. And honestly, it might be a better use of my time than sitting round here thinking about hanging baskets.'

'Hanging baskets?' repeated Ken, swirling the last bit of tea in his cup with a wistful gyration. 'They're not for me, putting a basket up where you can't see it properly. No, I prefer terracotta pots. Are you thinking of getting one? I could help you choose some plants if you like. Would really cheer your place up. I mean, I've not been there, I'm surmising, like.'

'It's just something I'm looking into at work.'

'Your insurance job?' said Mum.

'Yes, I have to assess any risks with them. I know it sounds ridiculous, but even a hanging basket can be dangerous.'

Ken's cup clattered as it dropped onto the table.

Una flinched. 'What?'

'It's something and nothing,' he said.

'Someone we knew had an accident with a hanging basket recently,' said Mum, gripping her orange beads with force.

Una sat forward, her mind ablaze. Was this the missing data in her analysis? Were hanging baskets systematically causing death and destruction at the seaside? A dodgy batch from the manufacturer? A pensioner TikTok craze gone too far?

'Really?' she said. 'That's unusual. Tell me more.'

'It was a friend of ours,' said Ken. 'Eileen. Tragic how she went. She used to be in our bingo circle.'

'Eileen?'

'Yes, Eileen O'Connor,' said Mum. 'Only recently, very sad. She used to teach at the same school as John, Jean's husband. You must have met Jean.'

'No idea who she is. But Eileen died because of a hanging basket?'

'Freak accident,' said Ken. 'No point dwelling on it. Shit happens.'

'Ken's right,' said Mum. 'There but for the grace . . .'

Could Eileen be the hanging basket accident in the mortality figures that Una was reviewing? It was such an unusual way to go. The data was supposed to be abstract, impersonal and confined to the world of work, not part of family chit-chat. And yet one of the cases from her research seemed to involve someone Mum knew.

She searched for 'death Eastbourne hanging basket Eileen' on her phone. Up came an article in the *Eastbourne Enquirer*:

Eileen O'Connor, a 76-year-old former history teacher, has died following a tragic accident. At around 4 p.m. on Monday 1 January, a hanging basket fell onto Mrs O'Connor while she was on her own doorstep. She lived alone in a two-bedroom terraced house at 19 Chamberlayne Road and had no close family. 'Such a shame,' said her neighbour, Rosa Boniface, 39, a hairdresser and part-time fashion student. 'She kept her garden lovely and she was a great neighbour – there was never a peep from her.'

'Well, we'd better get moving,' said Ken, leaping up from the couch.

'We're popping along to your dad's grave,' said Mum.

'Needs tending every so often to keep it tidy,' added Ken.

'You're very welcome to join us. It's entirely up to you, though. Only if you want to.'

Una sipped her tea. After four minutes of cooling, it was hot but no longer posed any significant dermatological risk. So, Ken was now currying favour with Mum through blatant acts of kindness. Whereas Una never visited the grave. Looking at mortality tables with aggregated figures every day was one thing, but graveyards were essentially raw data. Too raw.

Ken and Mum started to rummage and re-rummage, creating ziplock bags of ziplock bags that they packed into a tote bag in preparation for their trip to the cemetery, where Ken would be invading a precious family space. A space that Una ought to go to herself.

But this sudden development about Eileen had piqued her curiosity. She looked up Chamberlayne Road – it was only a short walk away. She could wander over and look at

Eileen's house in person while Mum and Ken were at the cemetery. Perhaps she'd discover some additional data factor that would explain the upward trend of accidental deaths at the seaside, or at least the hanging basket incident – dodgy brickwork, tremors from a nearby rail service, overambitious floral displays. It was a ridiculous approach for such a small sample of people who'd died in such different ways, but if she could find a connection that no one else had thought of, that might impress the management team.

This on-the-ground approach would be innovative and daring. Unorthodox. It felt transgressive thinking about one of her data points as an actual person. But it would be fine; it wasn't like she'd known Eileen. She'd simply act like a professional, a neutral observer, collecting more data to analyse with statistics.

Dad would have understood; he'd have wanted her to be a successful actuary. Well, he'd have said something about her doing whatever made her happy, as life was short. Technically speaking, life could only be relatively short compared to the median lifespan. But surely professional achievement would make her happy after all these years of dedication? And if there were risks to living at the seaside, she should investigate them for Mum's sake. That was something Dad would definitely have approved of; it was from him that she'd developed a healthy appreciation of everyday hazards.

She snatched up the binoculars, put them round her neck and strode to the hall table to get her coat. Ken was checking his phone by the front door.

'I think you're right, Ken,' she said. 'I'm going out to get some fresh air instead of logging into work. Mum, I'm going to take my new binoculars out and start on some urban birding.'

'Thought you'd like them,' said Ken, patting himself on the back.

'Have a nice time, Una love, see you later,' said Mum, wrapping some flowers on the coffee table.

'Hang on,' said Una. 'What about the news you mentioned last night?'

'We'll tell you later, when we're having our tea. As I said, nothing to worry about.'

# 3

# *Urban Birdwatching*

Una set out along the esplanade and passed by a tearoom that was full to the brim with Eastbourne's elderly. No obvious signs of reckless behaviour inside. Just the usual risks of tea-drinking: impalement on a broken cup shard, choking on a sugar cube – overall, pretty safe. She inhaled the sharp, salty air and glared at a man on the beach throwing bits of bread onto the shingle for the gulls.

As she hadn't grown up in Eastbourne, the streets felt unfamiliar outside specific routes to the station or the seafront. Mum and Dad had always planned to retire by the seaside and moved there after she'd already left home. For the first six months, it had seemed like a bad choice; leaving friends, family and local knowledge of the best parking spaces. But in the end, Eastbourne gave them opportunities to meet people their own age. Enjoy themselves. Until Dad became ill.

Una turned off the main stretch into a narrow residential street, following the route on her phone that led to Eileen's house. With lightning reactions, she swerved away from a local who was bombing down the pavement on a mobility scooter. She was forced to hug a privet. What sort of licence was required to drive one of these vehicles? What sort of ongoing checks were being made to maintain driver quality? Did they need insurance? Did she, the pedestrian, need insurance? By the time she'd exhausted these possibilities, she'd arrived.

She stood across the road facing Eileen's house. Her plan was to remain a calm, neutral observer, making sure not to attract attention. She'd review the house for any factors that could explain why the basket had fallen and get back before Mum and Ken returned.

The street was deserted, so she picked up her new binoculars to assess the front of the house. From her initial sweep, nothing seemed out of the ordinary. The doorstep, the tiles on the floor, just the same as the neighbouring houses. Two large black bins stood at the front like bouncers. And yet Eileen was now end of policy.

She focused on the brickwork just above the door frame. The hanging basket had been removed and she could see the holes where the fitting had been attached. What crazed soul had even invented the idea of a basket that would hang higher than eye-level directly above a doorway? At least it was less buttock-clenching than the red earthenware window box protruding over the rim of the second-floor window ledge next door. Was the insurance industry to blame? Did their customers take out life insurance and then become complacent, or even actively seek out death-wish horticulture?

She looked up the weather conditions for 4 p.m. in Eastbourne on 1 January. No rain, and a wind speed of 4, so unlikely that a freak gust had dislodged the basket. Shoddy workmanship? That could be something to consider for her insurance calculations. A third party might have been involved. A feral cat. A fox. Perhaps an escaped zoo animal, a leopard, had used its powerful hind legs to jump onto the basket, unaware of the knock-on effects.

'You a traffic warden?'

Una turned round and found herself facing an old man. Potentially a useful data source. Pavement-grey trousers, taupe anorak – she liked his style.

'No.'

'Why are you looking through those binoculars then?' he asked. 'You're trying to catch people out so they can't see you and drive off. Sneaky, I call that.'

She shook her head. 'No. I'm not a traffic warden. I'm . . . an urban birder.'

'What's that then?'

'Birdwatching in the street.'

Much as Ken irritated her, she had to admit the binoculars were proving useful for her undercover surveillance mission.

'I see,' the man said. 'You need Caulston Street for that. The lady at number 24 puts out one of those nut bags for the birds on a little table. Loads of the little blighters.'

'Okay, thanks.'

He pointed down the street. 'Just down there, first on your left.'

'I'll check it out. Thanks.'

The man shuffled off.

Clearly Una wasn't as well camouflaged as she'd thought. She was here to observe, not be observed. Her palms felt sticky against the binoculars. She looked left and right to check the street was clear, and then focused back on number 19, sweeping over the bins outside. There seemed to be something on the side of one of them, but as she adjusted the lenses to zoom in close, she sensed movement nearby.

A woman in her late thirties came out of the house next door to Eileen's and put a black rubbish bag into the bin outside her house. Una stood up sharply and thrust the binoculars inside her cagoule. What if the woman had seen her spying? She might get the wrong idea and call the police. She took out her phone, pretended to browse on it and went through some worst-case scenarios to calm her nerves. A few seconds later, the woman returned inside.

'Still here?' The old man was back, now with a pint of milk looped round his thumb. His eyes narrowed. 'Looking at that house, aren't you? You're not a birdwatcher, no, I think you're one of those property developers up from London, hoping to make a quick buck out of us. Am I right?'

Una couldn't continue her professional survey of the house with this sort of hassle. What kind of person would embroider all these ridiculous scenarios anyway? She'd play along with him.

'You've caught me out,' she said. 'Yes, I am interested in the house. Do you know who lived there before?'

'Eileen,' he said. He made the sign of the cross. 'But she passed away recently.'

'Sorry to hear that,' Una said, allowing herself a two-second reverential pause. 'How did that happen? I'm just asking in a mercenary way, in case it was due to dry rot or damp or some other structural issue that would affect the price of the house.'

The man pointed over at number 19. 'It was the basket, the hanging basket that used to be above the front door. Dropped on her. Very odd, it was. A basket like that.'

'Yes, it is odd,' said Una. 'I mean why hang up a basket?'

'No, no, lass. I mean it's odd because those baskets aren't even that heavy, and she got Tommo to put it up and Tommo's a reliable type. But accidents happen.'

'I see. So, you knew Eileen well.'

'Knew her? I was the one that called the ambulance.'

'What?'

The man shuffled closer and loosened the football scarf around his neck. 'She'd had all the usual gang around, just a small gathering, to show the pictures from her holiday. I hadn't had a formal invite, but I knew I'd be welcome, so I popped round late afternoon when I thought they'd be there. I couldn't believe it when I saw her lying on the doorstep . . .'

'But what about her other guests?'

'Already gone. The ambulance came, but there was nothing they could do.'

Una wasn't sure how she'd react in a worst-case scenario like that – it was one thing to spot one, quite another to actually be in one. 'I see. I'm sorry, that must have been a shock. Sounds like you did the right thing.'

'You going to move in yourself, then?' asked the man, performing a full loop-di-loop of the milk carton around his thumb.

'What?'

'The house? It'd be nice to have a new friend around here. Even if you are a money-grabbing you-know-what.'

'Well, I'm going to mull it over, check out the interest rates.'

'You do that, greedy guts,' he said, raising a hand and turning towards his front door. 'See you round.'

She waited until he was safely inside, then sidled over to the front of Eileen's house. Checking the coast was clear, she squatted behind the nearest bin. What would she say if someone found her here? Her body was in fight-or-flight mode, but her head was in analysis mode. On the side of the bin were two stick-on numbers, black on gold: a 4 and a 1, making 41. That was odd – the house was number 19. Perhaps the wrong bin had been wheeled back?

She glanced upwards to confirm there were no overhead leopards. Reassured, she got her phone out to take a picture of the numbers. Probably of no significance, but good to have a record. After taking a couple of shots, she heard someone attempting to whistle 'Smells Like Teen Spirit', and footsteps getting louder . . . Then the buzzer went for next door. As she crouched lower behind the bin, the binoculars case whacked the tiles below. She froze as the footsteps started to come towards her. She was going to get caught. What if this got back to work? She was sweating now, the moisture-wicking properties of her sports vest at full capacity.

Suddenly, the neighbour's door opened.

'Ken, looking well there. Love the scarf. Come in, come in.'

'Cheers, Rosa.'

Ken! What was he doing here?

Una's heartbeat was 20 per cent faster than its average resting rate. She waited until she heard the door close, then sprinted back to Mum's flat.

# 4

# *Nothing To Worry About News*

Back at the flat, Mum was polishing the Amazon Echo.

'How was your walk?' she asked. 'The fresh air will have done you good.'

Una slumped into the armchair. Her heart was still thumping as she recovered from nearly being caught out. 'It was fine,' she said. 'Can I do something to help?'

'No,' said Mum. 'You just sit there, I'm on a roll. And then I'll make you something snacky to eat.'

'I'm not hungry, thanks.' Her stomach was scrunched up with adrenalin. 'So, how did your trip to the cemetery go?'

'We ended up going for a coffee afterwards, in the new café on Dale Street, and I had a caramel latte.'

Una half listened to Mum's morning summary. But her focus was on what Ken had been doing hanging around Chamberlayne Road.

'Ken didn't come back here with you then?' she asked.

'No, he had some business or other to take care of.'

'What sort of business? Was he visiting someone?'

'He didn't say, now I come to think of it. And I didn't see any need to ask him, thank you. Anyhow he'll be back soon, he said.'

This so-called business of Ken's – why hadn't he told Mum what he was up to? Why would he be visiting Eileen's neighbour? Perhaps he was a bigamist. He had the face of a bigamist. Or a trigamist.

Una took out her phone and found the article about Eileen's death that mentioned her neighbour. *Rosa Boniface, 39, a hairdresser and part-time fashion student.* She'd check Ken's head for signs of a haircut when he returned.

Ken arrived thirty minutes later. He took off his leather jacket and hovered over the Echo, asking it to play The Clash. Una got up to scrutinise his head. No change of length or style, just the usual thick gelled mass of white hair, moulded into a slight quiff at the front.

'How was your walk?' he asked, huffing as he straightened himself up. 'Blown the cobwebs away?'

'Yes, I did some birdwatching,' said Una, stepping back. 'The binoculars were useful.'

'There you are,' said Mum, squeezing Ken's shoulder. 'That was a good present.'

'Did you see the crested grebes by the pier?' said Ken. '"London Calling"!'

'No,' Una said, 'must have missed them.' She had no idea what grebes were, or what being crested involved. Perhaps Ken was making up nonsense words to catch her out.

'Shame,' he said, hurling himself down on the couch. 'I'm a bit of an ornithologiser myself, you know. We had a busy morning. Went to your dad's grave. I tidied it up and your mother put out some new flowers. Daffs.'

Una sat on the edge of the armchair and worried at a wobbly button on the armrest. Ken had been performing valuable family duties, but she also had family duties.

'Why were you late back, Ken? Did you have to go somewhere? Visit someone?'

'Just had a few errands to take care of. No biggie. Followed by "Rock the Casbah" in your own time, Jeanette.'

'Errands?'

He pushed himself up from the couch. 'You know what, I could murder a cup of tea. I'll put the kettle on.'

'Ken, take it easy,' said Mum. 'We've still got the club tonight.'

'Don't worry, pet. Three teas coming up.'

And with that, he disappeared into the kitchen.

This was a suspicious response. Ken normally gave generous answers to questions, packed with unnecessary detail, so this concise reply was out of character.

When he returned with the teas, he sprawled on the couch next to Mum. 'I'm knackered,' he said. 'I was supposed to bed some bulbs today, tulips, but that's not going to happen.'

'Ken's got green fingers,' said Mum, patting his hand.

'I should see the doctor about that,' he said, laughing and spluttering spumes of tea over the couch.

Una picked at the wobbly button again. 'Sounds like gardening can be dangerous in Eastbourne, from what you said about your friend Eileen earlier. Are there many gardening-related injuries round here? For example, are her neighbours safe?'

'Safe?' said Ken.

'She takes after Bob,' said Mum. 'Always very careful.'

And what was wrong with that? From learning how to build a sandcastle with adequate foundations, to not opening shaken cans of Coke, Dad had done his best to prepare her for the world. A place where the only thing that was certain was uncertainty.

'What happened to Eileen was a one-off, a tragedy,' said Ken. 'Life's a roller coaster, Una. One minute she was going on that luxury cruise with the money she'd come into, and the next thing you know . . .'

'Yes, at least she got to see the fjords,' said Mum, sighing into her mug. 'Poor thing. To think we'd been round to look at the photos just before . . . you know. Just as well we all saw her that day. And the pictures were amazing, her camera had so many megapixels.'

'Hold on,' said Una. 'You were both there when she died?'

'Oh no, we'd left before it happened,' said Mum. 'On the way out, she said she was going to water all the plants, and then . . . Well, you never know, do you?'

The wobbly button was now hanging by a few strands. Mum and Ken had been at the gathering that the busybody on Chamberlayne Road had mentioned, and then Eileen must have somehow caused the accident when she was trying to water the plants in the basket. Una's on-the-ground investigation of Eileen's death had wasted time she could have spent on genuine roll-your-sleeves-up statistics to help fix the numbers. She had to avoid getting sidetracked.

'Anyhow,' said Ken, crashing his mug onto the table, 'are you both ready for two and a half hours of bingo? That's the big question.'

'I'm sure it will be very enlightening,' Una said.

29

Even though she'd agreed to go to the club out of a sense of duty, the evening might yield some useful information about unusual deaths in the local area. More pressingly, she could hunt down some details about Eileen's neighbour and the reason for Ken's secret visit to her.

'I'm so pleased you're coming,' said Mum. 'I'm really looking forward to this evening. You'll get to meet our usual crowd just as things are finally getting back to normal.'

'They're going to be better than normal, my angel,' said Ken, each arm encircling a cushion. 'I love bingo night. And I bet with all your maths knowledge, Una, you'll be a knockout at it.'

How could someone be a 'knockout' at bingo, a game of pure chance?

'Ken's been having a recent streak of luck,' said Mum. 'Won a wine rack last time.'

'There's no such thing as luck,' said Una. 'There is simply probability.'

'You're wrong there,' said Ken. 'There's times when luck is on your side. Look at me – feeling flush, got a machine that plays any tune ever made, and getting married to a wonderful woman. These are good times.'

'Married?' Una blurted out the word she hadn't expected to hear.

Ken put his hands to his face. 'Sorry, Sheila.'

'It's fine, Ken,' said Mum. 'Look, we meant to tell you when we were sitting down with the food.'

'You're getting married? To who?'

'We're getting married to each other, Una love. Ken popped the question last weekend when we had a run to the café at the garden centre.'

30

Mum lifted her left hand. There beside her usual rings was a new diamond ring, twinkling with an expensive sparkle. Una doubled over in the chair, winded, and then felt a hot, wet sensation over her stomach.

She looked down at her lap. 'I've spilt tea on myself. I never spill tea.'

'I'll get some kitchen roll,' said Mum. 'You should get out of that top, dab some cold water on yourself.'

Una stood up and bounded into the guest bedroom. She sat on the bed and took off her sweatshirt. The tea had left a faint pinkish mark. She applied some Savlon from her travel first-aid kit and put on the spare T-shirt she'd brought with her. She thumped the pillow three times, plumped it up and then sat staring at the Formica wardrobe door, taking in the news.

Why hadn't she predicted this situation when she spent all day trying to predict the worst things that could happen in the future?

'Sorry, Una,' said Ken, when she re-entered the lounge. 'That probably came as a bit of a shock.'

'So, what do you think then?' said Mum. She was perched on the edge of the couch, looking nervous. 'I didn't want to tell you over the phone, I wanted to wait until I could speak to you in person.'

'When are you actually getting married?' asked Una. 'I assume you're going to have a long engagement.'

'We've booked for the beginning of March. You'll need to take the Friday off. I made sure you weren't on any work trips last week on the phone.'

'A day off? And that's only six weeks away!' said Una. She needed more time to carry out checks on Ken – financial checks, criminal record checks, dental checks, and checks on his suspicious movements around Chamberlayne Road.

'We originally booked the reception for a Saturday in May,' said Ken, 'but then this slot freed up and we thought . . . that's fate. And they threw in a medium-sized ice sculpture.'

'Fate? But you haven't been going out together for very long; why rush?'

'I'm sixty-eight, Una, I can't dilly-dally,' said Mum. 'I know it's a lot to take in, but you know what? I've been doing some reading on the internet, and the *Daily Mail* said there's research that shows that married people live for longer. So, there you go.'

'I believe there is some research to support that theory, but it is contested.'

Even though she knew that Mum was manipulating her, Una had to admit this was an interesting argument. Marriage as a life extension strategy – she must look up the average number of years it would add to her life versus the time spent on dating sites and dating to achieve it.

If she was being objective, although Ken was extremely annoying, there were advantages to having someone around – if Mum was ill or stressed, for instance. And it wasn't as if she had provided much support herself over the last couple of years. She couldn't even bring herself to go to the cemetery with Mum today. But what if Ken was a bad apple? It was her responsibility to find any rot or bruising. And fast.

'It's going to be the best wedding ever,' said Ken. 'I've been spending big-time, making sure everything will be perfect, no expense spared.'

'Let's not get carried away, Ken dear,' said Mum. 'There's no need for you to overdo things and get stressed. The main thing is that we have our family and friends there.'

'You're right,' said Ken. 'As always, my precious. I just want everyone to have the best day possible. "Should I Stay or Should I Go", Jeanette.'

'And Una,' said Mum, taking Una's hand between hers, 'I'd like you to give me away at the wedding.'

'Give you away?'

'Walk me down the aisle. We're just going to the registry office, as Ken's not religious, and then a reception at a four-star hotel afterwards.'

'That's right. I'm spiritual but not religious,' said Ken.

'I'll be happy to give you away,' said Una, not able to look up at them. The news about the wedding was bad enough, but now she'd be publicly facilitating it. She'd have to work fast to audit Ken and find something on him.

'Anyhow, you're not losing your mother,' said Ken, straightening his Radiohead T-shirt over his portly frame, 'you're gaining me.'

'You know what,' said Mum, 'why don't we have some cava with our dinner to celebrate. I'm making a fish pie.'

'I meant to bring some with me,' said Ken. 'Forgot. Never mind, I'll pop out to Trunnocks and pick up a couple of bottles.'

'You need to rest, like Dr Santos told you,' said Mum. 'You're going to wear yourself out. It doesn't matter about the cava.'

Una knew that particular tone of 'it doesn't matter' from Mum meant the opposite, and anyhow, a walk seemed very attractive with her mind whirling at the news.

'I'll go and get the cava,' she said.

'You don't have to,' said Mum.

'It's no problem.'

'I can give you the money,' said Ken, scrabbling in his jacket for his wallet.

'I've got money,' Una said.

'I'll send you a piccy of the make we like,' said Ken.

A photo popped up on her phone of Ken and Mum with raised glasses, beaming at each other over a bottle, behind them other people leaning awkwardly to get into the frame.

'I'll get on with the dinner,' said Mum. 'We want to grab a good table at the bingo.'

Una headed outside and looked up Trunnocks on her phone. An evening chill had descended on the seafront, the waves were crashing over the shingle, and she drew the cords on the collar of her jacket tight around her neck. After scrolling through the search results to find the address, she noticed a local newspaper article from last November: *Pensioner Harry Reboot Makes Final Checkout at Trunnocks.*

She shivered as she read the story. Death by shopping trolley was another of the unusual causes of death that had ruined her research.

# 5

## *Supermarket Sweep*

Una's phone glowed under the darkening sky. The article revealed that Harry had been shopping at Trunnocks on 1 December when he'd skidded on a wet patch from a stray bag of frozen Brussels sprouts, which had started to thaw.

During the skid, Harry, 71, was jettisoned towards a shopping trolley that had been left unsupervised by graphic designer, Jada, 23, originally from Southampton. He put his hands out to grab the trolley, which flung him into a free-standing cabinet of sports energy drinks, off which he ricocheted head-first into a display of reduced-to-clear Prosecco. The cause of death was unclear. At the inquest, his brother Roger, a climate-change denier, ventured the opinion that late-stage capitalism had killed him. But the doctor said that shock was the most likely cause. Trunnocks issued a statement that lessons had been learnt. There is no record about what happened to the trolley and whether it is still in service.

As Una arrived at Trunnocks, the doors automatically swooshed apart. Open seven days a week, the supermarket stood at the end of a short parade of shops. There were jagged neon shapes in the window promising manager's specials and cheap booze offers. Her first instinct was to grab a basket, as she only needed a couple of bottles of cava, but then she saw the bank of trolleys. Using a trolley could help get her into the killer object's point of view.

What other sort of risks could there be at a supermarket? Falling tins, freezer cabinet doors open with corners that could clip your head if you stood up too quickly, fingers tourniqueted in the gaps of the shopping basket mesh.

She set off on her mission to locate the fatal frozen sprouts. She was simply an insurance professional collecting a few items of data as she went about her shopping.

The shop was arranged in a tight maze of long aisles with the tills at the end. She pushed past shelves filled with brightly coloured pulses and grains with different languages and typefaces on their wrappers. She continued on to tinned goods, some of them still in cardboard boxes with the fronts ripped off. There were a lot of tinned goods compared to her usual supermarket; if a catastrophic earth event wiped out all of humanity except for her, this would be an ideal place to come for food. Freshly made hummus from the artisanal deli near her flat in London wouldn't cut it in those circumstances.

She turned the corner, the narrow aisle requiring precision skills from her trolley, whose wheels appeared to pivot at random angles. Perhaps an intransigent trolley had been a factor in Harry's last spin. She wheeled slowly alongside the freezers, trudging her trainers along the slightly sticky floor to get a good grip, making an unpleasant rubber rasp. The cabinets beside her were arranged in two tiers – one at eye level, the other on the floor. The lower ones contained frozen vegetables: peas, carrots and of course the homicidal Brussels sprouts. But no trace of the tragedy remained – it looked like a perfectly normal chest cabinet on a clean enough floor. Nothing to suggest this was an accident blackspot.

Time to find the cava. She swivelled the trolley round to find the drinks section, but as she did so, she crashed into one of the shop assistants, a young girl in a grey nylon uniform, who was wheeling a pallet of 'Kitty Treats' along the aisle.

'Sorry, wasn't looking where I was going,' said Una. She was mortified. She was supposed to be a neutral observer, not causing accidents.

The girl looked at her. 'You should be careful with that trolley,' she said.

'I'm trying to,' said Una, 'but it's got a mind of its own.'

This sounded like something Mum would say, and she'd only been down here for eight hours.

'Yeah, well, we've been waiting for Tommo to come in and sort them out,' said the girl.

'Tommo?' asked Una. This was the second time she'd heard that name today.

'Local customer. Our odd-job guy. He's going to put some WD40 on a few of them.' The girl reached for the handle of the cart.

Una tensed – she needed to extract more data from this source. 'So,' she said, 'have you worked here long?'

The assistant's face reflected Una's own discomfort at this feeble attempt at chit-chat.

'A while,' she said, fidgeting with her lanyard. 'Why are you asking?'

'Just wondered, as a family friend had an accident here recently. Perhaps it's . . . you know . . . a place I should shop respectfully in.'

37

This was not going well. She was steering the conversation with less skill than she could manoeuvre a Trunnocks trolley.

'An accident . . .'

'His name was Harry,' said Una. 'I believe it was just here where it happened.'

The girl scowled. 'Look here, are you a journalist? Why all these questions? Or are you part of that Eastbourne True Crime meet-up group? They were the worst, with their stupid questions about motive and opportunity.'

'No, really, I just happened to be here shopping . . .'

'And nothing in your trolley? I think you people are sick. That poor man – I was here when . . .' The girl's eyes moistened and her bottom lip was trembling. Una felt herself going into panic mode.

'I'm sorry, I didn't mean to . . . I just popped in so I could get some cava. Look, this one.'

She took out her phone and brought up the picture of Mum and Ken beside the bottle. It was irrational, but perhaps it would reassure the girl that she wasn't some kind of murder hobbyist.

'That's Ken,' said the girl, pointing to the photo.

'Yes, it is,' said Una. 'And that's my mum next to him.'

'Okay. If you know Ken, then you're probably all right.'

'Really? You know Ken?' said Una. Any intel might help her save Mum from this hasty marriage. 'What do you think about him as a customer? Is he ever accompanied by a mysterious younger woman when he's in the shop? Anything else you've noticed about him that's, you know, suspect?'

The girl scrunched her face. 'Let me tell you about Ken,' she said. 'When Trunnocks was under threat by a big supermarket trying to take over the lease, Ken organised a flash mob outside to support us. Got the local newspaper involved too, and in the end the licence wasn't granted. Just as well. Trunnocks employs quite a few local people, whereas this new supermarket was going to be all computers.'

'But surely automation is a good thing,' said Una. 'Efficient, fast.'

'I'd better be getting on,' said the girl, going for the handle again.

Una had to stop her. She still had more to ask. 'I should have put it a better way,' she said. 'That was clumsy of me, sorry. About the incident with Harry. You said you were there?'

The girl stopped and looked at her like she was a dented tin of peaches. 'You don't give up, do you? What do you think? It was awful. Harry was such a lovely man. He and Ken were like a double act. When we went over to him lying next to that trolley . . . His last words were "Wrong number" – he mustn't have known what had hit him. It was terrible. Just as well that doctor was around, even though he's really annoying and says he only comes to shop here in an emergency when actually he's in here loads.'

'When you said Ken, you mean a different Ken, right?'

'No, Ken in that photo. And his friends, they were all at the flash mob that day, he invited everyone he knew. We were all excited about it, and then later, Harry . . .'

Ken knew both Eileen and Harry. They'd all been part of the same circle of friends. This was a coincidence, although perhaps it was not unlikely that a group of pensioners would have a cluster of accidents if enough samples were taken into account. But Harry's last words – what was this wrong number? A phone number? An address?

Una took out a bag of frozen carrots from one of the cabinets so she'd look like a functioning customer. 'Was there anything else?' she asked. 'Anything about the floor, the trolley or the cabinets that could have caused the accident? Would you say that your customers in general have a decent average life expectancy?'

The girl stood silent with folded arms. Numbers were so much easier to manipulate than people.

'I'll take that as a no.'

'Is there anything else I can help you with?'

'That's it, thanks. Oh, hang on, where's the cava?'

'Aisle before last.'

The girl pushed on with the cart. Having uncovered this new connection with Ken and his friends, Una decided to do one more pass over the freezer cabinets. She wanted to check thoroughly for all possible risks.

She crouched down, putting the bag of frozen carrots on the floor. Then she squat-walked along the lower cabinets to check for any unusual signs. As she squat-walked back for a second check, she slipped on the icy patch the carrots had made on the lino and fell backwards. There was a sharp pain in her coccyx and she sat for a few seconds to make sure she was still fully functional. Her neck had cricked at a funny angle and it was then that she spotted the fire safety notice on the wall above. Next to it were two perfectly placed numbers in the same gold and black as the ones on Eileen's bins. This time they made the number 37.

# 6

## *Full House*

The community centre where the bingo night was being held was an old Victorian school hall with a gable roof and brightly painted windows. Tonight it contained clumps of tightly packed pensioners, their white heads forming cauliflower florets. The walls and ceiling were plain except for fire safety notices and smoke alarms, which pleased Una. She was less impressed with the slightly sticky carpet. At least there was a reassuring whiff of bleach about the place.

She sat on a rickety plastic chair, next to Mum and opposite Ken, who was browsing a site called 'Groovy Grooms' on his oversized smartphone. She surveyed the potential portfolio of life insurance buyers in the hall. It was in the interests of Katapult that they lived as long as possible and kept paying their monthly premiums. Eleven per cent of them should smoke. She counted the smokers around the room based on the packets of cigarettes on their tables. Yes, that seemed in line with the expected figures.

Moving on to alcohol intake. Ken had already sunk a whole pint. He definitely wasn't helping the average life expectancy for Eastbourne. Una took a sip from her single gin with slimline tonic; a drink that hit the sweet spot between liver deterioration and brain rot on one hand and preventative dementia measures on the other. As a bonus, it was also mildly enjoyable.

'I'll go and get our books for the bingo,' said Mum, heading to the front of the hall and leaving Una and Ken alone at the table.

The revelation of the second pair of numbers had caused Una's brain to become an electrical forcefield. She couldn't stop thinking about them. Were they simply a popular brand of stick-on numbers? Some sort of farewell gesture from a grieving friend?

'I hadn't been to Trunnocks before,' she said. She looked around at the bingo crowd – tonight she would extract maximum data from them.

'They work their socks off, and the place is always well stocked,' said Ken. 'Tell me something you couldn't find there. You can't. It's like the Harrods of Eastbourne.'

'Yes, it was quite an experience. Although I fell over near the freezers, as the floor was slippery.'

Ken dropped his phone with a clatter. 'By the freezers? At Trunnocks? I can't believe it. I thought they'd be very strict on that now.'

Mum returned with three bingo books.

'Ken, are you okay?' she asked. 'You've gone a funny colour. I'll get you a glass of water.'

'I'm fine,' he said. 'Una said she slipped over at Trunnocks. I got a bit of a shock.'

'No! Like Harry,' said Mum, bringing out a scrap of kitchen roll from her evening bag and dabbing her eyes.

'And who's Harry?' asked Una, leafing through the book

of games to hide her interest, the grids of numbers only inflaming her need for data.

'Our friend Harry sadly had an accident at Trunnocks a couple of months ago,' said Ken, gulping from his pint glass, 'due to a spillage on the floor by the freezers. I'm going to write a letter to them; they need to sort this out or there'll be hell to pay!'

'It was my own fault,' she said, thinking of the unimpressed but competent shop assistant she'd met. 'Don't write to them. I caused a spillage and then slipped on it.'

'This isn't like you,' said Mum. 'You spilt your tea earlier, too, and now you say you fell over. Are you feeling okay?'

'I'm fine, it must be all the excitement about your big news. So, back to Harry. Was he part of your bingo crowd?'

'Yes, he sometimes came to bingo,' said Ken, 'although we originally met him through Jean and John at that book club they used to do before the bust-up.'

'He was a solicitor,' said Mum. 'Had his own practice and everything. He was thick as thieves with Ken.'

'Very down to earth, he was,' said Ken.

'Was he into numbers at all? Series of numbers?'

'Numbers? Why would he be into numbers?' asked Ken.

Una didn't meet his eye. 'And Eileen,' she said. 'Did he know Eileen?'

Ken leant towards her and looked directly into her face.

'Why are you asking about Eileen?'

'I don't know,' she said, struggling to provide a convincing answer. 'It just seems a bit strange that two people you know have died in unusual accidents recently.'

'Una!' said Mum, patting Ken's arm.

Ken stood up, his shoulders drooping and his chin on the verge of a wobble. 'Just popping to the gents. I'll get some more drinks in while I'm up. What are you both having?'

'I'm fine,' said Una. Mum tapped her wine glass to indicate she wanted another, and he bundled off to the bar.

'Please can you not talk about Eileen or Harry in front of Ken,' said Mum when he was out of earshot. 'He's already stressed out with all the big ideas he keeps coming up with for the wedding. I need him to stay calm, it's not good for him to get all flustered.'

'Okay, sorry, was he really close to them?'

'Yes, he was good mates with Harry and he'd known Eileen since she was knee-high – they were at junior school together.'

'Really?'

'He's already got himself in a tizz without you winding him up asking him about numbers, of all things. They were people to us, not numbers, thank you very much.'

'But I just want to make sure that Eastbourne is safe for you.'

Mum grabbed Una's hand. 'You're reading too much into things as usual. They were tragic accidents, that's all. Please change the subject.'

Ken returned with a man wearing a Deep Purple T-shirt underneath an elaborate waistcoat, whose long grey ponytail remained static even as he strode towards them.

'Tommo, just wanted to introduce you to Una, Sheila's daughter,' said Ken. 'Tommo used to work with me, he's my right-hand man. And he's also our bingo caller. You just about got here on time, the punters are starting to get restless.'

'Nice to meet you,' said Tommo, giving a slight bow of his head.

So this was the infamous Tommo, who'd put up the basket above Eileen's door as well as being the go-to trolley oiler at Trunnocks. Ken had had his own building firm, so Tommo would have the right skills. He took out an e-cigarette and started to vape.

'What's the flavour this week?' asked Ken, starting on his next pint.

'Kale. I've gone vegan this month,' said Tommo. 'Right, I'd better get started before this lot turn nasty.'

He strode off to the front of the hall and stood behind a trestle table, where he took out a yellow cloth from a glasses case and started to polish the top of the bingo number machine that was sitting on top.

'I must say, I like the look of my numbers tonight,' said Mum, smiling at her sheet for the first game.

'It's completely random,' said Una, 'providing the selection process has no bias.'

'Eyes down, game starting,' announced Tommo, holding up the first bingo ball. 'Two fat ladies, 88.'

Two fat ladies at a table nearby started nudging each other and giggling. Una inwardly tutted – having a BMI over 25 was nothing to smile about.

'A flea in heaven, 37.'

'Yes!' said Mum. 'That's on my card, brilliant.'

'All the threes, 33,' said Tommo.

'There you go,' said Mum, 'got that too. I'm on for a line.'

'As it happens, I have those two numbers on my card as well,' said Una, 'thanks to the laws of probability.'

45

The numbers continued. It was proving quite soothing to tick them off after the cataclysmic wedding revelation earlier.

'Sixty-two, tickety-boo.'

'Una, you've won,' said Mum. 'Look. Shout house.'

'House!' bleated Una.

Tommo stepped out from behind his table, collected her card and took it to the front to check. When he announced her win, there was a disgruntled murmuring across the room.

'Go up then,' said Mum. 'You've got to collect your prize.'

Una went up to the front desk and Tommo handed her a bottle of sparkling white wine with a high sugar content.

'Congratulations, Una,' he said, and performed a small bow. She could feel the eyes of the other bingo players boring into her and she looked down at the floor as she made her way back to their table.

'Well done,' said Mum.

Una thrust the bottle towards her. 'You can have this. Please.'

'Thanks, Una.'

'There you go,' said Ken, 'you're lucky after all.'

After the bingo games ended, two women from a nearby table came over. Mum introduced them as 'some very good friends of ours', Jean and Cassie, and Una recognised them from the background of the cava photo. The novelty of meeting so many elderly data samples in person was wearing off. Jean twitched about in her tweed blazer like a sparrow that had downed one too many cans of Coke, whereas Cassie, swamped in a black velveteen dress, was still and expressionless like a cushion.

46

Jean put her hand under Una's chin and rotated her head on its axis, sizing it up like a supermarket mango. 'So this is your daughter, Sheila. I can see you in her.'

'Yes, this is my Una. She works in insurance in London.' Mum turned to Una. 'Jean's husband, John, was a maths teacher – you'd enjoy talking to him.'

'John's in his shed tonight,' said Jean, 'working on some craft project, he said – saw him going in there with glue. Goodness knows what he's up to. I think he's still a bit upset about Tommo being picked as the new bingo caller when clearly my John is more numerate.'

'Tommo's doing a grand job,' said Ken.

'No Raj with you tonight then?' asked Mum.

'Yes, we're not a "full house" without him here – where is his nibs?' said Ken.

Jean shrugged. 'I did ask him, but he doesn't like the bingo night, says it's full of old people, thank you very much. No, he's popped down to London, to see Simon Russell Beale in a play. You know Raj, he's very into culture. And yet he, amongst others, helped destroy my book club.'

'Now, now,' said Ken.

'I see you've already won, Una, you must be lucky,' said Jean, purse-lipped, picking up the bottle of sparkling wine to read the label. 'Typo on that label, lack of attention to detail.'

'I don't believe in luck, there is only probability,' said Una.

Mum cleared her throat. 'How's the hip, Jean?'

'Playing up a bit, Sheila, perhaps because the weather's changing. They've put me on some new tablets, so we'll see how that pans out.'

47

'I'm on new tablets as well,' said Mum. 'For my blood pressure. Statins. Have to keep remembering to take them.'

'I didn't know about that,' said Una. Why wasn't she up to date with Mum's medication?

'Have you told her the big news yet?' said Jean, shifting her weight from one comfi-fit shoe to the other.

Una girded herself for wedding talk.

'Yes, we told her today,' said Mum.

'You must be thrilled,' said Jean.

'It certainly was a surprise,' replied Una.

'And I'm the best man,' said Tommo, who had pulled up a chair.

'We're looking forward to the wedding after all the bad news recently,' said Jean. 'John's getting a new shirt and tie.'

'We were talking about poor Eileen and Harry with Una earlier,' said Mum.

'As it happens,' said Una, 'I'd be very interested to hear if there have been any other unusual deaths round here. For example, any garden accessory deaths you're aware of.'

'Why do you want to know that?' said Jean.

She just wanted a simple answer to a simple question. Google never questioned her motives. She bit her lip and summoned all her patience.

'Just to help me when I'm choosing stuff for my flat,' she said. 'I'll certainly avoid hanging baskets.'

'We've never had any problems with our hanging baskets in all these years,' said Jean.

It was at this point that Cassie piped up. 'It's not baskets you should be worried about, but Una's right, you should

48

all be careful. I see darkness approaching. I see a jagged, monstrous claw. And . . . I see garden furniture.'

'That's a lot to see,' said Ken, swilling the last drop in his pint glass.

'I see danger,' Cassie went on. Her reedy voice had taken on a misty quality.

'You always see danger, Cassie,' said Ken, slamming his glass down on the table. 'When is this big event supposedly happening?'

Cassie raised her wiry arms skywards. 'In about a fortnight's time.'

Following her announcement, Cassie swept off. The rest of the group fell silent.

'What was that about?' said Una. 'She basically said something bad is going to happen quite soon.'

Why did people choose to retire here? The constant drama was exhausting. And spotting risks was her domain. What data sets was Cassie using to make these sorts of claims?

'Take no notice,' said Ken. He shook his head and corralled the glasses on their table into a neat circle. 'That was just Cassie being Cassie. Me and Jean were at school with her; you just have to get used to her little ways.'

'She has the gift of second sight,' said Jean. 'Well, had. She used to read people's palms on the pier, but then she started to lose the gift and her customers, so she had to shut up shop.'

'Load of old tosh,' said Ken. 'She couldn't predict if there was going to be a "y" in the day. Her mother used to come

49

round our house reading tea leaves for my mother. Generations of codswallop.'

'She's het up about us getting married, that's what it is,' said Mum. 'She didn't predict that, did she?'

Una felt an uncomfortable twinge in her stomach. She too was having her predictions questioned at work. Of course, she had used expertly sourced data and the latest statistical models rather than bogus magical insights, but if she carried on getting bad reviews from the internal audit team, perhaps she would end up derided by her peers, like Cassie.

'She's harmless enough,' said Jean.

'She's trying to put us on edge, winding us all up,' said Ken. 'It's not right.'

'I'm thinking, Ken, perhaps we should postpone the stag do,' said Tommo. 'That's in two weeks' time. She said her gift is coming back, didn't she? I don't want anything to happen to you before the wedding.'

'You're the best man,' said Ken, 'you're supposed to be supporting me. I'm not going to listen to her superstitious twaddle. Let's face it, her recent track record of predictions hasn't been all that. The stag do will go ahead.'

He huffed loudly, then turned to Una. 'And of course you're invited. It's a week on Saturday. It'll be a great laugh. I'd love you to come along, and not just because I'm a feminist. It would be good for my Anton if there were some people there his own age.'

A stag do! She might be expected to take part in dangerous activities that would require additional insurance. On the other hand, it would be an opportunity to observe Ken and find out if there were any chinks in his double-denim armour.

'I'll have to get back to you on that, Ken,' she said. 'See how work goes.'

'Well, I'm off,' said Jean. 'John's outside. I'll have a word with you-know-who tomorrow morning, try to calm her down.'

It was coming up to 10 p.m., and the group were putting on their coats and making their goodbyes. Una felt a hand grip her shoulder.

'Look who's here.'

She turned around. It was the old man who'd harassed her when she'd been watching Eileen's house; same anorak, same chirpy expression. Her stomach curdled. If he'd seen her crouching behind the bins, that would be tough to explain.

'Arthur!' said Ken. 'Hang on, do you two know each other?'

'Saw her this morning, eyeing up Eileen's house,' said Arthur.

'Why were you at Eileen's house?' asked Ken, zipping up his blouson leather jacket.

'Thinking of a buy-to-let, isn't she?' said Arthur. 'I've been reading about these money-making schemes on the net.'

'I happened to pass by on my way back from birdwatching,' said Una, staring at him fiercely. 'I thought I saw a sparrow.'

'What,' said Ken, 'you're looking to buy somewhere here? But Eileen's house, that's a bit creepy.'

'I'd keep tabs on her, Ken,' Arthur said, bumbling off.

Did Ken suspect that she knew about his furtive trip to Chamberlayne Road? She studied his reaction carefully, but got nothing.

'Who's Arthur? Don't remember you mentioning him,' she said, hoping the old man wasn't going to keep popping up.

'He's all right,' said Ken. 'He's not really part of our little group – I mean, he's harmless, but he's always sticking his nose in. It's Eileen he knew really, lived opposite.'

'I see.' Una stored this information about Arthur's curiosity – he might be a good source of data on the other bingo-goers.

Ken jangled keys in his pocket. 'You know, I could help you look for somewhere. I'm sure there's other places more suitable.'

'Honestly, I'm not looking,' she said. 'He must have got the wrong end of the stick.'

'That would be typical Arthur,' said Ken.

But Mum knew Una too well. When Ken wasn't listening, she leant closer for a discreet but pointed message. 'What happened to Eileen was an accident, Una, and that's that. You don't need to worry about it and you shouldn't poke your nose in where it's not wanted.'

Una aimed for an 'I completely agree' nod, to keep the peace. She'd arrived in Eastbourne with a professional interest in the unusual deaths, but as two of those deaths were linked to people Mum knew, her interest had become personal. The sensible thing to do was to go back to her tried-and-trusted methods, but her analytical reasoning was being hijacked by the mysterious black and gold numbers.

## 7

## *The Game is a Foot Spa*

The next morning, Una woke to the sounds of frantic bustle in the living room. Mum was packing brightly coloured dresses into a bag for life and there was a whiff of dated perfume.

'Morning,' she said. 'Just making a start on the clear-out.'

'Clear-out?' said Una. 'But don't you have enough to do without tidying the flat up? It looks fine to me.'

Mum smiled. 'I need to make space for Ken's stuff, as he's moving in after we get married.'

'He's moving in here?'

'Yes, his house is too big for just the two of us, so he's sticking it on the market and we'll live here. He's doing a clear-out too, and Anton's coming down next weekend to help. Ken says he's going through a bit of a rough patch, just split up from his girlfriend, but that'll keep him busy. And while I'm on the topic, it would be good if you could sort out that cupboard by the front door – it's full of your old stuff.'

The reality of the wedding was now hitting Una with full force. Afterwards, Ken would be a permanent and inescapable feature of family life.

'Okay, Mum, I'll do it next time I'm down. But are you going to get a pre-nup agreement? You want to make sure you don't get diddled out of your flat.'

Mum huffed. 'Una, I'm not Kim Kardashian off the telly. No, I'm not getting a pre-nup, thank you very much.'

Una strode to the sink and put the tap on full blast to fill the kettle. With everything else going on, she'd stalled on her plans to dig deeper into Ken's spending habits. 'Make sure you don't throw out anything that's collectible,' she said.

'I don't think these old dresses are worth much,' said Mum, 'so perhaps you could drop them off at the charity shop on your way to the station. You need to go to Tread Softly on Radcliffe Street; it's pedestrianised round there, so it's very safe. Jean's the manager. You'll probably see her, she's normally in on a Sunday – very dedicated. Gets in a nark if any of us so much as look at another charity shop.'

'What sort of charity is Tread Softly?' said Una. 'I've never heard of them.'

'It helps old people. That's as much as I know.'

Una searched for the shop's website on her phone. It looked like some sort of scam site, with its old-fashioned font and colours and a stock photo of a group of pensioners. There was very little information on how the charity actually helped old people. *Tread Softly – where everyone counts*, said the banner at the top of the page. That was promising – perhaps they promoted numeracy? She could really get behind that. But then she noticed some unusual messages from an anonymous troll in the comments section:

*Support young people not old ones*

*Population should be shaped like a triangle not a square*

*Old people clogged up the condiments aisle at Waitrose this morning – again*

Someone clearly did not appreciate the contribution of the older community in Eastbourne.

Mum knotted the bags and pushed them towards her.

'No problem, I'll take them,' said Una. 'I'd better get ready to go.'

'Come here,' said Mum. Una shuffled towards her and was enveloped in a close hug as well as a strong whumph of Madame Rochas perfume.

'Well,' said Mum, finally releasing her, 'it was nice having you up this weekend. Perhaps you could pop back and help me with the wedding prep? There's a lot to do and I want you to feel part of it.'

'I'm pretty busy, Mum, but I can help from London – most of it can probably be sorted out online.'

'Okay, that would be something.'

With all the distractions this weekend, Una had spent very little time looking over her research, but tomorrow she'd stay late at work and focus on it. She was annoyed with herself for getting swept up on a wild numbers chase; she'd even felt unnerved by Cassie's predictions last night, even though they were complete nonsense.

She left early for the station to allow time for the detour to Tread Softly. It was a chilly, overcast morning, and as a nod to her health, she walked at a brisk pace that would still allow her to have a conversation with someone, not that she had any intention of doing so. She found the pedestrianised area where the charity shop was located. People, pushchairs and bikes filled the street with a noisy hubbub. Tread Softly was situated between a 'Bath and Body' store and a shop selling jewellery for teenage girls. There was another charity shop a few doors down, which supported young people.

A bell rang as Una entered, and she was confronted with the sensory overload of the shop. It was cluttered with stuff. Used stuff. Stuff that had been handled by many people. She had her antibacterial gel in her backpack, so that was a comfort. The floor space was packed with round racks of clothes, and along the walls were rows and rows of books whose spines had broken into white creases. There was a lightly sweet scent of mildew, mustiness and mothball.

'Look who it is,' said Jean from behind the counter at the back. 'Fancy seeing you again, Una love.'

'Just bringing in some stuff, dresses from Mum,' said Una. 'Where do you want me to put them?'

'Bring it all over to the counter here. We could do with more dresses.'

There was a pause while Jean peered inside the bag.

'I noticed you've got a rival shop a few doors down,' Una said.

'They are not a rival,' said Jean, pulling one of the dresses out and smoothing it on the counter.

'Sorry, I guess you're all trying to raise money for good causes.'

'Their window displays are distinctly second-rate,' said Jean, pursing her lips, 'as is their choice of stock.'

'You do indeed have a lot of stuff in here.' Given how easy it was to wind Jean up, Una decided that sticking to short factual statements was the way to go.

'I hope you didn't get the wrong impression of us last night,' said Jean, putting the dress back in the bag and balancing it on top of a mound of other bags and boxes behind the counter. 'We're very close knit as a group normally.'

'Aren't you worried about that woman predicting that there's danger coming soon?'

'Cassie? You know what, in her own way, I think she's trying to help us.'

'I'm just surprised that you all see her as a close friend,' said Una, 'when she's coming out with all these dark visions.'

'I just let it go over my head,' said Jean. 'We all cut her some slack. Her gift, as she likes to call it, went off the boil a while ago, and then her son went off to New Zealand and she hardly ever sees him because of the cost. Shame.'

Una checked her watch. She still had time to get to the station, so she drew nearer to the counter. Cassie's son might not be around to keep an eye on his mother, but she was going to step up and protect Mum.

'Talking of costs,' she said, 'Ken seems to be a generous sort of person.'

'He's always been a bit flash, has Ken. Mind you, it's very useful for the shop, as he gets tired of things quickly. He brought in a new lot of stuff a few weeks ago, along with some things from poor Harry that his daughter had put aside. Some of the books weren't suitable, so I had to find another home for them. But look at that foot spa over there, next to that pile of his old jumpers. Harry only used it once, and it's got three heat settings.'

Una followed Jean's line of sight to the box on a shelf.

'It's our manager's special, if you're interested?'

'I'm okay, thanks,' said Una. A second-hand foot spa was a worst-case scenario in itself, and this one probably still had traces of the recently departed Harry's feet. 'Ken must be well off if he can buy all this stuff, right?'

'You're just like my daughter. She thinks us old folk are all as rich as Croesus because of our pensions and the price we paid for our houses. Well, let me tell you, I worked hard all my life, and so did Ken. Hope that's answered your question.'

It hadn't. It had only raised the possibility of Ken cluttering the flat with bric-a-brac. Time to move on to her next audit point.

'Another thing,' she said. 'I was talking to Ken at the bingo about how it was a bit odd that he knew two people who'd had unusual deaths. It didn't seem to go down well and he went a funny colour. Is he okay, health-wise?'

Jean sighed. 'He probably was a bit uncomfortable about that, yes, as he was behind both events. He insisted that Eileen had a photo party to show off her cruise snaps, and then he came up with the flash mob idea for Trunnocks. I said we should do a petition, but he said that wasn't Instagrammable enough.'

'I see. I mean, sort of.'

'So I think he feels a bit guilty, even though there's no way those accidents were caused by all of us having been around. In fact, I see it as a blessing that we were with them both near the end. In any case, best not to bring it up in front of him; he's a very sensitive soul.'

Una formulated more questions about Ken as she looked more closely at the jumper next to the foot spa. It was white, with some kind of red pattern knitted into it. She opened it out with the tips of her fingers – there were a couple of red snake squiggles or perhaps 2s along the front hem. She wondered why Harry had picked that design. If they were numbers, there was no obvious link with the numbers she'd seen yesterday by the freezers. That's if there was any link at all.

'Jean, do you know what the pattern is on this jumper? Is it a number?'

Jean was forensically filleting a blouse with a coat hanger. 'I've no idea. Might be some trendy brand. Perhaps it was a special number for him – you'd need to ask John about that, he's the numbers expert round here. Don't know if he'll pop in this morning. Left first thing, didn't say much, but then again that's what attracted me to him, his air of mystery.'

As Una replaced the jumper and took a step back, there was a blood-curdling scream. Something was gripping onto her leg, a warm presence that was pulsating like an alien heart. She looked down. The tabby face of a cat with large amber eyes glared up at her as it clung on.

'A cat. There's a cat. I think I might have frightened it,' she said.

'Don't worry,' said Jean, 'that's just Pedro, Cassie's cat. I don't encourage him to come into the shop, of course, but I've known him since he was a kitten. We're one of the stops on his daily circuit.'

'It's got its claws into me. Can't you call it off?'

'Here, Pedro, here,' said Jean, shaking a bag of the Kitty Treats Una had seen at Trunnocks. The cat bounded over to her and started to gorge itself on the treats that she'd scattered on the floor.

'That cat is a menace,' said Una. She rolled up her jeans and looked at the claw marks. If she squeezed her calf really hard and waggled it, she could make some tiny traces of blood come out. Disaster. She'd have to keep a close eye on this injury. 'I've got wounds from its claws.'

'Oh!' said Jean. 'I'll get the first-aid kit, if I can find it.'

Una baulked at the idea of Jean applying donated bandages to her leg. She'd have to quiz her about the black and gold numbers some other time.

'It's fine. I'll see to it myself. Got to dash.'

She tried not to put weight on her wounded leg, which actually didn't hurt that much – was that a bad sign? Was her body in shock from the attack and responding by numbing her leg? Whatever the case, she was treading softly as she left Tread Softly.

After hurrying to Eastbourne station with only thirty minutes spare to catch her train, she got a seat in a relatively quiet carriage and returned to London. She'd purchased her one-bedroom flat five years ago, after considerable fretting about taking on the huge loan. She was ready for independent living after years of sharing with friends, strangers or insurance colleagues, living in rentals where she couldn't be sure that her flatmates had turned off the hob or not overloaded their plug sockets. Places in areas of London with serious subsidence issues that could cause the house to collapse as she slept. By the time her professional exams were over and she'd spent a few years establishing herself at work, she'd built up a deposit and found an up-and-coming area with relatively appealing crime statistics for her budget. Balham.

The development she'd bought in was an old jam factory that had been converted into flats while preserving some of its original features. It had solid brick walls and a sturdy intercom. Her flat was on the third floor, reducing the chance of outside entry. She'd kept the default neutral decoration, and the tiny kitchen was part of the main living room, which was great as it meant she could glance over to make sure there was no unexpected smouldering from the toaster or flooding from an overflowing sink. She rarely saw any of the other residents, but she'd established a healthy nodding relationship with a family who lived at the end of her corridor.

She checked the communal letter boxes in the lobby – just one pink envelope, handwritten address. It was a wedding invite, from Mum and Ken. Upstairs, she heated up a small portion of the frozen Thai vegetable curry that she'd batched during the week and started her monthly video chat with her friend Amara, who lived in Leeds with her husband and daughter, having stayed on there after they'd finished university together.

After a few pleasantries about Naz and Ela and Amara's parents, Una cut straight to the dramatic events of the weekend.

'I get it, you're not happy about the wedding,' said Amara. There was a short burst of dog barks. The blankness of the background in Una's chat window contrasted with the clutter of books and pictures and general stuff in Amara's.

'Of course not. I just don't know enough about Ken,' said Una. 'They should go slower. Today I found out he'd arranged various meet-ups with his friends, and shortly afterwards two of those friends died in unusual accidents. Statistically significant unusual accidents from my point of view.'

Amara winced. 'The poor guy. No wonder he's looking forward to the wedding.'

'He's not exactly lucky to be around, is he?'

'I thought you didn't believe in luck. If you're that bothered about him, why don't you spend some time getting to know him?'

'That's exactly what I intend to do. I'm going to run every check I can on him.'

'No, I meant talk to him, get to know him as a person.'

Una muted the phone while she sighed.

'It sounds like your mum is ready to move on with her life,' said Amara.

'Move on? But she might move on to something worse than her current situation.'

'Everything you've told me, all the little presents, the way he speaks to her, he seems like a nice guy.'

Amara was being both reasonable and irrational. Ken was an unknown.

'You're speculating based on minimal information,' said Una, over more barking. 'How is he funding all these presents? And I haven't told you yet that I saw him go into a house owned by a younger woman.'

'And?'

'He gave no explanation when I grilled him about it.'

'Grilled him? I bet he didn't. It's probably just a family friend or a relative or something. Sounds like you're the one who's speculating based on minimal evidence.'

That was a good point, and now Amara leant forward, her head filling the frame of Una's laptop. Una looked away, down at the small window that showed her own face onscreen. She was starting to look like Mum. When did that happen?

'Perhaps you should move on with your life too,' said Amara, in a gentler tone.

'I've put myself forward for a promotion at work actually.'

'I saw a new dating site for mathematical people,' Amara went on, drawing her daughter onto her lap. She clasped Ela's pudgy hand in her fingers and waved it at Una. Una's wave back felt a bit forced too, to be fair.

'Already been on it. Filled out the questionnaire in great detail and specified that I only wanted to see people I was a 99 per cent match with. So far, zero matches.'

'That's a shame,' said Amara. 'By the way, Jules has got hitched.'

'What!'

'Yeah, to Rach. They got their spaniel to deliver the rings on a tiny tray. It's all on Facebook.'

Jules had been so independent at university, and now she had a spaniel. What had happened to female solidarity and staying as empowered individuals for the rest of their lives?

'You know, Una, I was thinking about what you said. And this is just a suggestion.'

Una knew this was a codeword for delivering something challenging. 'Okay, go on.'

'Why not do something to include your dad, you know, at the wedding? You've said it before: your dad would want your mum to be happy. He wouldn't want her to be on her own, would he?'

Una's lungs fully deflated. 'How would that work?'

'You could include some photos of him and your mum, or read a favourite poem. But nothing, I repeat, nothing that tries to make Ken look bad in comparison.'

Not even Una's ergonomic desk chair could ease her out of this discomfort zone. 'I'll think about it,' she said, glancing back at Amara's concerned expression.

Amara moved on to *Line of Duty* and her theories about each character. But her suggestion about the wedding was now eating at Una's thoughts like lichen eroding a window frame on the path to a building insurance claim.

# 8

## *Ken is a Random Variable*

It was Monday, a normal Monday, the sort of Monday that wouldn't stand out in a police line-up of Mondays. But as she composed, forwarded or replied to emails, Una churned over everything she'd learnt in Eastbourne. She opened up her analysis and tried to focus on reviewing historic trends in seaside deaths, using the standard methods that had served her well for so many years. The promotion decision was looming and she needed to gain an advantage over Tim, but all she could think about was Ken.

The wedding announcement had turned him from someone she'd mentally swept under the carpet into someone personally significant. But his furtive visit to Rosa and his organised gatherings just before Eileen and Harry died also meant he was becoming statistically significant. Was Ken some sort of variable that affected the aggregated data in her spreadsheet?

The wedding would take place in less than six weeks' time, and Una *had* to use that time to find out how solid Ken was. She went back over what she'd found out about the accidents over the weekend, to see if any patterns emerged.

One connection was in the dates of the unusual deaths. Harry had died on 1 December, Eileen on 1 January. She checked for astronomical phenomena, phases of the moon, national festivals and TV schedules, but couldn't see any obvious correlations. There was the unlikely input of Cassie's prediction at the bingo hall. Something about a monstrous claw and garden furniture. How was that supposed to help? She could warn Mum to avoid bistro sets. 1 February fell a week on Thursday.

From a professional point of view, the whole exercise was a waste of time. She'd put together a ridiculously small sample of data from which she could extract no credible analysis. But one question kept drawing her back. What was the significance of the numbers she'd found at the house and the supermarket? Years, anniversaries, favourite bingo numbers, house numbers? 41 and 37 were both prime numbers – perhaps local mathmo John had a fixation on them, and who could blame him? One number was easy to explain away, but two sets in similar format, each at a grisly scene of death, were troubling.

Her leg started itching, a good time to check on the wound Pedro had inflicted. She couldn't afford to get an infection when she needed to be on top data-analysis form. She grabbed her mug and walked over to the first-aid box in the kitchenette. Swinging her leg onto a box of A4 photocopy paper, she applied antiseptic cream and a plaster.

'Good to see you're making use of the first-aid box. Heal thyself, right? What happened?'

She turned her head. Neoliberal Tim was doing squat

thrusts next to the fridge while swinging a two-litre carton of protein powder.

'I got attacked by a cat.'

'What sort of cat? You talking big game?'

'No, just a pet cat.'

'Ah, *Felis catus* ... Hang on, it's not Bring Your Pet to Work Day today, is it?'

'No, that's ages away.'

'So where did this happen? I'm allergic to cats, they bring me out in a rash.'

'I was dropping off some stuff at a charity shop and a cat there bit me.'

It all made sense in Eastbourne, but not so much back in the insurance heartland of the City of London.

'It looks like a very minor scratch to me,' said Tim, leaning in for a closer look.

Una rolled her trouser leg back over the plaster.

'And please don't think popping into a charity shop counts as corporate social responsibility,' he added. 'Since you asked, I'm training hard for my Ironman to raise money for anaemia sufferers to go on a Tim-funded fun day. I'll send you the donation link.'

'Thanks. I've already got it. Twice.'

For the last six months, since splitting up with Gareth in Pet Insurance, Tim had immersed himself in charity stunts. Whatever happened to the sponsored silence? Why had low-risk fundraising gone out of fashion?

'Just wondering,' she said, putting back the first-aid kit. 'Have you made any progress on the seaside resort analysis? I've been working on my own theory.'

'Good for you. But probably not a great use of your time, given my own review. The firm's view on outliers is too conservative, and by applying a small adjustment factor, the model is still okay. It's just a weird run of events.'

'Just a weird run of events?' she said, her jaw tensing. This was too much – Tim dismissing her research again. 'I see. Well, I predict there will be another unusual death on 1 February in Eastbourne.'

'Based on what?'

'My own data research drawn from deep analysis of the local area.'

Had she given away too much? She turned to put a peppermint tea bag into her mug so that Tim couldn't see her reaction.

He put down his protein powder and focused on her. 'Oh really? That's a very specific prediction, and you sound pretty confident.'

'Sure. I can predict with some certainty when another unusual death will occur – I'm just not sure who or how.'

'I mean, it's possible, but highly unlikely,' said Tim. 'And I don't see any way you can have modelled this – these unusual causes are all completely different and not linked to each other. If there was a link, I would have found it.'

Una blasted the tea bag with boiling water. 'We'll see who's right,' she said. 'Perhaps it will show that my research methods are more sophisticated than yours, and that will impress Ajay.'

'Perhaps. But let me inform you, I'm going full Bayesian on this if I have to.' Tim gripped the edge of the sink to perform a set of tricep dips.

She completed the tea steeping process by expertly tossing the sodden tea bag into the recycling bin with a flourish, then headed back. In the short journey from the kitchenette to her desk, a moral dilemma had started seeping through her like a herbal infusion. She had boasted to Tim about her insights into the next death, insights gained from two of Mum's friends dying in tragic accidents when Ken was in the vicinity. She should be using her skills to check on why Ken appeared to be a risk to those around him and therefore a potential risk to Mum. Was he simply a very unlucky person to be about at the beginning of the month? Was he sticking up those black and gold numbers as a curse and happening to get an excellent curse conversion rate? Or was it something more sinister?

There was no choice. She would go back to Eastbourne next week and offer to help Mum with the wedding plans.

She sipped her tea and it burnt her lip – mint tea needed more cooling time. Going to Eastbourne might expose her to danger too, even if she was just there as an observer. The best way to mitigate against this unknown risk was to prepare as well as she could. There was no need for complex data clustering; she simply focused on Ken and Mum's inner circle of friends and the data points she'd extracted at the bingo evening:

Jean, 72, former English teacher, married to John. Was at school with Eileen, Cassie and Ken. Bingo-goer. Keen on grammar. Set up a book club that no longer exists.

John, 76, former maths teacher. Met Jean when teaching. Two children – one lives with his family in the US, the other in Kent somewhere. Does craft in a shed.

Tommo, 70-something, former plumber. Friend of Ken's, worked together. Widowed, one daughter in Sheffield and son in Portsmouth. Bingo-goer. Put up Eileen's hanging basket.

Raj, 68, retired doctor. Knows Ken, Jean and John from a former book club. Appears to enjoy going to the theatre.

Cassie, 72, mystic and former fortune teller on the pier. Son living in New Zealand. Bingo-goer. Has made an ominous warning with unclear parameters about an undetermined event in two weeks' time.

Ken, 72, used to run his own building firm. Divorced twice. Has a son, Anton, and a daughter, Chrissie. Bingo-goer. Spendthrift. Possible philanderer.

She stood up and strode to Ajay's office.
'Quick word?' she asked as she entered.
'Hi, Una, how can I help?' said Ajay, with a slight slouch behind his standing desk.
'I was thinking about all that holiday you wanted me to use up. I wondered if I could take next week off. I realise it's short notice, but I can log in if needed and I'll do some extra hours this week. I want to spend some quality time with my mum, as she's getting married and I thought I could help out with the arrangements.'

'Getting married? Good for her. Send her my congratulations. You take that time off. I appreciate the option of contacting you, but seriously, just relax.'

'Thanks, Ajay.'

'And can I just say,' he said, 'I'm so pleased that you've listened to my feedback. You know, that's something I've mentioned a couple of times in your annual review, that you don't seem to listen to feedback.'

She couldn't remember Ajay mentioning that at any of her annual reviews. He gave her a single deep nod. That was a sign that the meeting was over as far as he was concerned, but there was still the matter of the upcoming promotion decision.

'One last thing,' said Una. 'I've been speaking to Tim about the seaside figures.'

'Great. I was going to suggest that you pair up and give me a joint update when you're ready.'

'Okay,' she said. 'And I just wondered, has there been any more news about the role managing the Life Insurance special projects team?'

'Still under discussion, but we'll have everything decided in the next few weeks, as we need to sort out a transition plan. Got a call now, sorry, appreciate you closing the door on your way out.'

That meant there was still enough time for her to sort out her research. She'd focus on that once she'd sorted out her concerns about Ken.

On the way back, she passed by Tim's desk. To avoid looking at his Young Actuary trophy, she glanced at his triple monitors. One of them showed a timetable of trains to Eastbourne. Was Tim going into the field too?

# 9

## *Clue of the Day*

The following Saturday, when Una arrived back at Eastbourne station, she sat on a bench in the airy ticket hall, facing a Cornish pasty shop. The sun was blasting through the narrow panes of the glass roof, making a complicated criss-cross of shadows on the floor. She'd got an early train on Mum's instruction, the same one that Anton was also getting from London, with the intention that they'd meet up on the station concourse. She didn't know what he looked like, so she put her mobile phone on her lap in case he texted.

Sitting next to the pasty shop was a single figure on a bench like hers. He had a prominent pointy nose and wiry blond-grey hair that led into a wispy beard on his chin. He reminded her of Tumbleweed, an Airedale terrier who'd forced her out of her short-lived paper round with its yapping. He was wearing a tweed jacket, loose jeans and some serious-looking boots, with a late-thirties face resting on top of it all. He looked at her and started to text something. If he was Anton, she needed to get her text in first. As she sent, *Hello. This is Una. I'm waiting on a bench in the foyer*, she received an *Is that you?* back. After an awkward shuffle, they met in the middle.

'Una?' he said.

'Yes.'

'I'm Anton.'

They hadn't made eye contact yet, and she watched his right hand twitch to offer a handshake, and then back out and return to its original position.

'Right,' she said.

'Shall we head off?'

'Okay, yes.'

They left the station and set off to meet Mum and Ken at Dino's restaurant in the centre of town. Saturday shoppers vied for pavement space and they struggled to walk side by side while letting people past.

'So, what do you do, Una?' asked Anton, his large leather messenger bag slapping against his side, out of sync with his slow stride.

'I'm an actuary,' she said.

'Oh, that's something to do with insurance, right?'

'Yes, I specialise in life insurance.'

'I see. That must be why I feel safe walking next to you.'

Una couldn't tell if that was a joke or a compliment, so she put on her most all-purpose smile. They turned into a narrower street, which was one person width, and had an awkward inverted power battle of who wasn't going to take the lead.

'And what do you do?' asked Una.

'I do various bits and pieces. Photography, bit of video work, some web content.'

'Okay,' she said, struggling to think of a follow-up question. 'So do you make films?'

'Short ones. In fact, I'm going to be doing the wedding video. Not my normal thing, but when Dad said he had a job for me, I was made up. Usually, Chrissie would be all over any family event, telling us what to do, but she can't get here until right before the wedding. I just need to work out how to put my own slant on it. Make something a bit different.'

Amara's suggestion came back to her. It somehow bypassed the rational part of her brain and blurted out of her mouth.

'I was thinking about whether it would possibly be an idea to include some old family photos at the wedding,' she said. 'A friend of mine suggested it, though it's probably a bit cheesy.'

'Yes!' Anton dragged his hands through his hair several times. 'We could create a montage. Splice photos from the past with scenes of social and political change at that time, layered with the relevant chart music.'

It sounded an ambitious plan – Una couldn't even work out how to do dynamic arrows on her monthly slide decks for Ajay.

'I don't know how much I can help on that,' she said. 'But I can give you some of our family photos.'

'Leave it to me,' said Anton. 'I know Dad's usual crowd, I can message them to send me stuff. It will be an amazing surprise for him. Thanks for suggesting it.'

'I can pick up the photos,' she said, her voice volunteering her to help before her brain could shut it down.

'What?' said Anton.

The thought had suddenly come to her. Meeting with the bingo crowd to collect these photos could be a good opportunity to interrogate them about Ken and establish any more links with Eileen and Harry.

'I'm off work this week. It'll give me something to do. A lot of the older photos will probably be physical copies, right?'

'If you're okay with that,' he said, 'but can you make sure you get some context for each picture?'

'What sort of context?'

'The mood, what music was playing, was anyone wearing a distinctive scent. I'd like to re-create something of the atmosphere.'

'But this will get shown when people are tucking into their dinner,' she said. 'We'll be lucky if they even notice the photos.'

Anton scowled. 'I'm making it to my standards, not theirs. Anyhow, I'll take you up on your offer, thanks. We can be co-producers. I'll send out a message now on Facebook to tell everyone you'll be in contact.'

They'd arrived at Dino's, with its striped green awning that precluded any hanging baskets. Inside, it was a noisy, bustling place with red and white check plastic tablecloths that looked practical to wipe down after a messy pasta meal. Mum and Ken were already sitting at a table that was just big enough to squeeze the four of them round. After much fussing over their arrival, Una found herself sitting on the chair that backed onto other tables, which meant that people were constantly pushing past her. There was silence as Ken, Mum and Anton reviewed the menu and peered at the specials on the blackboard.

'Not looking at the menu, Una?' said Ken. 'Do you need a vegetarian menu? I can ask.'

'No, I don't need a menu because I know what I want.'

'You looked online or something before we came?' he asked.

'No, I always have the same thing at Italian restaurants. Spaghetti carbonara. Saves time on decisions. I like to make sure I'm using my mental energy on important things.' Best to get this out of the way now, so hopefully it wouldn't rear its head again at any future meals.

'Well, blow me down,' said Ken. 'I never have the same thing twice.'

'I agree it's efficient, Una,' said Mum, 'but what are you saving all this time for?'

'I quite like the look of the sea bass,' said Ken. 'Anton will know what to order. He lived in Italy for a while and then came back over here with his senorita.'

'Until she upped and left,' said Anton, glowering.

'Poor thing,' said Mum, patting his arm.

'Just after you'd completed on that house as well,' said Ken. 'Heartbreaking.' He patted Anton's other arm.

Anton was pretending to read the menu. Una could see that he was looking at the blank frontispiece on the first page and not the actual list of offerings.

'Perhaps you'll find someone at the wedding,' said Mum.

'One's company, two's a crowd,' said Anton, snapping a breadstick in his right hand.

'Don't you worry,' said Ken. 'I told your mother I'd take good care of you while you're here.'

Anton bristled. 'I'm quite capable of—'

'I won't take no for an answer,' said Ken. 'You'll be getting a banana flax smoothie every morning. I could probably crush diamonds in that blender, it's so powerful. QVC Special Value.'

The waiter came for their orders.

'I'm going for the special, chicken in Parma ham,' said Mum.

'Sea bass for me,' said Ken, 'with a side of rosemary-encrusted potatoes, ta.'

'Fettucine al vongole,' said Anton, with an impressive Italian accent.

'Spaghetti carbonara,' said Una.

'Sorry, the carbonara is not on the menu today,' said the waiter. 'We've run out of pancetta. It's a very popular dish.'

Everyone looked at her. There was no time to reassess each option properly. She was going to have to be spontaneous.

'I'll just have the same as Ken,' she said.

Ken was beaming. Una felt deflated, as if in some way she'd handed him a victory in a battle that she wasn't even aware she'd been taking part in.

'I'm sure you'll enjoy it,' he said.

On the plus side, fish was brain food. On the other hand, there were bones – small but hardy bones that could enter a mouth hidden in a Trojan Horse of fish flesh, only to pop out and look for somewhere to lodge themselves, in particular her oesophagus. She'd have to chew carefully. Potatoes, even rosemary-encrusted ones, seemed comparatively safe. Try as she might, it was difficult to see danger in a potato wedge.

'This is nice,' said Ken. No one replied, but he seemed undaunted as he turned his attention to tucking his serviette into his polo shirt collar and telling everyone how he always got stuff on himself because he'd never been to finishing school.

He was clearly a silence-phobic. Una had noticed that people at work with this disorder were often promoted to be middle managers to provide a carpet of sound at strategy meetings. But she could use this to her advantage.

'So, Ken,' she said, 'what have you got planned for later this week?'

'Busy, busy, as usual,' he replied, getting out his phone and scrolling through his calendar. Una strained forward, trying to read his schedule for 1 February, but the text was too small. There was probably a minor moral transgression involved with looking at Ken's personal data. Certainly there were plenty of privacy policies to remember at work. But if it meant she could link the numbers she'd seen, then it would be fully justified. She needed to get hold of that phone.

She stared at the wall for inspiration. There was a corkboard covered with photos of the restaurant's owner, Dino, with various people she presumed were local celebrities.

'Why don't I take a photo of us all?' she suggested.

'Good one,' said Ken, removing his napkin.

'I can use your phone, Ken, as it's probably got the best camera.'

'Hold on . . .' said Anton, offering his own phone, which he'd cushioned in his cupped hands. 'Use mine, please.'

'Una's right,' said Ken, 'mine's got tons of megapixels, best one on the market. But I could get one of the waiters to take the picture so you can be in it.'

'That's okay, I've got the best light from over here.' She picked up Ken's phone.

'You just need to press the white button onscreen,' said Ken.

She bought time by getting the group to huddle in a more horseshoe shape. Her heart was thumping. She looked for the calendar app.

'Hurry up,' said Mum. 'The food will be here soon.'

She took two photos and then pretended that she was checking them at different angles. She opened up Ken's calendar and found an appointment on Thursday 1st that said *DIY store*. At least she now knew one of his destinations that day. Then she felt the phone being wrested from her grip.

'Let's have a look at these pictures then,' said Ken, frowning at the screen with his calendar still showing. The food had now started to arrive, which she hoped would deflect his suspicions.

'Sorry, Ken,' she said. 'I was trying to find the album on your phone to make sure the photos had saved.'

'No worries,' he said. 'I'm an open book. And what are your plans this week, Una? House-hunting?'

'House-hunting?' asked Mum.

'No, I'm helping Mum with her wedding prep,' said Una, avoiding Ken's eye. 'Can you pass the pepper, please?'

'That's right. So much to do. Dress fitting, what flowers to choose,' said Mum. She was beaming over her chicken. 'I'm so chuffed that you're with me for the rest of the week.'

'This wedding's going to be perfecto,' said Ken.

'What about the prediction of doom and gloom from that eccentric friend of yours?' said Una.

'Eccentric?' said Ken.

'I think she means Cassie,' said Anton.

'Cassie loves winding people up with her visions,' said Mum. 'Although we did get our own back a bit at that Halloween party, when she said she saw dark things in the offing just before a load of fireworks went off.'

'Perhaps we did go a bit far making fun of her, and Harry was too harsh on her,' said Ken. 'I know he was a stickler for the rules, but I should have stood up for her a bit more.'

'You're too soft on her,' said Mum. 'She's been muttering stuff about the wedding as well. If I hear anything, I'll be giving her an earful.'

'It'll be fine, love,' said Ken. 'She can't think anything bad's going to happen at the wedding – she accepted the invite.'

'Yes, and I can imagine what sort of present we'll be getting,' said Mum. 'It'll be something knitted. A woolly plant pot or a mohair Nespresso machine cover.'

It was out of character for Mum to bad-mouth someone like this. As she had said, Cassie's forecasts were winding her up. Coming back this week had been the right decision.

'The wedding will all go fine. She must need some Mr Sheen on her crystal ball or something,' said Ken, chuckling at his own joke.

At the end of the meal, Ken settled the bill, serving up his silver credit card with a swagger.

'Let me know about the photos.' Anton leant across to whisper to Una. 'Looking forward to starting work on our film.'

Una nodded. 'I'll get on the case.'

'Nice to meet you both today,' he said, straightening up but still mumbling through his beard.

'And you,' replied Mum, wrestling with the zip on her coat.

'Hope we'll be seeing you at the stag do, Una, if not before,' said Ken.

'That reminds me,' said Mum, 'I need to see how Jean is doing on sorting out my hen do.'

'Make sure you don't get a stripper,' said Ken.

'We won't.'

'Get two,' he chuckled. 'Anyone having these mints?' he added, sweeping the mints off the receipt and into the pocket of his slate-grey blouson leather jacket in one continuous movement. Mints contaminated with urine, dust and potentially harmful bacteria.

'All yours,' said Una.

# 10

## *Skew-whiff Antimacassar*

'If you could leave your shoes on the rack. We had new carpet put down in the living room last October.'

Una wriggled out of her trainers and felt thankful she was wearing her non-slip socks in order to gain sufficient grip on the laminate flooring in the hall. She followed Jean through to the lounge. The room smelt of vanilla and she suspected a scented candle was lurking somewhere, spewing out the sickly-sweet aroma. There was a row of objects on the mantelpiece above the imitation fire – she'd never seen so many snow globes before and she went over to look closer.

'We recently went on an Antiquities of Egypt cruise,' said Jean. 'Have you been to Egypt?'

'No. Not yet.'

'Fabulous,' said Jean. 'Once in a lifetime.'

There was a snow globe containing the Pyramids of Giza at the end of the line.

'Would you like a cup of tea?' asked Jean.

'Yes please.'

'What sort?'

'Have you got English Breakfast? If not, any tea is fine, honestly.'

'I've got that, I've got the Twinings one. Sit yourself down. Milk?'

Una nodded and sat down on the two-seater velvet sofa, her back resting against the snout of a West Highland terrier embossed on a cushion. She noticed that an Extremely Difficult Sudoku had been started in the newspaper resting on the table. Jean returned a few minutes later and placed a mug of tea on a beaded coaster in front of her.

'How are you enjoying it here?' she asked. 'It's very different from London. You've got everything there. *The Lion King. Phantom.* Everything.'

Una was not the best at chit-chat, and chit-chat about popular West End musicals had emerged as yet another gap in her conversational arsenal. This plan to interview the bingo crowd was a mistake. She felt completely out of her comfort zone.

'I'm not really into musicals, so it's not that much of a plus. Anyhow, I arrived back yesterday and thought I'd pop round since you replied so quickly. Thank you. I'm looking to create a photo montage of people Mum and Ken know, to play during the wedding meal. Anton's going to help put it together. I wondered if you had any special photos of them or of all of you together that we could use?'

'Yes, of course,' said Jean. 'I've started to root some out, although our most recent ones are on the cloud now.'

'Even better.'

Una blew on the tea as she considered how to turn the discussion to death. Jean was on tiptoe at the bookcase. She shimmied out a photo album and then came to sit beside her, her bony knee jabbing at Una's thigh.

'Here we go. John's seventieth, we had it at the Centre.' She pointed to a photo of a group of friends sitting at a table holding up their glasses. Una recognised many of the faces from the bingo night.

'And can you just run through who they all are?'

'Well, that's us, then Raj, Ken, Cassie, Eileen . . .'

'Eileen?'

'She's no longer here, I'm afraid.'

Una nodded to hide her guilt about having to question Jean. 'Of course, I heard about that. Was she a good friend? Should I include her picture as a gesture, or would it be inappropriate?'

Jean was silent for a moment. 'Why not,' she said eventually. 'I think that would be appreciated after all that's happened recently.'

'And what was she like?'

This was it – Una was hoping to hear that Eileen had been a thrill-seeker whose devil-may-care attitude culminated in her reckless need for a precarious hanging basket.

'Eileen? Well, we were at school together. She was always smartly turned out, lovely handwriting. But she was in the habit of putting in apostrophes where they had no business being, no matter how many times I corrected her.'

'Why's that important?' asked Una. 'You can just run things through a grammar checker. No one needs to actually know the rules any more.'

Creating order was good, but best done with numbers rather than words.

'Do you mean one of those computerised things? Don't mention those to me. Grammar indicates a tidy mind, a

84

disciplined mind. I abhor sloppiness. I mean, if people can't take the time to punctuate correctly, then . . . then perhaps they deserve what's coming to them.' Jean straightened the square coaster under her cup until it tessellated snugly with the corner of the table.

The front door opened and shut, followed by the sound of feet frantically scuffling back and forth on the doormat, and John appeared in the room. He was tall and imposing, especially as he was wearing an outsize khaki rain poncho. It gave him the look of a retired superhero.

'Hello, ladies,' he said. He crossed the room, his hand outstretched. 'And you must be the Una everyone is talking about. Sheila's daughter – down for the week, right?'

'Where've you been?' asked Jean. 'You're back much later than you said.'

'I . . . Well . . . there was a huge queue at the cash machine,' said John.

'You've been very unreliable this last week,' said Jean, standing and heading towards the kitchen. 'I'll get you a cup of tea. Una wants to do a montage at Ken and Sheila's wedding. She's asked us for some photos.'

'A montage? Is that what they do in London now for weddings?' asked John.

'Anton and I just thought it would add something personal,' said Una.

John removed his poncho and folded it into itself until it formed a tiny purse. Then he sat in the armchair with his fingers steepled and lightly touching. Chit-chat time again.

'Who's the Sudoku fan?' she asked, pointing towards the paper. She knew that ex-maths teacher John was the prime candidate. But her Unconscious Bias training at work must have kicked in.

'Guilty as charged,' said John. 'I bet you must be good at them. I've heard you're a fellow maths bod.'

'I like number puzzles, but I'm not that into Sudoku.'

'I also hear you're into birding; Ken said. You should join Raj and myself while you're here. We go out quite often, up on the cliffs.'

Finally, an opportunity to meet Raj, who was the only person who hadn't replied to Anton's message. On the other hand, there were risks. She knew nothing about birds, and she didn't like the idea of walking along a cliff; a cliff that plummeted down to jagged rocks that sliced human flesh like butter.

'Sounds good,' she said.

'Why don't you join us on our trip on Tuesday morning? I'll send you the details. And Ken says you might be coming to the stag do.'

'Might do.'

'I'm seeing him on Thursday, but I won't mention the montage,' said John, tapping his nose.

'Thursday? The first? What are you doing with Ken then?'

'Not sure,' said John. 'He said to keep the morning free. Why?'

'No reason.'

Una didn't want to alarm John, but hanging round Ken on the first of the month was a high-risk strategy. She couldn't work out how to tell him to avoid the trip to the DIY store that she'd discovered during her phone snooping.

Jean returned with John's tea and then continued to go through the photo album.

'I think these two will be ideal, as they have all of us in. The seventieth one I showed you before, and then a more recent one from a dinner to celebrate our Tony's engagement. You can see all the usual suspects in this one, including Sheila.'

Indeed, the picture did have all the people Una was interested in, sitting round a table – Ken holding Tommo's head in a vice-like grip for fun, Eileen's face poking out of a chunky jumper, Jean and John leaning forward like photosynthesising plants seeking a light source. Next along was Mum, sitting next to Raj, who was holding his chopsticks with expertise, while the final person, at the back, was reading a spy novel and not looking at the camera, their face obscured by the book.

'Who's that?' said Una, pointing.

'That's Harry. He's no longer with us,' said Jean.

'Of course. Sorry. And what was he like?'

Excellent, Una thought, finally some information on the elusive Harry.

'As you can see, always had his head in a book,' said Jean. 'Usually quite commercial books, page-turners, although we were a very broad church at the book club until . . . Well, I mean, of course I don't want to speak ill of him. Or Eileen. And Raj egged them on, quite frankly.'

'What happened?' said Una, desperately plundering her mind for book club risks.

'He got on famously with Ken,' said John, suddenly darting forward in the armchair. 'They were always off to the pub together.'

'And did Harry know Eileen?'

'Well, of course. They could have continued to meet at the book club, but hey ho,' said Jean. 'Apart from that, I don't think he ever went to the bingo nights, whereas she was an aficionado. Why do you ask?'

Una sipped her tea. If it wasn't the bingo that connected Harry and Eileen, perhaps the book club fallout needed more investigation. She didn't feel she was going to get any more out of Jean on that topic, but she had plenty of other interviews coming up.

'Was he grammatically correct?' she asked.

'Good question. He had a fantastic grasp of plurals and semi-colons,' Jean said. 'But he was slapdash about the Oxford comma and missed out the full stops in Latin abbreviations, for example e.g. It makes me angry just—'

'I must get a new light bulb for the recess where the dishwasher is situated,' said John, giving a cough like a punctuation mark. 'I can't remember whether it's a bayonet or screw fitting.'

'Screw,' said Jean, tweaking a skew-whiff antimacassar into position.

There was a pause. Normally Una liked quiet times during a conversation, as she could focus on something more useful, but she detected that this was a 'go away' kind of pause.

'I'd better make tracks,' she said, aware that she was now starting to sound like one of the bingo crowd. 'I'm meeting Mum for lunch. I'll just take a couple of photos of the photos so you can keep the originals safe.'

She took out her phone and quickly checked for mail, out of nervous habit. Cassie had replied on Facebook to say she'd be free tomorrow afternoon. That would be interesting – two professional prediction-makers meeting face to face. She carefully captured Jean's photos on her phone, then got up to leave.

'Thanks for popping round,' said Jean.

'I'll give you a call,' said John, 'when we go to the cliffs next. Make sure you wear stout boots. Especially if it's a windy day; you'll need a good grip.'

Una nodded and headed to the front door. As she reached for the latch, she felt a tap on her shoulder, and turned to find Jean's face very close to her own. Jean's eyes were laser-focused; her breath smelt of plain digestive.

'And please tell Ken that if anything happens to my John at that stag do, I'll have his guts for garters.'

That would definitely be an unusual way to go.

# 11

## Bubbles, Bubbles, Toile and Troubles

Una rarely wore dresses. She never wore pastel colours. But she had to accept that for two, possibly three hours on 1 March, she would be wearing a lavender dress with a peplum feature in front of a large group of people she barely knew.

The wedding dress shop was situated in a dead-end street off the main stretch, a street that had seen better days. One of the other shops in the row was closing down, according to neon posters in the window that said, *Everything Must Go*. But *did* everything have to go? Una's theory was that some things, some people, could go on for ever, if they were really, really careful.

Next door to that was an empty shop with clouded windows that displayed a council notice in print that was too small to read. But between that shop and a charity shop at the end of the row stood Bridal Dreams, and as an indicator of those dreams, three beige mannequins gestured in white lace wedding dresses in the window.

Una was still in a buoyant mood after completing her interview with Jean and John yesterday. She wasn't the deskbound insurance worker that Tim and the others had pigeonholed her as. She opened the shop door with gusto and a bell rang. A tall lady in her late fifties with pink hair, pink jeans and a silver sequinned top cooed like a pigeon with a barm cake as she walked towards her open-armed.

'Sheila, who is this lovely young lady who's entered my store?'

'This is my Una I was telling you about,' said Mum from somewhere further back in the shop.

'Una, love! Lovely to meet you. Your mum's told me all about you. Welcome to Bridal Dreams.'

'She works far too hard,' Mum said. 'But I've got her for a whole week!'

Una detected a hint of irritation in Mum's voice. Her investigations meant that she and Mum hadn't actually spent a huge amount of time together yet. She'd already had to come up with an excuse about going to an internet café for work to cover her trip to Jean.

'I'm Lilah. Glass of fizz, Una? We love our bubbles in here.'

Una took a seat next to Mum on one of the ornate sofas at the back of the shop and Lilah handed her a glass of Prosecco. The shop's perimeter was lined with frothing lace dresses.

'Shall we get started?' said Lilah. She came up close and gripped Una's jaw in her right hand, so that Una could feel the scrape of long blue acrylic nails on her face. 'Lavender isn't really your colour. You've got more Mediterranean looks.'

'Like her father,' said Mum with a smile-nod.

Una couldn't meet her eye.

91

'Hmm,' said Lilah. 'Would you consider a contrast colour, Sheila?'

'I'm under orders from Ken to stick to the colour scheme he wanted, and also we've sent the swatches to Chrissie.'

This was a good point. At least Ken's daughter would have to endure wearing one of these awful dresses as well. A public humiliation shared is a public humiliation halved, as the saying went. And now that she'd met Anton and found him to be so unlike Ken, perhaps Chrissie would turn out to be bearable too.

'Let's get you into your dress then and see what alterations we might need to make,' said Lilah.

She ushered Una into a corner of the shop, where a curtain on a rail struggled to create a private changing room. Thrusting the lavender dress at her, she swung the curtain across. Una shrugged out of her clothes and wriggled into the dress, desperately avoiding knocking into the curtain, the only thing concealing her from the brightly lit shop window beyond.

There was a loud clump as a pair of strappy silver shoes were dropped underneath it. They were slightly too small, and she attempted to create the least painful arrangement of her foot flesh. A toe loop at the top was trying to separate her big toe from the next one along.

'Try those on,' said Lilah through the curtain at her. 'They're like slippers, you can wear them all day.'

Finally Una stepped out. There was no mirror in sight – Mum and Lilah were to be it.

'You know,' said Mum, 'it looks better than I thought. Not bad at all.'

'Perhaps a necklace will break it up,' said Lilah. 'Or a scarf.'

Una flinched as Lilah came towards her with a purple pashmina fashioned into a lasso.

'It's that neck we need to sort out,' she said.

As she watched the reflection of Lilah in the shop window approaching her with the monstrous purple scarf, Una was distracted by someone walking past outside. That was all she needed, more of an audience. She could see the figure waving at someone further down the street. But then he looked in, saw her and walked briskly on. She recognised the shock of grey hair and the poncho; what was John doing down this alley? The only other place to go was the charity shop at the end. He'd already scuttled away. She was due to go birdwatching with him and Raj tomorrow; she'd add that to her list of questions.

She stood still as the scarf was draped around her in various configurations. After five minutes, Lilah removed it.

'You know, she looks better without it,' she said. 'I must have just got used to it.'

Suddenly the bell went and they all looked towards the door. Under the shop lights, the doorway framed Ken like some biblical figure forming a bridge between the earthly and celestial worlds, only somewhat marred by the large *Choose Ken* message on the T-shirt that protruded from his suit of double denim.

'Hey, I've got all the guys with me,' he said, looking back over his shoulder. 'Guys, come in!'

Una froze.

'Only joking. You look great, Una. Let's get you ladies home.'

'You took your time,' said Mum.

'Busy on something,' said Ken, waving his hand vaguely as he moved forward to greet them all.

Una rocked back and forth in the silver kitten heels she'd be wearing at the wedding. How long would she be able to stand them before her big toes dropped off? Then she noticed a long brown hair that stood out against Ken's white T-shirt. It annoyed her, and she instinctively plucked it off and dropped it onto the floor.

'Were you visiting someone?' she asked. It had just occurred to her that the hair might be Rosa's and she'd got rid of the evidence.

'Just a few more errands for the wedding, that's all.'

Another of Ken's mysterious errands.

'I wondered if you had a lot to organise for the stag do,' said Una. 'If you need any last-minute help, I'm free on Thursday.'

'You're all right there, thanks. Tommo is sorting it all out. And I'm going to spend Thursday at DIY City, getting in some bits and pieces to start on the changes to your mum's place,' said Ken, beaming. 'Unless you want to help us get some shelving.'

'DIY City?' she said. 'I'll have a think about it.'

She went back to the changing room to absorb this news. She'd need to do a risk assessment of the DIY store. But at least she could now track Ken on Thursday and find out whether he was the fatal number-setter.

When she re-emerged, Ken was trying on various wedding hats to amuse Mum and Lilah. They all left the shop together, and Una fell back and looked at the charity shop

94

next door. It was called Age Against the Machine, and was a charity that raised funds for older people, which meant it was a direct rival to Tread Softly.

So why had John been waving at someone in there and putting himself in danger of Jean's wrath?

# 12

## *Risk It for a Biscuit*

Cassie lived in a low-rise local-authority block in the centre of town, near to the high street. Her flat was two floors up and Una hurled herself up the stairs and walked along the balcony. Most of the neighbouring flats had been personalised in some way – one with a white plastic patio set, one with a giant palm plant that curved over the door. She could hear the sound of chatter from the residents on the corridor below.

Back in Balham, Una avoided talking to any of her neighbours. If she was about to leave her flat and heard someone in the communal corridor, she'd linger inside until they were out of the way. It was a dutiful mix of social anxiety and politeness that meant she had absolutely no idea who she was living next to.

When she got to Flat 35, an undercurrent of daytime TV rippled through the front door. She rapped the knocker. Second day of interviews. She wondered if Pedro would be lurking behind the door, ready to pounce. She'd managed to stick some shin pads under her jeans in preparation.

After a few seconds, the sound of television disappeared and she heard a shuffling sound. Cassie opened the door wearing a purple velveteen gown with tiny round mirrors sewn into it. Una scanned the hall: no sign of Pedro.

'Hi, Cassie. Just popping by to see you about the photos.'

Cassie's thin voice drifted towards her. 'I've been expecting you.'

Una had anticipated that she'd say something like that. It was a shame that someone who claimed to predict the future could be so predictable themselves. But she had to focus on her goal – how did Cassie fit into the pensioner death nexus? And how had she conjured those uncanny visions about the future?

She followed Cassie into her lounge.

'Cup of tea?' said Cassie.

Una wasn't going to fall into that trap. Tea leaves could provide an opportunity for Cassie's necromancy.

'I'd prefer coffee, if you have any.'

'Yes,' Cassie said. 'But it's the instant stuff.'

'That's fine, thanks.' Una took in the lounge. It was filled with a blue leather two-seater sofa and matching armchair that formed a pincer movement around a nest of tables. An astrological chart hovered over the mantelpiece. She flinched at the sound of smashing glass, but it was only the beaded curtain across the arch on the back wall that led into a small kitchen where Cassie was now filling the kettle. 'Where's your cat, by the way?'

'Pedro?' said Cassie mistily. 'Oh, he'll be out and about at this time.'

She came back with two mugs of coffee and some milk chocolate Hobnobs, which she set down next to a crystal ball.

'Biscuit?'

'Yes thanks,' said Una, shimmying one out of the packet. 'These are my favourites.'

'I sensed that about you,' said Cassie, nodding and easing herself back into the armchair. 'So, I expect you want to ask me some questions?'

Una had to be on her guard here and avoid any giveaway body language, so she put down the half-chomped Hobnob and sat upright with her arms by her sides, to achieve a neutral posture that would be difficult for Cassie to read.

'What makes you say that?' she said. 'I'm simply here to see if you have any photos you'd like to contribute for a video we're putting together for Ken and Mum's wedding – happy memories, special occasions, that sort of thing.'

She was really starting to nail this chit-chat business. Admittedly, it was chit-chat tailored to septuagenarians who faced imminent but interesting deaths in a seaside resort, but it was a start.

'Let's take a look,' said Cassie. 'Can you get to the dresser behind you?'

Una turned round, making an unpleasant squodge on the leather sofa, and found a pine cupboard with a glass door. A forlorn shepherdess ornament pleaded at her from the top of the cupboard; beside it was a slightly yellowed photo of a boy in school uniform with one of his front teeth missing.

'I've got my photo album in there,' said Cassie. 'Bottom drawer if you can reach.'

Una could feel unusual muscles pulling as she made the difficult twist to reach into the drawer. She started to feel around with her hand for something square with a lightly padded cover, and there it was, just behind a spiky object that jammed into her thumb.

'Ouch!'

'Watch out for the needles, by the way,' said Cassie.

'Needles?' Una hated needles. Blood tests, injections were challenging for her. Her fingers retracted into her palm, adopting a sort of foetal position.

'Only for my knitting,' said Cassie, smiling and snapping a Hobnob in two.

Una carefully extracted the photo album and handed it to Cassie, who placed it on the nest of tables between them. They both leant forward as Cassie flipped over the pages. The section at the start was filled with black and white photographs.

'Here's one of us as kids – Jean, Eileen, me, and of course, Ken.'

Jean was very neat, with her white socks pulled up to the same height. Eileen was wearing some kind of headband and Cassie was frowning at the camera. Ken, at the centre of the group, had a shiny black quiff that caught the sunlight, and his shirt collar was turned up.

'Ken was always an attention-seeker,' said Cassie. 'He was the football captain at his school. Even here you can see he's going to turn into a bit of a heartbreaker.'

'Really?'

Cassie stayed silent and continued to gaze at the photo.

'And Jean and Eileen, what were they like?'

'Jean thought she knew better than everyone else, used to correct the teacher if she got the opportunity. Eileen was a bit of a swot, top in history, geography and maths, a rule-follower. I was pretty good at maths myself, I liked the problem-solving, but no one encouraged me, it wasn't seen as a girls' subject.'

'That's a shame,' said Una. This was exactly the sort of thing she could share with the Women in Statistics chatroom.

Cassie skimmed forward in time through the album before smiling and stopping at another photo.

'This was when my son, Kevin, was over from Auckland and we all went for dinner. There's Jean and John, Ken with Diane, his first wife.'

Una wasn't sure that Mum would like a photo with Ken's first wife in it at the wedding, but she had a good look at Diane, who looked exactly like Anton but with a perm and no beard.

'Does your son still live in Auckland?' He could be a useful data point to question if he was local.

'Yes.' Cassie sighed. 'You're lucky you're just a train ride away from your mum. I'd love to see Kevin, but I don't have much in the way of savings and he's been out of work for a while. It's not the same over a video chat.'

Una felt uncomfortable about this diversion into Cassie's family problems. She had to redirect the conversation back to the here and now.

'Have you got any with my mum in?' she asked.

Cassie flicked through the book again. 'Here's a fairly recent one I took at Dino's.'

Ken was at the centre, working his angles in the spotlight, with Mum beaming next to him.

'Yes, I'll use all of them, if that's okay?' Una pulled out her phone to take pictures of them.

'Now,' said Cassie, piercing her with an all-knowing stare. 'Anything else you wanted to bring up? I predicted you would want to ask questions.'

Una considered telling her that predictions were made by analysing past data; what she was doing was guessing. But she kept her tone level as she said, 'I'm curious about these strange deaths – Harry and then Eileen. I just want to make sure that Mum's safe. It seems to be a bit of a dangerous area for her to live in.'

Cassie gave a dainty shrug. 'I did tell everyone that there was trouble coming, but no one listened. Perhaps there are scores being settled that are coming from a higher power.'

Or perhaps, as Tim had proposed, an additional risk factor would fix Una's errant insurance model. But that didn't explain the numbers, the black and gold numbers.

'You talked about Eileen, but what about Harry?'

'Didn't know him that well, thank goodness. Typical Leo. Had to be in charge of things, throwing his weight around. Was very rude to me last year but,' Cassie inhaled and exhaled deeply, 'I've let that go. He used to go to the book club until he did something to split it up.'

'Jean's book club?'

'Yes. I mean, she could pick a fight in an empty room when it comes to books. It was like that at school. She used to bully the boys who read comics, telling them to read proper books instead.'

'But what happened at the book club?'

'I've no idea, wasn't there that night. It wouldn't take much to make Jean fly off the handle.'

This was in line with what Una had seen of Jean's fanatical grammar adherence. She put her mug down.

'So nothing odd happened concerning Harry before he died?'

'He was too busy going on about the new fancy Velux he'd had put in to take notice of my advice.'

Una had very little time for Cassie and her predictions, but she could see that if they had one thing in common, it was that they were both fighting a battle against those who doubted their predictive powers.

Time to try a different way in. 'At the bingo night, you said that you had seen dangerous events in the future,' said Una. 'As a fellow predictor, I'd be interested in knowing more about that.'

'Thank you, dear, that's appreciated,' said Cassie.

'So, do you know who's next?' said Una. 'To have an accident?'

'I can only repeat what I said before,' said Cassie, tucking in the loose wrapper on the Hobnobs.

Una's patience was wearing thin. 'A jagged, monstrous claw and garden furniture.'

'Well remembered. Shame other people aren't as conscientious.'

'Perhaps there is something I can do to stop it happening.'

Cassie closed the album and leant back in her chair. 'I don't think so. But feel free to confide in me. I can see there's a pattern here and I think you can too. '

'I want to do something about it,' said Una, 'but the thing is, I'm worried something will happen to me too.'

'I'll try to help you if I can. I could try doing a reading.'

'I thought you'd given that up?'

'It's been difficult,' said Cassie. 'Work dried up at the pier, so I tried to embrace the latest technology. I started doing readings online, asking people to place their palms on their iPad screens and what have you. But I couldn't do it like that; how can you connect with someone's soul through an iPad? Recently, though, I've started getting visions again and they're coming true. In time, people will have to take what I've got to say seriously.'

Una didn't believe in this gift Cassie spoke about, but she knew what it was like to start to doubt your own abilities and wanted to give her some encouragement.

'Maybe,' she said.

Cassie moved forward and took Una's right hand, bringing her face close to it so that Una could feel her breath on her palm.

'Here's what I can see. You are not safe in Eastbourne,' she said with certainty, but then she frowned. 'And wait, I see something else. Don't go into the graveyard. There are dark forces there.'

Very sensible advice that Una would absolutely be following but for her own reasons. She decided to push further. Her investigation could be making her into a target, and Cassie was in a similar position.

'What about yourself?' she said. 'Aren't you worried that you're putting yourself in danger by publicly declaring these gloomy predictions?'

Cassie drew back and then looked at Una directly. 'I'll be okay, but thank you for asking. The only thing I need to watch out for is a vision I often have that the entire town will fall on top of me. But that doesn't make any sense, does it? How could that happen?' She seemed to be questioning herself rather than Una. Just as well, as it sounded like complete nonsense.

She stared into the imitation log fire that flickered half-heartedly in front of them. It was time for Una to leave.

'Thanks for the biscuits and the photos, Cassie,' she said. 'I'm going to head off now.'

Cassie started pressing on the arms of the armchair to hoist herself up.

'No, don't get up,' said Una. 'I'll let myself out.'

She took the mugs into the kitchen, setting off the beaded glass curtain, and rinsed them out. She noticed that there was a pile of Kitty Treats sachets stacked in the corner, an unwelcome reminder of Pedro. When she went back into the lounge, Cassie had reseated herself and was reaching behind the sole velveteen cushion on her armchair to bring out a piece of knitting.

'Just getting on with the wedding present. But it's a secret.' She raised her finger to her lips.

Mum was right after all about Cassie's woollen wedding gift.

'Are you following a pattern?' asked Una.

'Of course. Everything has a pattern,' said Cassie, focusing on the needles moving like a tiny factory at her fingertips, 'but not everyone can see it.'

# 13

## *Graphite Club*

The next morning was sunny and the sky was clear of cloud. Perfect birding weather, Una speculated. She put on her sturdiest trainers and got the bus to Beachy Head, arriving at 10 a.m. on the dot. Raj was already standing by the path up to the cliffs. He was wearing a technical jacket in the sort of colour that would increase the probability of that jacket being part of a technical jacket sale in a mountain equipment superstore in an out-of-town retail park. On his feet were a pair of overly functional walking boots – adequate for trekking to the South Pole, more than adequate for bird-spotting in Sussex.

'A pleasure to meet you,' he said. 'I've heard a lot about you. Shall we make a start?'

'Aren't we waiting for John?' said Una. She wanted to ask him why he'd been outside the wedding shop yesterday.

'Got a text earlier. He said something had come up last minute. Very unlike him. He's normally a punctilious sort of person. Never mind, I'm sure you'll do as a substitute.'

They started up the short path to the top. The visitor centre was the only building for miles, and as they went up the slope, there was just grass, sky and then the sea appeared. Most of the clumps of tourists and walkers around them wore headphones, and it was almost silent. Occasionally an aeroplane tore through the sky or the sounds of people on the beach below carried upwards.

'So it won't be all seagulls up here then?' asked Una.

Raj puffed up with irritation. 'No! That is a total misconception about the avian variety that Eastbourne offers to the birder.'

She decided not to ask any more bird questions in case Raj uncovered her lack of knowledge – if in doubt, she could ask her most reliable friend, Google.

'So, Raj, how long have you known all the crowd I met at the bingo game? Did you meet them through Ken?'

'Absolutely not. I was a regular attendee at a book club that Jean set up. It was a great place for me to meet people after my divorce, got me out of the house. And even though the book group ended as it did, we all kept in touch. I mean, I don't have a lot in common with some of them, but they mean well and have even helped me out on a few occasions. Ken did a good job on those shelves I wanted in my eaves. Somewhere to display my first editions.'

'Ken put up your shelves? Is he short of money?'

'Goodness, no! He charged me "mate's rates", as he put it. Yes, he's definitely, shall we say, solvent.'

Una wanted to extract more from Raj on this topic but couldn't see a way to continue.

'It's a shame the book club ended,' she said instead. 'Did you run out of ideas for books or something?'

'There was a disagreement about the vision and future direction of the group, and after that, there was no going back.'

'But what was the—'

'Lapwing at two o'clock.'

A brown bird was hopping by a bush in the direction that Raj was pointing.

'A female, with drab plumage as you'd expect,' he said.

Una found it difficult to imagine that the female lapwing saw Raj as an enticing mate in his equally drab get-up.

Raj swung his binoculars round and stood swaying slightly as he observed the bird. She also focused her binoculars as best she could on the creature, trying to keep it in shot as it pranced around. It seemed to expend a lot of energy for no purpose.

'Good that you've kept in contact with them,' she said.

'Yes, we do try to keep in touch, keep each other going.'

'I heard there've been some difficult times recently, after Harry and Eileen passed away.'

Raj stopped looking through his binoculars and held them with reverence. 'Both former patients of mine. Given the mix of medication that Eileen rather ostentatiously took each day, and the various organs that Harry had had replaced or zapped, it was surprising to see them go from non-natural causes.'

'Surprising?'

'Yes, I mean they were hardly the sorts of death I'm used to seeing, but there you are, one never knows when The End will come.'

'You don't know,' said Una, 'but you can predict it with a fair degree of accuracy.'

'But you never know for yourself. That's why you should live life to the fullest, take risks, enjoy the pleasures of life,' he said, taking out a Mars bar from one of the many pockets in his jacket and a Swiss Army penknife from another.

'Slice of Mars bar? Keep you going,' he said.

She took a slice and they chewed in silence. Another birder waved over at Raj, a lady with a solid helmet of gold hair who was wearing a cherry-red cagoule. She was smiling and shaking a tartan flask at him.

'Anthea,' he said. 'Pleasant enough, and keen, but she startles the starlings with her garish plumage and is always after a chat. It's not a social club. Let's get further up before she comes over and forces her sugary supermarket-own-brand tea on us.'

They continued on, Raj pointing out various birds along the way – a few seagulls, a fulmar and two crows. Even when he saw yet another gull flitting about, he swung his binoculars up to take a look.

As they approached the edge of the cliff, he paused, then turned abruptly to face her. 'So let's cut to the chase, Una. There's something you wanted to ask me.'

'Was there? Yes, about the wedding. I'm collecting photos for a montage I'm putting together with Anton, to play during the meal.'

'A montage? Isn't that a bit nineties?' said Raj.

'Maybe it is,' said Una, 'but do you have any group pictures you'd like to contribute? Or any stories you'd like putting up?'

'Not a big fan of weddings, to be honest,' he said. 'I'll show my face, of course, but I no longer feel cheered by that institution. I'll have a look for some. JPEG okay?'

'Thanks, yes, any format will do. I'm not a fan myself either. Of weddings, that is. I still have to think of something to get them as a present as well. I've no idea what to give them. They both have their own places full of stuff as it is.'

Raj put down his binoculars and lowered his head. 'Don't you feel they're a bit old to be getting married?' he said. 'Don't you find yourself mildly disgusted by it?'

They were now at the edge of the cliff. Seagulls hovered above, the vultures of the seaside, squawking at each other. No way would Una be removing her protective glasses today.

'I mean,' he continued, 'people nowadays still think of themselves as young at seventy, able to do what they want providing they shove loads of pills and medicine down their gullets each day. Even worse is someone like Tommo trusting in homeopathy. But they're taking funding from younger people; it's them we should be investing in, not the old ones.'

'But what would you do with them?' said Una. 'And perhaps they can still do stuff.'

'Yes, perhaps some of them can, but nothing truly productive that adds value to society. They're gradually dwindling physically and mentally.'

She stared at him. 'Wow, you're really ageist.'

'I'm a realist,' he said. 'Is it right that we support an ageing population with their expensive medical needs just to prop up a deteriorating quality of life? The population chart should be like a pyramid declining upwards not downwards.'

This last statement sounded vaguely familiar.

'Perhaps scientists will discover a way for people to stay younger and healthier for longer,' said Una. 'Death will be abolished.'

As she said this, she felt a terrible gaping feeling in her stomach, something she'd briefly and rarely experienced before. A vertiginous plummeting sensation like she imagined you would get from falling off the edge of the sort of cliff face they were now so close to. What was this feeling? All she knew was that she wanted science to keep her alive for ever; she didn't want to die.

'Scientists should be focused on ways to make young people healthier and save the planet,' said Raj, 'not on keeping some gasping old biddy in an electric wheelchair going so she can watch mindless television and dribble over a ready meal. It should be about quality of life, not quantity.'

'And who would judge what counted as sufficient quality?'

'Common sense,' he said.

'And what would happen if it was decided that you were no longer living a good enough life?'

'You should make a graceful exit rather than being assisted to simply keep going. That would be my way to deal with all these old people.'

Una could see a potential issue with Raj's viewpoint. 'But you're not exactly that young yourself,' she said. 'Does that mean you feel *you* should make a graceful exit?

As she said this, she glanced over at the edge of the cliff. It was very near; within a person-hurl away from her.

Raj turned towards her. His puce face clashed with his technical jacket. 'Me? I'm only sixty-eight and a half! I've got at least twenty good years left. My BMI, my blood pressure, my cholesterol level, my glucose level, my gut bacteria levels are all far superior to other people of my age. The sort of people who clutter up the pantry section at Waitrose.'

110

And then she remembered.

'Is it you leaving those messages about old people on the Tread Softly site?' she asked. As the words came out, she wished they'd stayed in thought format.

'What!' Raj stepped towards her with purpose.

In her peripheral vision, Una sensed a figure in the distance looking over at them with binoculars, just a silhouette darting behind a nearby gorse bush. Another birder, no doubt. If only she could alert them to her predicament. She sent her legs strong signals to move, but they ignored her commands and remained rooted in her trainers.

Raj was holding something in front of him. She was relieved to see that it was only a pencil rather than the Swiss Army knife, and yet there was something sinister about the way he brandished it. It was sharpened to a fine point, and his face was angry as he stealthily approached to within sketching distance. So close that the tip of the pencil was hovering over Una's anorak in the vicinity of her heart. His medical training would mean he'd have pinpoint precision in identifying her major organs.

Time had slowed down, which was irrational – one second lasted the same as another. She shuffled backwards, aware of the cliff edge nearing. Her heart was galloping somewhere near her neck. She was so close to the edge, a sudden stumble would be a disaster. The waves were crashing in jagged white lines on the rocks below. She was going to be pigeon fodder.

She felt a tap on her shoulder, and everything went black.

# 14

## *Second Opinion*

Una opened her eyes and saw the blue of the sky above. Am I dead? she wondered. Is this it?

A face appeared. The face of Neoliberal Tim. What was he doing in the afterlife?

'She's back,' he said.

Raj's face also came into shot. 'How many fingers am I holding up?' he asked.

'Does a thumb count as a finger?' said Una.

She felt a hand pushing into her back to bring her to a sitting position. It was Tim holding her up.

'You fainted,' said Raj. 'Have you been doing that often? Right near the edge, too. I'm shaking, look. You gave me quite a fright. And you, sir, should not have surprised her like that.'

'I thought she was too close to the edge,' said Tim. 'I don't like to call myself a hero, but I pulled her back for her own safety, no doubt saving her life.' He had stopped holding her upright and was now preening his hair.

'Nonsense,' said Raj. 'I know these cliffs very well. She had plenty of room there. She's too cautious – she's clearly not cut out for birdwatching. Disappointing, but to show

112

there's no hard feelings, let me order you a taxi to take you home.'

'I can take charge now, thanks,' said Tim. 'I'm the sixth-floor first-aid rep.'

Raj was unfazed by Tim's power play and held up one hand as a stop sign while he was on the phone. 'The taxi will be here in five minutes, by the bus stop,' he said. 'After all this fuss, I'm going to go and say a quick hello to Anthea. Send my regards to your mother.' He struck out across the clifftop.

'Tim,' said Una, quietly, 'what are you doing here? Sneaking up on me like that.'

'I was curious about what you were up to. You seemed so confident that something was going to happen here. So I told Ajay that I'd work from home today as I didn't have any meetings. And as for sneaking up on you, I was worried. You looked petrified.'

'I was. I froze.'

'Well, there you go,' said Tim. 'I had to act. Even if it brought considerable danger to myself. For a Tuesday.'

'But how did you know I'd be up here?'

'I simply scrutinised your social media feeds and I saw that Raj had tweeted about coming here with you this morning.'

'That's impressive if a bit unsettling. Anyhow, we need to talk. Let's go somewhere.'

Even though Tim had nearly shocked her into a cliff plunge, she was grateful that he'd saved her from her confrontation with Raj. The close shave had alerted her to the fact that she was putting herself in danger simply by asking so many questions. Perhaps an outsider like Tim could help her uncover who was behind these numbers – he had the right skills and knowledge, after all.

Raj, for instance, definitely warranted further investigation. He knew both Harry and Eileen and their medical histories. And he was clearly a bit sensitive on the subject of ageing – was he trying to reshape the demographic, one by one? So far, she'd placed all her suspicion on Ken, but here was one of his friends not exactly looking innocent.

She headed off in the taxi with Tim. She needed coffee, and lots of it, to calm her nerves. She looked up a café on her phone. KeenBeanz was a little way out from the main shopping area and would be unlikely to attract any of the suspects. Its two internet reviews were 'A bit quiet for my liking' from DinaDoors, who'd given it 3.5 stars on TripAdvisor; and 'Good if you like quiet' from Jedi42, who gave it 4.5 stars. Overall, these reviews suggested somewhere quiet and slightly unpopular – qualities Una admired in both people and independent cafés. She paid the taxi driver when they arrived at KeenBeanz to reassert her executive presence in front of Tim.

The café was empty apart from a woman rocking a pram in the middle and a man holding his head in his hands over a laptop as he perched on a high bench next to the front window. Tim chose a table at the back.

'Cappuccino, no chocolate on top,' said Una to the barista before calling over to Tim, 'I expect you'll want one too?'

'Thanks for saving my life, Tim,' said Tim. 'Yes, I'll have an espresso, please.'

She collected the coffees and sat down opposite him.

'If I say thank you,' she said, 'then you must never mention any of this at work.'

'Okay. I mean, I wouldn't anyway. I don't think it would look good for either of us, snooping around the seaside when we're supposed to just look at the data about it.'

'Thank you,' she said, very quietly and quickly. 'But now I have something serious to discuss. Numbers.'

Time to put aside promotion worries. She took Tim through her suspicions about the group she'd met at the bingo night and the data she'd collected on them, and showed him the photos of the numbers she'd found on the bins and at the supermarket.

'Only two numbers,' he said. 'Not exactly a series, is it.'

'But look, they're exactly the same type of sticker. It can't be a coincidence.'

'I'm not convinced, Una.'

'You'll be convinced on Thursday,' said Una, 'when the next one happens. I was thinking perhaps we could join forces and find out who's behind this – we might even save the next victim.'

Tim knocked back his espresso in one. 'Are you joking?'

'From the pattern so far, I think there'll be another unusual death on Thursday and some numbers placed nearby. And what's more, I'm worried that my mum's recently acquired fiancé is involved. I'm going to follow him round all day, and it would be better if you were there in case things get nasty.'

Tim raised his eyebrows. 'And what do you expect me to do if someone does carry out an attack?'

'We could stop them and save someone's life.'

'I repeat, are you joking?'

'I realise it's dangerous and you'll be taking a risk, but don't we have a duty to help?'

'I'm not concerned about the risk,' said Tim. 'Let me bullet-point why we shouldn't get involved. First, if we go round saving people from dying, we're effectively influencing the data in the mortality tables – that seems an ethically dubious thing to do, right? Plus, saving this whoever-it-is might make your model less wrong.'

'Oh, I see. So you're more worried about your ego than helping save a poor old person from prematurely dying in a dodgy accident.'

Tim shook his head. 'You're crossing a line, Una; you're starting to see them as human beings rather than data points.'

He was right. She'd lost her distance from the data. But didn't he understand? She had to find out who or what was the link between those numbers. What if her mum was next?

'I don't care what you think,' she said, 'I'm going to follow Ken on Thursday. I already know some of his schedule. It would be better if there was someone else there as well to help guard potential victims, someone who's good at assessing risks. But I guess I'll have to make do . . .'

Tim frowned at his empty espresso cup. 'I think you've become a bit paranoid,' he said. 'You're reading too much into things. Although I have to admit there does seem to be something odd about the pattern of deaths. I've been over them myself and it's certainly an outlier. But it could simply be a coincidence – the new risk factor adjustment that I'm working on should sort it out. These are two small anomalies within terabytes of mortality data. We're trained to handle anomalies.

Perhaps you need to step away. All this planning for your mum's wedding, maybe the stress of it is affecting you.'

She put down her coffee; Tim being thoughtful was unsettling.

'You could be right. But what about the numbers? Someone put them there for a reason. So do you want to help me solve the case?'

'I just don't think there *is* a case, as you put it,' he said. 'Look, I'll try to come along on Thursday – I can use it as cycle practice. If something does happen, I can make sure myself that nothing odd is going on and that the new proposal I'm working on for Ajay is solid.'

As Tim drained the last dregs of his espresso, the café door opened and Anton walked in carrying a copy of *Wired* magazine and a pack of neon highlighter pens. He spotted Una and froze.

'Una, what are you doing here?' he asked.

'Hi, Anton, just having a coffee and a chat with Tim. I don't believe you've met.'

'Hi there, I'm Tim. Colleague of Una's. Happened to be in the area and thought we'd catch up on some work stuff.'

'Hi, Tim. Anton. I'm, well, I'm a family friend.'

Tim performed his arm-wrestling-strength handshake on Anton, to assert his dominance.

'Was just looking for a quiet spot to read,' said Anton, waggling his hand. 'You know how it is.'

'We were just leaving,' said Una, wanting to avoid the cognitive dissonance of work and non-work people colliding. And Tim might mention her suspicions about Ken to Anton.

'I see. There was something I was going to ask you, Una,' said Anton, 'but I can do that some other time.'

'Oh, right,' said Una. 'Well, I can stay for a bit.'

'That's okay,' said Tim. 'I have to get back anyhow, got a nuclear yoga session booked. I'll see you on Monday.'

'See you, Tim,' she said. 'And thanks for helping me on that matter today.'

'Bye, Anton,' said Tim. 'Nice to meet you.' He gave Anton one of his polished intranet profile smiles and headed out.

'Are you okay?' asked Anton. 'You look a bit dazed.'

'Work's stressful at the moment, that's all,' Una said. 'Can I get you a coffee? I'm going to have another one.'

Anton put down the magazine and the pens. 'A latte, please,' he said, twirling his beard. 'No, a matcha latte.'

'Okay, I'll see if they can do that.'

'Actually,' he said, 'we could share a beetroot brownie. I couldn't manage a whole one.'

'Why not?' said Una. After surviving the cliff edge, perhaps she could afford to be indulgent and live a little.

'I'll pay,' he said, handing her his card. 'I've asked for the most expensive things.'

She returned with the coffees, cake and a knife. Anton hovered the knife over the centre of the brownie to cut it roughly in half.

'Let me,' said Una. She bisected the brownie diagonally and ushered half towards him. 'Much better chance of equal sizes with this method.'

'I was going to give you the bigger half anyway,' said Anton, 'but I appreciate the thought.'

Una suppressed her irritation with the concept of a 'bigger half'. 'So, what's up?' she said. 'I've made a good start on the photos.'

'That's great, but actually I wasn't going to hassle you on that. It's about something else. Dad's asked me to do a reading at the wedding, a poem he's selected. I hate speaking in front of people, but I couldn't say no. I wondered if I could read it out to you first.'

Una knew well the dread of public speaking. At a recent presentation she'd given to the global team, she'd got page fright and made the audience stare at a bar chart for two minutes while she'd collected her thoughts.

'Of course,' she said. 'I'm glad I don't have to speak at the wedding. It's a shame Tim's gone, he loves all that stuff. I'll ask him if he's got any links or articles he can forward on.'

'Yes, he looks like a textbook alpha male. So, this Tim, he's a friend of yours?'

'He's just a colleague who happened to be in the area. Total coincidence.'

'Came a long way to see you,' said Anton. 'Why would he be here about work stuff? In Eastbourne of all places?'

There was no way she could tell Anton that she was trying to find out whether Ken was a crazed serial killer, but that meant him thinking there was something going on between her and Tim. But why did it even matter to her what Anton thought? She'd open up to him about the suspicious numbers once she'd made sure that Ken wasn't the one placing them at each scene.

'People think working with statistics is a deskbound job,' she said, 'but you'd be surprised.'

# 15

## The Plumber with the Numbers

Una got off at the bus stop nearest Chamberlayne Road, the rain hitting her as she stepped out. She normally enjoyed a bit of rain, cleaning up the general surface of things, but this was a downpour, combined with a head-on wind, and her compact umbrella was struggling. At least her waterproof jacket was earning its 4.9 star rating and only her face was exposed to the elements.

She could feel her calves nagging as she strode into the wind. No one was out on the street; no sounds came from inside the houses. She glanced over her shoulder to check behind her. All quiet except for the wind harassing the flimsy trees and her. When she got to Eileen's house, she paused. The black and gold numbers were still on the bin.

She crossed the street and rang the buzzer for number 22. She was shaking out her umbrella when Tommo opened the front door to Arthur's house wearing paint-splattered blue overalls, his long mane of grey hair firmly tied back from his face.

'Hi, Una. Still raining, is it?'

Water dripped from her nose onto her top lip. 'Yes, that's right.'

'Let's get that coat off you, I'll hang it up to dry. Sorry to drag you out here. Could have done another day, like I said, or over Zoom. But an emergency call from Arthur, what can you do?'

Una attempted to mop up her face with her wet palm. 'No problem at all. I wanted to catch you before the weekend and I thought it was better to do it in person. It won't take long and it was only a short bus ride; well, it would have been if there were fewer stops.'

She handed him her jacket and shimmied out of her wet trainers, which she slotted into the plastic rack in the hallway next to two pairs of highly polished black lace-up shoes with threadbare soles.

Tommo was halfway up the stairs. 'Up here, leak from the bathroom sink.'

She followed him. The Anaglypta wallpaper was worn in places and the stair carpet was made from a nylon mix – she must avoid touching any metal objects. She stopped herself. This was the type of domestic criticism that she would hate if a stranger wandered around her flat.

The bathroom was windowless and dank. Tommo had taken the left tap off and wedged a towel around the base of the avocado sink. Una peered into the basin – she'd want to wash her hands again if she washed her hands in that.

'Where's Arthur?' she asked.

'Gone for some blood test that he didn't want to rebook. It's fine, he gave me a set of keys – easier without him hanging about for a small job like this. Don't know why he doesn't spend a bit of his cash to do it up, it's a decent-size bathroom.'

Una nodded, thinking of the tiny shower room in her own flat. 'Well, thanks for letting me pop round,' she said. 'As I mentioned, I'm putting together a set of photos to play at the wedding dinner as a surprise for Ken and Mum.'

'It's a smashing idea,' he said. 'I've dug some out for you.'

He handed her his phone and she flicked through the photos. Some new, some from the same events that she'd got from Jean and John but at a different angle. She copied them all – the more data the better.

'That's Eileen,' said Tommo, following her line of sight.

'Did you know her well?'

'Not that well, only through Ken. He knew her from when she was knee-high. Eileen was great, a bit on the cautious side, but her heart was in the right place. I helped out on a few jobs that needed doing round her house. I don't like looking at pictures of her. Not after what happened.'

'Oh yes,' Una said, 'the accident with the basket.'

Tommo's passive expression changed into a frown. 'Can't understand it. I'd put up that hanging basket only a couple of weeks before. How it came down I'll never know. I checked it myself, gave it a good wiggle. Anyhow.'

Una jolted. She was alone in this house with Tommo, who had put up the basket in Eileen's house over the road and maintained the supermarket trolleys at Trunnocks. No one knew she was here. But she wanted to complete the last of her interviews before the stake-out tomorrow; forewarned was forearmed.

'And what about Harry?' she asked. 'I've not got many photos of him yet and I'd like to include some. Any memorable occasions?'

122

'Again, he was more Ken's friend. Ken knows everyone. I met him out and about at different events – he liked a good laugh. I sorted out his washing machine for him last year, limescale. Just before I tried out that book club.'

'Book club? Wasn't there some big argument there?'

Tommo was focused on putting the tap back in place. 'I only went the once, not my cup of tea, and yes, there was a big row that I tried not to get involved in. Something about the book that Harry had chosen.'

So far this had been a waste of time. Dangerous or not, she needed to extract as much information as she could.

'Was he the sort of person to take risks at a local supermarket?'

Tommo looked up at her. 'He was a very level-headed man,' he said. 'But I don't think it's appropriate for you to be prying like this, Una. You could upset people asking these sorts of questions.'

She'd gone too far – what if they were all discussing her visits between themselves?

'Sorry, Tommo, it's because of my job. I'm always looking into the detail. I should be a bit more respectful.'

'You're in insurance, aren't you? I don't have any myself, I don't see the need. I mean, *que será será*.'

Una baulked at this provocative statement. 'What?' Her goal of remaining neutral was being tested. This was blasphemy.

'I mean,' he continued, 'you can never tell what the future will bring, right? You can try and control everything, but what's the point? Take Eileen, she couldn't have planned for whatever brought that basket down. Best to live your life. You only have one.'

It was because she only had one that Una decided to not get into an argument with him.

'The way I see it, you go when you go. Take Ken.' Tommo was on a roll now, pointing a spanner at her. 'He does his Pilates, he did a vegan cleanse month, but he's got family history, heart problems, had an op last year. He's already on plenty of medication. "Ken," I've said to him, "you can't change your fate." And yet there's people like me who've drunk and smoked all their life and I'm fit as a fiddle. Any problems, I seek out alternative therapies.'

Mum hadn't mentioned that Ken had health issues. Should she be marrying him if he was seriously ill? Una would have to find a good time to raise this with her before the wedding.

'I noticed that you were the bingo caller,' she continued. 'How did you get into that? Do you enjoy numbers? Any numbers in particular?'

'Well, it used to be Donny, but his eyesight started going and I said I'd pitch in. Jean stuck her oar in, said that it was time they had someone professional doing the numbers, and John piped up saying he'd been a maths teacher, but Ken, Harry and Eileen were all keen for me to have a go, so in the end he was outvoted. Put his nose out of joint, me beating a teacher. I don't even really care about the numbers themselves; I mean, it could be apples and oranges I'm pulling out.'

She was at a dead end. Tommo clearly didn't have a mania for sequences of numbers.

'I'd better head off, Tommo, let you get on. Thanks for the photos.'

'No problem. I'll see you at the stag do on Saturday, right? Eleven o'clock sharp at the rendezvous point.'

'Still not sure if I can make it,' she said. 'Are you planning anything . . . risky?'

'Well, it's a secret, so don't mention it to any of the others. But we're going quad biking.'

Una pondered quad biking's potential for risk. After a relatively short period of pondering, she came to the conclusion that its potential was rather high.

'Unfortunately, I'm not qualified to ride a quad bike,' she said. 'Besides, don't you need special insurance for that?'

'The centre where I've booked will sort all that out, and anyway, no point worrying,' said Tommo. 'As I said, when it's your time, it's your time. I'll just get your coat.'

Downstairs, he disappeared into a room and returned with her jacket, still damp. 'There you go. See you on Saturday? Go on, it'll be great fun. Let me dig out the address for you so you can check them out.' He took out his wallet and flicked through a stack of cards. Una noticed a scraggy ripped-out page of notepad peeping out from one of the pockets in the wallet, with its corner curled over. On the part that was visible were three numbers written in biro – 37, 41, 43.

The door buzzer went.

'More visitors,' said Tommo. 'I didn't realise Arthur was so popular.'

She had to find out about this scrap of paper before the new person arrived. It contained both Eileen's and Harry's numbers, and a new one.

'Tommo, I just wanted to ask about those numbers in your wallet.'

'What numbers?' said Tommo, opening the front door.

She pointed towards the half-hidden scrap of paper. 'These numbers . . .'

Ken's large head appeared around the door.

'Only me!'

# 16

## *A Smashing Time*

Ken flung open the door. He was carrying a wodge of parcels under his left arm. Not a speck of rain sullied his trench coat or his Dr Martens boots.

'Hi, Ken,' said Tommo.

Ken lifted his trilby to return the greeting. 'Una? What are you doing here?'

'I . . .' She scrambled around for something to say.

'She had some ideas about modernising the bingo calling process,' said Tommo, 'something related to her work, so she thought she'd go through that with me and then I ended up having to pop out here. Very interesting, thanks, Una, but it went a bit over my head, sorry.'

Una was underestimating Ken and his friends.

'I see,' said Ken. 'I think that's great. Let's not stick to the old ways; we should embrace the future. Anyways, sorry I interrupted, you were asking about some numbers?'

There was no way she could ask about them now. If that was the sequence, then Ken would know she was on to him. Perhaps he was in cahoots with Tommo – they'd worked together before, and she had no doubt that an experienced plumber could bring transferable skills to designing unusual deaths.

'It was nothing,' she said, putting her damp coat on, which made her colder rather than warmer. 'We were just talking about bingo, like Tommo said. I was about to leave.'

'I'll run you back,' said Ken. 'It's chilly out there. You don't want to catch a cold.'

Una wasn't looking forward to waiting at the bus stop in the rain, but she also knew that being out in the cold didn't give you a cold.

'That's fine, the bus stop is a short walk. You've come all the way to see your friend.'

Ken removed his trilby. 'Your mother would never let me hear the end of it. You're getting a lift. I was just dropping something off. You said you needed clear sealant, young Tommo – well, you're in luck. I can get some more tomorrow anyway.'

Tommo's face split with a smile. 'Brilliant. You're a star. I said to Arthur, you're unlucky getting a leak the day before I'm going to restock.' He tossed the can of sealant into the large canvas bag at the foot of the stairs.

'What's that?' asked Ken, pointing to a brown paper package peeping out of the bag. 'Someone sent a present?'

Tommo scrunched the parcel at its edges. 'Yeah, arrived just as I was leaving. No idea what it is. I haven't ordered anything. Hand-written address.'

Ken stretched, causing a cracking sound. 'Well, we'd better let you get on,' he said. 'Got much left to do?'

Tommo sighed. 'I've nearly sorted out the leak. Then I've got to load up the van with some stuff he wants taking to the tip.'

Ken rifled through the assortment of bric-a-brac at the end of the hall. Old suitcases, ornaments, stacks of paper

– receipts, bank statements, newspapers, and collapsed cardboard boxes. 'You could just load the whole house up. It's full of old tat.'

Tommo nodded. 'I can't even take much of this little lot in to Jean.'

'You might catch a medieval disease off it,' said Ken. 'Look at this monstrosity.' He wiggled a gold-framed landscape from out of a tall, thin crate. 'You can hardly see what it's of, it's so dingy, and are they wormholes? Andy Warhol prints all the way for me, thanks.'

'He wants to send that picture to some relative in the States, as a token,' said Tommo. 'No one here to hand stuff on to.'

'Lives on his own, doesn't have much family,' said Ken, picking up and discarding old copies of *Reader's Digest*. 'Guess that's why this place has gone to rack and ruin. Now then, this is pretty decent, if it had a bit of a polish.' He picked up another gold frame, this time a landscape of the Eastbourne coast.

'View of the cliffs,' said Tommo.

Given Una's recent experience at the cliff edge, it was the last thing she'd want to look at. Far preferable to have the murky one that couldn't provoke any chilling flashbacks.

'He'd be better sending this picture,' said Ken. 'More cheerful. No wormholes.'

'That's not your decision to make, Ken,' said Tommo, shaking his head.

'But he can't afford to lose what family he's got, right? Be doing him a favour.'

While Ken and Tommo were bickering about the picture, Una sneaked past them and peered into Arthur's living room. He wasn't part of the inner circle, but there might be some useful photos on display. She did a 360-degree turn round the room – no photos visible, but then she didn't have any in her own flat. She projected her own life forward in time and imagined her flat like Arthur's place, dark and damp and lonely. She quickly reversed it back to the present.

'Una, what you doing in there?' asked Ken from the doorway.

She scuttled backwards into the hall and kicked over a dusty floral vase, which teetered to right itself and then smashed on the tiled floor.

'Oh no!' she said. Her horror was tinged with the delight of finding a new worst-case scenario.

'Serves you right for nosing around,' said Ken. 'You're a bit like Arthur like that.'

Una gasped for breath. 'What shall I do? Will his third-party cover take care of this?'

Tommo shook his head. 'Valuable family heirloom, that was.' He lifted his hand to his mouth and snickered. 'It was going off to the tip anyway.'

'You've probably added value to the house by smashing it,' said Ken. 'As for you, Tommo, do you want a hand getting these into the van?'

'Don't be daft. Not with these biceps.'

'See you tomorrow morning, Popeye, bright and early,' said Ken.

'Looking forward to it, Bluto,' replied Tommo, saluting him.

Una got into Ken's teal Toyota Prius, which he'd parked outside Rosa's house. Perhaps he'd paid a visit before heading across to Arthur's?

130

She put her seat belt on automatically – it was protection in the event of a crash, but it made her vulnerable to a sudden attack by Ken. She ran through all the reasons why that wouldn't happen, and reassured herself that even if he was behind the deaths, the next one wasn't due until tomorrow.

He got in next to her and put Radio 2 on. He was panting like a worn-out spaniel.

She took out her emergency bottle of mineral water, unscrewed it and offered it to him. 'Have some of this,' she said.

Ken sipped at the water, making unnecessarily loud appreciative sounds throughout. 'Thanks,' he said, wiping his mouth on his leather jacket sleeve and handing the bottle back. 'That's just what I needed.'

'You can keep it, in case you need a bit more.'

'Got out of puff there,' he said. 'Shifting all those pictures about. Need to conserve my energy for the stag do.'

Or to do away with another of his peers, Una mused.

'If you're so tired,' she said, 'perhaps you should rest tomorrow instead of doing all this DIY business?'

'Oh, don't you worry, I'll rest when I get back. I love going to DIY City. It's like Aladdin's cave.'

'At least have a lie-in tomorrow.'

Ken was breathing more normally now. 'Thanks, Una, appreciate the concern, but I want to get there when it opens. Need some space to check everything out. Let's get going.' He started the car. 'You should get yourself a reusable water bottle instead of using plastic, you know. Think about the environment. I follow Greta on the

Twitter, but she hasn't followed me back yet. I guess she's busy.'

Una looked up DIY City on her phone to check the opening times. A one-stop shop of personal endangerment. An arsenal of unusual death causes openly stocked on shelves for the general public. She'd have to venture inside if she was going to keep tabs on Ken. Who knew what he'd use . . . strimmer, spade, superglue? She'd make one more effort to keep him from going there in the first place.

She put down the phone and turned towards him. 'You should be taking it easy. With the wedding coming up, I can't see why DIY is a priority over your health.'

Ken shrugged. 'I need to paint the main bedroom in my house, freshen it up to help it sell.' He was now bopping to 'Shake It Off', thumping the steering wheel to the beat. 'Good to spend a bit of one-on-one time like this, get to know each other. Go on, ask me anything!'

Una frowned. Right now, her only request was to arrive at Mum's flat in one piece. 'Thanks for the offer, but I don't want to distract you from your driving.'

'I'm curious,' said Ken. 'You seem to be a careful, cautious kind of person. Nothing wrong with that, especially in your line of work. But have you always been like that? You don't need to answer. I'll understand if you feel I'm crossing a line.'

What sort of chit-chat was this? Would it make sense for her to ask him at what point he'd become so 'Ken'? She held her tongue – if asked, he would probably have a long anecdote about his defining moment of Ken-ness.

She felt the G-force of a corner that he was taking at speed. Back on the straight, stomach settled, she attempted an answer. This wasn't a good time to upset Mum's husband-to-be/a potential serial killer/her designated driver.

'Well,' she said, 'I don't think there was any incident in particular. It's just that I was always aware that life was short and so I should avoid doing things that made it any shorter.'

This was terrible – she was spouting unverifiable statements about herself.

Ken nodded and turned the volume down on the stereo, 'You are so right! But for me, I see that as "make the most of now because you never know what tomorrow brings". Whoa! Look at this guy walking out in front of us. Unbelievable! Perhaps it was something that happened in your childhood. Losing someone in your family? A family friend?'

'No.'

He sighed. 'I remember Nanna dying as if it was yesterday. What about a pet?'

'No . . . Okay, there was a pet that I got upset about,' said Una, 'but correlation does not equal causation.'

'Gotcha,' said Ken. 'I'm being a nosy nelly. Anyways, I'm glad you're getting along with Anton. He's been a bit down in the dumps since his break-up, and every time he comes down here to visit, he ends up spending his time with us oldies. Good for him to have a friend his own age around. He said he was going to text you about something. Something you have to send him about Facebook or something.'

Una brightened. At the start of the week, the photos had simply been a means to getting access to the suspects, but now she was thawing towards the ridiculous wedding montage. 'That's right,' she said. 'You can let him know that I'll message him.'

Ken pulled up outside Morningview Mansions. 'Well, take care. See you Saturday, I hope, bright and early. Make sure you have a big breakfast to set yourself up, as we'll be having a few drinks.'

'Thanks for the lift,' Una said.

She waved at Ken as he headed off, then fished out her phone. As well as a scam text from a bank she'd never heard of, there were two texts from Anton:

*Gentle reminder – SEND PHOTOS AT ONCE!!*

*That was a* ☺ *btw.*

She'd now completed her mission to collect the photos from Ken and Mum's friends. She just had to email them over to Anton with some notes on when and where they were taken. Job done.

Except, she realised with a jolt, she didn't actually have any of her own family.

Back in the flat, she waited until Mum decided to pop out to Boots for toothpaste, and then took out some old albums, with cushioned covers and gold inlay. She opened one at random – *Bournemouth 1991*. On the first leaf was a photo of her, Mum and Dad at the beach. Its heightened tones and lack of sharpness dated it and made it more like a memory of the holiday. The objects on the beach were like impressions, and the sea was only distinguished from the sky by its shiny rough texture.

Dad was standing, hands on hips, wearing navy swimming trunks with a white cord at the waist. He had black hair and was thinner than she'd remembered. She was squatting at his feet, bottom almost touching the sand, guiding a yellow spade into a red bucket. A frilly sun hat had been placed on her head – already she was showing a flair for risk monitoring, by protecting herself from UV rays. She wasn't looking at the camera, but was focused on filling the bucket for a sandcastle.

She tried to connect herself with this tiny fat form, struggling to think of any distinct memories of the holiday. She remembered going to a fun fair and Dad winning a giant teddy bear for her, which burst on the journey home, its orange cubed sponge stuffing strewn around the boot. Mum was delighted that she could use the special attachment on the vacuum cleaner that helped justify going one-up to a more expensive model.

Una took out her phone to take a picture of the photo and looked at it onscreen. Dad must have been about the age she was now. Already a grown-up man with a family to support. Now that he was no longer here, Una resolved to be more grown-up herself and look after Mum.

When Mum returned thirty minutes later, Una had just finished putting all the photos together to send to Anton.

'You sit down,' she said, heading into the kitchen, 'I'll make you a hot drink.'

'Thanks,' Mum said. 'They had a three-for-two on cotton wool pads, so you can take one pack back with you.'

'Okay.' Una battered the tea bag with the back of a spoon to make sure it was a strong brew.

'Ken was on the WhatsApp. He said he bumped into you earlier.'

Una dreaded having to make up a story about going to see Tommo, and she focused on placing the tea on a coaster on the coffee table in front of Mum to buy some time.

'I'm glad you're making an effort with Ken,' Mum continued. 'I know it's a big change. It's a big change for me too.'

Una perched on the arm of the sofa next to her. 'I just want to make sure you're doing the right thing,' she said. 'That you're going to be safe. Now that ... I need to look out for you, that's all.'

'I appreciate that,' said Mum, leaning over to rest her head against Una's arm, 'but everything's going to work out fine. Hang on, have you been in the dresser?'

'Yes,' said Una. 'I was looking for something.'

'That's fine, just remember to close the drawer after you've been in it. Don't want you to trip over it.'

While Mum drank her tea, Una sent the photos off to Anton.

*PHOTOS ATTACHED AS REQUESTED! Montage required urgently lol.*

Yes, she'd be more grown-up and give Mum the support she deserved.

# 17

## *Hardware Nightmare*

By 9.15 the next day, Una was waiting in the queue for DIY City to open. She'd put her hood up, so that Ken and his friends wouldn't spot her before she'd had a chance to stake out the store and find a good vantage point. There were two others in the queue – in front of her was a short, stubby man wearing slack jeans and an even slacker leather jacket, and behind her was a man with a shaved head and a mythological creature tattooed on his arm. Neither had been in the bingo hall, but she knew there could be any sort of unknown connection at play behind the numbers: a kitchen extension that had caused a fracas, a leylandii grown too high – the accumulated triggers of daily life.

At 9.30, the assistant opened the doors and Una and the rest of the queue entered without incident. There was no sign of Ken or the others yet. She decided to walk the perimeter to get the measure of the store, noting the contents of each aisle, whose tall shelves dwarfed her. What a place! It seemed to contain the very things needed to make itself, through an act of building self-reproduction. Everything was a potential risk: nails, hammers, weedkiller. Many of the products were keen to stress that they were not suitable for eye proximity, but in font so small that her eyes had to be super close to find that out.

By 10 a.m., surveillance in a DIY superstore was losing its novelty. She headed to a patio set in the outdoor furniture section and slumped into a white plastic chair, where she could keep an eye on who was coming into the shop and wait for Tim to arrive. Almost immediately, she felt her body go tense and leapt up. Cassie's warning had mentioned garden furniture. She stepped away from the patio chair.

A few seconds later, she spotted Tommo striding into the foyer and rattling a metal shopping trolley free from its line, his grey ponytail swinging to and fro. He proceeded towards the small appliances section. Una wandered over to door hardware, which gave her a full view of both the entrance and Tommo, and picked up a gold-effect letter box to blend in.

Ken and John entered next and dawdled by the entrance before heading to the paint section. With no sign of Tim, she had to choose between keeping an eye on Tommo and tailing Ken and John. She chose Ken. He was about to marry Mum, after all, and she needed to be sure about him.

She hurried along the far wall, stopping at each aisle to check if it was Ken-free before continuing. Reaching the paint aisle, she slowly peered along it to find Ken and John standing with their backs to her. Ken was holding a small tin in his hand. John was leaning over, flipping through a colour chart hung up on the shelf. Una wanted to hear what they were saying, but she was too far away, so she decided to cut up the aisle next to them and try listening in from the other end.

During her diversion, she spotted some racks of stick-on numbers in gold and black on the bottom shelf of the aisle. They were just like the ones on Eileen's bin and at the supermarket. She noticed that someone had put a 4 on the rod that held the 5s. She had to fix that. She encouraged the 4 from its metal hook and wiggled it onto the front of the other 4s. Then she stood back and looked at them. Had someone put that 4 back in a rush? Perhaps someone who had come in to prepare for their next killing and in their haste had dislodged the numbers?

She continued to the end of the aisle and peeped around the edge.

'No, not magnolia,' said Ken, huffing at John. 'That's old hat. I want something like Farrow and Ball. But cheap.'

'Dawn Suggestion?' said John, pointing at the paint chart.

'Too pink.'

'Pelican Dreams?'

'Too grey.'

'They all just look like white paint to me,' said John.

'I've got a painterly eye,' said Ken. 'It's a blessing. And a curse.'

John straightened up and stretched. An uncomfortable cracking sound came out. 'I think I'm going to check out the light bulbs. I can't shilly-shally today, I'm afraid. Got some stuff planned for this afternoon.'

'You okay, John? Got a problem? You only have to say, I'm here for you.'

'I'm fine, Ken. Nothing I can't handle.'

'Well, see you in a bit,' said Ken. 'I won't be long.'

John wiggled his flat cap on his head and strode off, leaving Ken and Una an aisle apart. She was getting an ache in her calves and lower back from her static position, but she knew she needed to stay hidden. Ken put down the small tin of paint and selected a larger tin. He held it by its handle and started to swing it gently to and fro as if testing its weight. This could be a weapon – it was basically like a kettlebell, a piece of gym equipment that she'd studiously ignored, favouring a light resistance band.

There was too much at stake. She was going to have to disarm him, but how?

Ken had stopped swinging the tin and was nodding slowly. Una didn't like the look of that nod; he could be psyching himself up to act, to follow John and whack him with the tin. She needed to act before he did. Many scenarios played through her head: Ken chasing her, Ken throwing the can at her, Ken throwing the can at the shelves to cause an avalanche of paint tins to fall upon her – yes, that was more like it. But there wasn't time to plan a mitigation for each of these cases. Perhaps she could shock him into dropping the tin?

She inhaled deeply, her lungs expanding and pressing against her thumping heart, then jumped out.

'Boo!'

Ken turned round. He had gone very pale – not far off the colour of the paint in the tin he was still gripping tightly, Alaskan Bridal Suite. 'Una?' he gasped. He was panting now, slumping against the shelves.

Una was stumped. He didn't look in a fit state to chase anyone. And then she heard the scream. Ken glanced up at her, looking as confused as she felt.

140

It had come from the gardening implements and barbecues section. Una set off, aware that she was running towards danger without anywhere to hide. She should be running away from that hideous cry, not heading towards it as quickly as she could.

'Help!' she shouted, coming round the corner to the ornamental pots. 'Help, there's someone in danger.'

She stopped at the gnomes.

There at her feet was the body of a man in a green parka with a fur-trimmed hood, sprawled across a wall of grow-bags, a scythe sticking out of his back at a rakish angle. A Breville toaster, part of the 20 per cent off mid-season sale, lay abandoned just out of reach of his outflung right hand. She knelt down and checked for a pulse. But time and toasties had stopped for this customer.

'Help! Help!' Her voice was very faint, but she'd caught the attention of two of the staff, who were now running towards her.

One thing was undeniable – Tommo was dead.

# 18

# *Where is the Number?*

Una shuffled back from the body as the staff swooped in. A tickly chill ran down her spine. She'd spoken to Tommo only yesterday. That could have been her sprawled on the floor. She scrutinised the crowd – she'd just missed the killer. They were probably still here. Was that a blur of movement in the corner by the slug pellets?

She inhaled deeply, but the fumes of creosote and disinfectant failed to clear her confusion. She wouldn't have long to look for clues before the scene was closed off. The staff were already putting up a barrier around Tommo. A small crowd had formed at the scene, but their gentle murmuring couldn't hide the sound of trainers squelching as they pounded the concrete floor. She looked round; it was Tim.

'There you are. Where have you been?' she said.

Several store assistants stood in the cordoned-off area around the body. One of them had googled for health and safety advice on scythe accidents and was muttering it to the others. A manager gently threw a tarpaulin over Tommo.

'Is he . . . end of life?' asked Tim, catching his breath.

Una nodded and shuffled towards him. 'See, it happened, just as I said. Do you really think these are accidents?'

'Look, there's a metal toolbox on the floor over there,' said Tim, pointing over towards Tommo. 'He could have just tripped over it and fallen backwards onto that scythe, although I admit there is a small possibility of foul play.'

'Oh please,' said Una.

Sweat dripped from Tim's cycling helmet. 'Sorry I'm late, by the way. I got lost using the route on my phone. Looks like I missed all the action.'

'So did I,' said Una. 'I only came over after I'd heard him scream.'

'Who is he? Do you know him?

'It's a guy called Tommo. He's a friend of Ken's. He was supposed to be best man at the wedding.'

'Perhaps we need to factor "knowing Ken" into our life insurance models,' said Tim. Una nodded, stopping as she realised that category included her. 'And what about the numbers? What are they this time?'

'Ambulance is on its way,' said a voice over the tannoy. 'Can you all stay in the store in case the police want to speak with you. Please proceed to the kitchenware aisle in an orderly fashion and congregate there until further notice.'

Some of the assistants began ushering the crowd away from the scene.

'I didn't look,' said Una, kicking a nearby shelf and regretting it. 'I forgot. I'm in shock.'

'Oh no!' John had joined them. He was holding up a 60-watt light bulb in his right hand like a candle.

'Hi, John,' she said.

'What's happened?'

'There's been a bit of an accident,' said Tim. 'With a scythe.'

John looked at the tarpaulin in horror. 'Is that a body?'

'It's Tommo,' said Una. 'I'm afraid he's . . . you know . . .'

'He's reached his expiry date,' said Tim, solemnly removing his cycling helmet.

'No!' John clutched the light bulb tight, the colour draining from his face.

'Did you see anything?' said Una. 'Were you near him?'

He shook his head. 'No, I just heard someone saying "Help" over and over.'

'That was me.'

'Where's Ken?' asked John, fumbling for his mobile. 'Is he okay?'

She'd forgotten about Ken. Ken was annoying, Ken made furtive trips to Chamberlayne Road. But Una had to admit it didn't seem possible that he could have caused Tommo's death. He'd been in her direct line of sight when she'd heard the scream.

Unlike John; after staying to watch over Ken, she'd lost track of John and his whereabouts.

She turned to Tim. 'We'd better find him. Come with me in case he's angry.'

'Why would he be angry?' asked Tim.

'I kind of leapt out at him, as I thought he was going to clock someone with a tin of paint.'

They jogged towards the paint section. Ken was where she'd left him, sitting on the floor, his back against the shelves.

Una crouched down beside him. 'Are you okay?'

'You gave me a shock,' said Ken, struggling to speak between breaths. He was still gripping onto the paint tin. 'Wasn't expecting to see you here.'

'Tim here. Can you feel your hands and feet?' said Tim, loosening Ken's collar. 'What is your name?'

'Yes,' said Ken. 'I'm fine. I'm Ken. I'm resting.'

'He's talking okay,' said Una. 'Although perhaps I should mention that he had a heart op last year.' She was starting to feel a bit panicky. There was no one to blame for Ken's present condition except her and her faulty reasoning.

'He doesn't look good,' said Tim. 'I'm the primary first-aider for Floor 6, remember. I'm taking charge of this situation. Are you getting any pains in your chest?'

'No, I'm not, don't make a fuss,' said Ken. 'I'm just getting my breath back, that's all. I had a couple of puffs of my inhaler and I'm waiting for them to kick in. Anyways, what was that horrible scream all about?'

'Never mind that for now,' said John, joining them still accompanied by the light bulb. 'You don't look too chipper, Ken. I'm going to run you back.'

'Thanks, John. Take me to Sheila's, will you?' said Ken.

'Are you sure you're up to moving?' asked Tim.

'I'm as fit as a fiddle,' said Ken, trying to push himself up against the shelves, 'and I don't mean some old fiddle like a Stradivarius either.' He gave a weak smile.

Una and Tim took one side each and helped him to his feet.

'Come on,' said John. 'Let's go and give our details to the police, so you don't have to hang around, and then I'll drop you off on the way home. I need a brandy after that.'

'Police? What's happened?' said Ken, perking up.

'I'll tell you on the way,' said John. 'Una, are you coming with us?'

'I'll see you there in a bit,' said Una. 'And I'll take Ken back in a taxi, no need to put you out. I'm sure you just want to get home to Jean.' Leaving him with John was too much of a risk.

'Okay,' said John, 'if you're sure.'

John and Ken shuffled slowly towards the police, who had gathered customers by the tills, away from the accident scene. Una was keen to maximise the short hiatus to see if she'd missed something about Tommo's accident. Besides, she wanted to put off facing Mum, who'd be furious with her about jumping out at Ken. Using her so-called risk analysis skills, she'd misjudged Ken and failed to prevent Tommo's death.

'Let's see if we can get near the barriers and find the numbers,' she said to Tim. 'Help me look.'

They hunted around the section, ending up where the garden implements were stored. The scythes had been barricaded off.

'I can't see any numbers and I've got better than twenty-twenty vision,' said Tim. 'Perhaps there wasn't enough time for this purported killer to leave them, as you got here so quickly? Or perhaps the numbers aren't connected at all, as per my proposal? Fair play, you did predict an unusual death and that is what has happened. But I continue to asseverate that it's just a series of unlikely events.'

Una's right thumb started wibbling back and forth as if she was holding a phantom comfort biro.

'What if I'm next?' she said. 'I must have been close to whoever did this. I could be in danger too.'

'You're in shock,' said Tim. 'We study mortality all day, but we don't usually have to see the goods up close like this.'

John and Ken were now shuffling back. Ken's face had turned Polar Bear Blush, which was reassuring.

'I'm off,' said John, extracting his compressed rain poncho from his jacket. 'Una, I'll leave you to get Ken home as soon as you can.' He bowled off.

Una was relieved that Ken was John-free, but Ken wasn't talking; in fact Ken was focusing on his breathing.

'I've got to go soon as well,' said Tim. 'So make the most of me.'

'But I needed to speak to you more,' said Una.

'I'll get myself a taxi,' said Ken. 'No need for you to come with me anyhow. I've got cash on me.'

Una could see a problem with his offer. 'But—'

He gave them a wave. 'Honestly, Una. You stay and speak to your friend if he's come all the way out here. I need a moment anyway. Just can't take it in.'

'Mum will—'

'See you back at the ranch,' said Ken, saluting her. 'Nice meeting you, Tim.'

'Likewise,' said Tim, as Ken hobbled off towards the exit.

'Well, you have to stay for a bit now,' said Una. 'I'm already going to be in trouble with Mum, so it can't make things any worse for me.'

'Okay, I can spare you a little more Tim time.'

'I need a coffee,' she said, keen to take control. 'There's a café at the far end. Let's go there to debrief, and then we can give our details and scram.'

'Good call,' said Tim. 'God, I hope they have soya milk. I mean, we're outside the M25.'

They walked together along the main aisle.

'Keep looking left and right for sharp implements,' he said. 'Remember, this shop has form.'

When they got to the café, they found the least wobbly table in the safest-looking corner. With no queue, it was fast work for Una to get the coffees. Time for analysis.

'Thanks for looking after Ken,' she said.

'My first-aid training just kicks in,' said Tim. 'It's like a reflex.'

'Ken definitely isn't behind this,' she said. 'He was at the scene of the crime for the third time. But he was nowhere near Tommo when he was attacked. Unless he rigged it up in some way. But I was one of the first ones in and I was watching him most of the time. He wouldn't have had a chance.'

'I don't see how he could have constructed that kind of set-up at a distance anyway,' said Tim.

'I've failed,' said Una. 'I completely focused on Ken as the culprit and I still haven't got the right prediction. Perhaps Tommo would still be alive if I'd worked harder.'

'It's not your job to save people,' said Tim. 'You work in life insurance. We're supposed to model data about people, not stop them from dying. Besides, if anyone is primed to be a have-a-go-hero round here, it's me.'

'Your analysis wouldn't even have told us someone was

going to die today,' she said. 'You can hardly have a go at saving someone if you're not around.'

'There is nothing wrong with my analysis,' said Tim. 'You got lucky with the date. And yes, it's an unusual death, but the problem is that it's completely different to the other ones you think are linked.'

'This isn't luck,' she said. 'You have to help me sort this out – every one of these deaths has happened on the first of the month. And they're all part of the same group of friends. Mum and Ken's wedding is on 1 March; that's when the murderer will strike next.'

'If you're so sure, why not go to the police?' said Tim.

'I don't see how they will buy into the numbers theory, especially as I can't even find any this time, and there's no proper evidence to show another person is involved.'

'We don't really know that there is,' he said. 'In fact, I'm glad I made the effort to cycle all the way here. I feel reassured that my new proposal to adjust the outlier limits based on the context will cover what happened today, so I don't really need to consider any extreme alternatives.'

'We need to find evidence,' she said. 'We need to go back over everything I've found and you need to help with making sure the wedding goes ahead safely. I definitely need to pay more attention to John. It's odd, you know, Cassie was right, sort of. Sure, it was a pretty rough-round-the-edges prediction about how and when it would happen, but still . . .'

'Nonsense, it's just like someone doing a horoscope,' said Tim. 'She gives vague details that can be adapted to any situation.'

Una kept quiet. Cassie had offered to help her find the links between the unusual deaths, but she didn't want Tim to know she was interested in her input – it was hardly the sort of information an actuary should be taking into account.

'Let's set up a meeting on Monday if you really feel there's more to discuss,' said Tim. 'Just check my calendar for a free slot. Hope Ken is okay.'

'Thanks, Tim,' she said. 'Perhaps I should get him a present to say sorry.'

'Well, it's not my business,' said Tim, 'but you could have caused serious harm to him. I understand you acted with the best of intentions, but it wasn't very professional, put it like that. I'd better head off.'

He strode out of the café.

How would she explain her Ken ambush to Mum? After giving her details to the police, she looked at the signs above the aisles, seeking inspiration on what would please Ken. She walked back to the paint section and saw his chosen tin still on the floor. That seemed like a good start, so she bought it and headed back to the flat.

Back at Mum's, Ken was lying on the couch and Mum and Anton were in the two armchairs flanking him. Anton gave her a look like an angry Airedale terrier when he saw her. Mum's was more like a disappointed Labrador.

'Hi, Ken,' said Una, creeping into the lounge. She avoided Mum and Anton's gaze as she put the paint tin on the floor next to the sofa. 'Hope you're feeling better. Look, I got you the paint you wanted.'

'I'm good, thanks,' he said. 'A fuss about nothing.'

'Sorry about earlier,' she said. 'I didn't mean to give you such a shock.'

'No problem, Una. And thanks for the paint. I'm going to redecorate the bedroom. Spruce it up for the sale.'

Una smiled weakly. 'That sounds good. I'll get on with clearing more stuff out.'

'Appreciated,' said Ken.

'And sorry about Tommo.'

Ken's face was wrestling against the effort not to well up. 'Just terrible. And we were so close. Oh Tommo, I can't believe it. He was always tripping over his own feet, but why did they have sharp tools out like that? It's a disgrace.'

A good point. Personally, Una would have put approximately 85 per cent of that shop under lock and key.

'I only saw him the other day . . .' said Ken.

Anton turned to Una. 'What were you doing there anyway?'

'We could have gone round the shop together if I'd known you were about,' added Ken.

'It was a last-minute thing,' she said.

But he didn't seem to be really listening. 'I can't believe it,' he said again. 'Harry, Eileen and now Tommo. I can't understand it. It's like a curse. And every time, I've been nearby.'

'You're reading too much into it,' said Mum, squeezing his hand. 'It's just terrible all you've had to go through recently.'

'At least you have the wedding to look forward to,' said Anton. He was deliberately not looking at Una.

'That's if we all make it,' said Ken. 'It's been one thing after another. Perhaps I should have listened to Cassie after all. Perhaps I should ask her what she can see next.'

Anton had started twirling his tiny beard again. 'This isn't like you,' he said. 'She'll only try to stir things up.'

'You're right,' said Ken. 'I just need some time for everything to sink in.'

'Would you like me to ring round and cancel the stag do?' asked Anton. 'I don't want you to be stressed. You need to rest this weekend.'

Ken got to his feet and pulled his T-shirt down tight. 'No! Tommo wouldn't want us to cancel. We'll reschedule it. It will go ahead as a tribute to him.'

'Are you really sure that's a good idea?' asked Anton. 'What about his kids? Karen and Mike, right? They might think it was a bit inappropriate.'

'I'm going to ring them this afternoon anyhow. I'll see if they're okay with it. We can have a seat spare at the pub and put his usual stout on the table as if he was there. And you can ring up the farm to let them know we're a space down.'

'Why are you going to a farm?' said Mum.

'For the quad biking,' said Anton.

'Kenneth, you are not going quad biking in your condition. That's an order,' said Mum.

Una could see that her scare today had reduced Ken's Ken-ness. Even his quiff had wilted and now lay in a spongy grey lump on his forehead.

'Okay, love,' he said. 'We could just go for a quiet drink at a pub.'

Since the stag do had now been de-risked, Una thought it was the perfect opportunity for her to make amends with Ken.

'You know, I think I'll be able to make the stag do after all,' she said. 'If I'm still invited?'

'Of course you are,' said Ken, beaming with only 60 watts of his normal 90-watt power. In his shoes, she wouldn't be so keen on socialising with someone who'd recently ambushed her in a DIY store, but then again, she would never wear a pair of neon Adidas Gazelle trainers.

'I can reserve a table somewhere,' said Anton.

'You're a good lad. And Una, why don't you invite that friend of yours, Tim, along? He tried to make sure I was all right at the store. I'd like to buy him a drink as a thank you.'

'Tim?' said Anton. 'That guy who was in the cafe? The ego with the handshake. He came up to see you again?'

'I'll ask him,' said Una. Although Tim was sceptical about the deaths being connected, perhaps she could get him to help collect more information by talking to the other stags.

'I'll get you another cup of tea,' said Mum. 'You can come with me, Una.'

They went into the kitchen and Mum shut the door quietly. 'So what was all that about today?' she said, shoving the kettle towards Una. 'Ken's not in great shape and you sprang out at him for no reason. He's already on edge because of Eileen and Harry passing away. And now his best friend . . . I expect better from you.'

Una filled up the kettle to avoid looking at her. 'I'm sorry,' she said. 'It was all a misunderstanding.'

Mum frowned. 'What's going on, Una? I feel like I've barely seen you since you've been here. You've been really secretive this week, and now I hear your colleague has been visiting you. Have you been working all this time?'

Una arranged four mugs in a line on the counter. 'There's a big project going on at work,' she said. It wasn't exactly a lie.

'You're meant to be having time off!' said Mum. 'It's not healthy, you working all the hours God sends. And I thought you were going to help me with wedding prep ... Look, I know it probably feels like Ken and I are moving a bit fast. But it has been a while now since your dad passed, and—'

'You're right, Mum,' Una interrupted. 'I'm sorry I haven't been more helpful. I'll make it up to you. And to Ken.'

Her visit two weeks ago had been intended to make things up to Mum, and since then she'd managed to unmake even more things.

'Well, you can start by helping me with the table plan,' said Mum. 'I've got to make sure no fights break out because we've sat people in the wrong place.'

'Sure. Whatever you want me to do,' said Una. 'But about Ken ... I mean, if he's so fragile, do you think you should be rushing into marrying him? What if something happens to him? Or you? It's true what he said about the deaths all happening in close proximity to him. What if he's right and he is cursed?'

'Oh Una, it's not like you to believe in stuff like that! They must be working you too hard. And Ken's had the all-clear and he's taking good care of himself.'

'But—'

'Any of us could go at any time,' continued Mum. 'Look at poor Tommo today. But Ken can't afford to have any stress on top of the wedding; he's already going over the top on that. No more sudden shocks for him, please.'

Una was only making things worse, and retreating seemed like the best option. 'I'm going to head back to London now, so you can have a quiet weekend together. But I'll come for the stag do and we can sort out the tables. And I'll clear out that cupboard as well.'

'That would be a big help,' said Mum. 'There's so much left to do for the wedding.'

Yes, thought Una. Produce the table plan, choose the flowers, find a killer.

Back home in Balham, Una unpacked, loaded the washing machine and called Amara. She couldn't wait until Sunday to offload and she provided a heavily edited version of the day's events at DIY City.

'Okay, okay, I mean it's good to hear that Ken's got the all-clear,' said Amara, 'even though it's not obvious from what you've said what triggered his funny turn. But why were you skulking round a DIY store at all? It sounds like the last place you'd go.'

Una dithered. 'I was just looking for some decoration ideas for the flat. It was fine – sure, there were hammers, patio cleaner and air fryers, but they were all carefully stacked on the shelves with clear warning signs as appropriate.'

'You're up to something,' said Amara. 'Back in the day, when we had that shared house on Hyde Park Road, you tested all the smoke alarms at 8 a.m. on the first of each month . . .'

'Not sure where this is going?' said Una, who, to be fair, had an inkling.

'. . . and when we had a barbecue, you made us buy a fire extinguisher and blanket,' Amara continued. 'And you had to go out of the house and sit on the wall at the front whenever I changed a plug. Yet now you're voluntarily hanging round DIY stores. Have you really changed that much?'

'People do change,' said Una. 'I'm getting quite bold these days.'

'Is that right? When you come up here,' said Amara, 'you can give me a hand putting up some shelves.'

'Sure,' said Una. 'I can wield an Allen key no problem, and even lift books onto the shelves, providing I keep a straight back and bend at the knee. It should be fine.'

Amara shook her head. 'These are going on the wall – I'll need to drill into it, so we'll have to check for any hidden electrics first.'

'Baby steps,' said Una, and moved the conversation to possible dates for her visit to Leeds.

# 19

## *The Bank of Tim*

It was a typical Monday morning, cutting and pasting chunks of data between spreadsheets. The cheese on toast of office life. But the long fingers of Eastbourne were soon tapping on Una's shoulder. She refreshed her inbox to find an email from Mum confirming that the stag do had been rescheduled for a week on Saturday, and giving the details of Tommo's funeral service the day before.

On a practical level, the funeral could provide lots of useful data. All the relevant suspects were likely to be there, enclosed in a small perimeter and in a state of high emotion, which she could use to provoke extra information from them. And with just under four weeks before the wedding, and Mum not taking her concerns seriously, she had to use all opportunities to work out the pattern. A funeral, though. An unwelcome reminder of post-life insurance policy oblivion. And it was being held at the same chapel she'd been to two years ago.

She messaged Tim to meet her in the kitchenette. In an open-plan office, face-to-face discussions between colleagues at their desks were frowned upon, even those involving murder prevention. When she arrived, he was already there, auditing his Tupperware lunch boxes in the fridge, each one neatly taped with his name.

'We need to plan, Tim,' she said. 'The next death is due on 1 March. We need to get this knocked on the head, as it were.'

'I have some doubts after the DIY store,' said Tim.

'But everything happened just like I said, when I said.'

He filled up a cone of water and glugged it down. 'I know,' he said. 'But there were no numbers this time, right? That was one of the main things you had that linked the deaths and suggested that they were planned. Perhaps they're just a series of deaths that appear to have some correlation but don't. Someone put the wrong bin back. The supermarket put up a number to show how many boxes of goods to order. These cases are already non-standard, so you may be subjectively looking for patterns that aren't there.'

'No way,' she said. 'Someone deliberately planted those numbers and arranged those deaths. I need to find out who that is and why they did it.'

'Una, Una, Una, you are getting into dangerous territory here. You're on the slippery slope to talking about motive. We are not going to stray into the quicksand of human psychology. We can't see inside other people's heads. I mean, we can do MRI scans, but we can't use those to detect these sort of intentions. We must stay professional and model the data to find the truth. Even if there is a murderer, the answer is not to start looking for reasons why someone would kill all these oldies; we simply need more data and the truth will emerge.'

He was right. Linking the deaths with personal motive was a waste of time.

'Okay, I agree,' she said. 'We need more information. Why don't you come with me to Tommo's funeral? I could do with some moral support – it might be dangerous – and you're the only person I've told my theory to.'

'Funeral? I don't think so. When is it?'

'A week on Friday. So you'd have to take a half-day off.'

'I can't spend time going to funerals because of a wild goose chase. And they're depressing. By the way, I didn't see anything from you yet on my funding page for my Ironman challenge.'

'I've sponsored loads of your stuff in the past.'

Tim had now stacked all of his lunch boxes in a pile. 'May I remind you, I'm the London rep on the philanthropy team – it's like a bear pit at those monthly meetings.'

'Okay, okay. I'll put something in for you,' she said. 'But perhaps you can show some support for me – we're supposed to be a team, remember.'

'Look, I'm just concerned that it was a false positive about the dates and you read too much into it. This theory about the numbers and Ken might just be a bit of wishful thinking. There were no numbers at the DIY store, and Ken was gasping for breath nowhere near that guy.'

'That's true, but—'

'For total transparency, I should tell you that I've submitted my new proposal on seaside mortality trends to Ajay this morning. As expected, all that was needed was a less conservative approach to some of the model assumptions.'

Una blinked back her disappointment. With all the drama of interviews and stake-outs over the last week, she'd lost focus on the promotion battle. And now Tim was one step ahead.

'But surely you can see there's something more sinister going on?' she said.

'Where's the evidence?' said Tim. 'What I'm proposing fits the figures.'

She felt compelled to purchase a giant Kit Kat from the vending machine. She watched its chunky frame topple into the collection tray.

'Well then,' she said, 'I understand you don't want to take a day off for the funeral of someone you don't know. But why not come along to Ken's stag do on the Saturday, the day after? He invited you as he wants to say thank you for looking after him, making sure he was okay. And you're so good at getting analytical information, you might spot something I've missed.'

This was bad – she was so desperate for Tim's help that she was now paying him compliments. But she couldn't face such a potentially dangerous situation on her own, not after seeing how Tommo was dispatched. She wanted to link the numbers, but she didn't want to become a statistic herself.

'Look, I'd love to help out,' said Tim, 'but there isn't anything in it for me, especially now that I've put in my report.'

'You know,' said Una, 'teamwork isn't about making everything into a transaction.'

'It is, actually,' said Tim. 'Favour culture. I maintain a spreadsheet where I keep tabs of coffees bought, interviews helped out on, presentations reviewed. I'm long on favours and I come in here every day knowing I can call them in any time I like.'

Una evaluated her options. The alternative to negotiating with Tim was to tell Anton about her theory, but he was still frosty with her for jumping out at Ken at DIY City.

'Okay. Let's deal,' she said.

'What have you got?' said Tim.

She had to find something that would appeal to him, and that meant something that would further his goals at work.

'I'll go round the pet insurance group on the fifth floor to increase your Ironman sponsorship,' she said.

'Interesting.'

'I know you won't approach them because of Gareth, but I could pop down there for you.'

'It's not about Gareth, for your information,' said Tim. 'The pet lot are really cliquey. They always do fundraising as a team.'

'It would boost your total,' she said.

She could see she was winning him round. 'With a bit of an uplift, I might raise more individually this quarter than they do as a team,' he said, wavering.

'So what do you say?'

'Deal. And anyway, I'm warming to the idea of Ken thanking me for saving his life.'

Una snapped a bar off the Kit Kat, annoyed that Tim was overinflating his contribution to Ken's welfare. Not that she would tell him so.

'Great,' she said. 'We can split the people at the stag do between us, and I expect you to be thorough in getting them to talk. In return, if you do a good job, I'll hit the fifth floor.'

Una and the Kit Kat headed back to her desk. Two meetings and ten emails had taken advantage of her kitchenette trip.

Ajay waved her over from his office.

'Hi, Una!' he said. 'How was your time with your family and friends? Everyone keeping well?'

'Good, thanks.' As well as could be expected with an integer-fixated psychopath picking them off one by one.

'Great, great. And for your information, we are now 100 per cent on our vacation scorecard pillar thanks to your time off last week.'

'Glad to hear that,' she said. 'I need to take Friday 16th off as well, though, sorry. A funeral for a family friend I need to go to.'

'Of course, my condolences.'

'Thanks.'

'Well, on to boring old business,' continued Ajay. 'Tim's sent me a draft paper outlining his recommendations for dealing with the type of outlier issue that came up with the seaside modelling. He said he'd spoken to you about that, kept you updated on his progress, which all sounds good. Great to see you working together as a team.'

'Yes, and I'll continue to look at the data in my own time as a learning experience.'

She knew that Ajay particularly liked that phrase, 'learning experience'. Tim's paper was total nonsense – there were clearly more sinister forces behind the statistics. It was a let-down that there hadn't been any numbers at the DIY store.

162

'Great stuff,' said Ajay. 'I mean, it's a shame about your research being slightly out like that, but it is what it is. I'll take everything into account when we do the restructuring.'

'When will that happen?'

'Sometime before the end of the month. I'll let you know.' He gestured for her to leave. 'Anyway, good to have you back. And can you close the door on your way out.'

If the team reshuffle was happening at the end of the month, she still had a few weeks to provide an alternative proposal for the seaside figures and revive her professional reputation. If she could prove that a murderer had thrown off her data, her model wouldn't be dismissed. No one on the team would make provisions for a serial killer.

For now, she would focus on finding out who the next target was, so she could act to prevent anything happening at the wedding. And there was John to investigate, too. He'd been at DIY City when Tommo had died, and she hadn't kept tabs on him.

She loitered by the lift entrance and rang Mum to tell her she'd be going to Tommo's funeral. The phone rang ten times, and she imagined Mum looking for her new phone around the flat and finding it next to the fruit bowl with the spare keys.

'Hi, Mum.'

'Are you okay?'

'I got your email. I'm going to come down for the funeral.'

'Ken will appreciate that,' she said. 'And I appreciate it too. I know you don't like that sort of thing. Funerals. And in Dad's chapel . . .'

Una swapped the phone to her left ear.

'Ken's been trying out that paint you bought him, by the way,' said Mum, when Una stayed silent. 'He's very happy with it.'

'That's good.'

'And he asked if you were inviting your work friend to the stag do, as he needs to know numbers.'

'Yes, he'll be there.' She still had over a week to think of a list of questions for Tim to cover.

'And you're going to help with the table plan, remember,' Mum said.

'I haven't forgotten. I'll come up on the Thursday evening, I'm sure it won't take long.'

'Great. I'll ask Ken to come round. It will take his mind off the funeral – he's been fretting about it.'

Una was also fretting about the funeral. Was it one that she could have prevented?

# 20

## *Nine Times Tables*

It quickly emerged on the Thursday evening before Tommo's funeral that working out the optimal table plan for the wedding was the sort of thing that might have flummoxed Alan Turing. Una had felt sleepy after she'd taken the train to Mum's flat and dumped her backpack in the little bedroom, but the challenge of arranging the guests had fired her up. There were so many rules!

At the front of the hall there would be a single-file table for the wedding party, which consisted of six people: Ken, Mum, Ken's daughter Chrissie, newly promoted best man Anton, Una herself and an honorary seat reserved for Tommo. The guests would be placed at nine round tables, each seating six people, and the room provided physical constraints on how the tables could be arranged. So far, so good; the tables fitted into the space and allowed a modest amount of room for getting in and out. But then came all the conditions.

The tables nearest the top table were considered the most desirable, as they reflected the closeness of the guests' relationship with the bride and groom. In addition to indicating the actual importance of each guest, however, the seating had to take into account their own perceived importance level combined with the likelihood of their being offended by getting the wrong seat. Their position at the table itself also had to be carefully calculated, making sure they were not sitting next to someone they hated. Finally, any single people had to be sat together, so that they didn't feel downhearted at attending the romantic occasion and would hopefully find someone to partner up with, to avoid the freedom, independence and emotional stability of staying single.

'Would you like me to create an algorithm?' asked Una. This was an opportunity for her to show Mum the sort of thing she did at work. Her professional life wasn't going so well, and she needed a boost.

'I don't think so,' said Mum. 'We can just work it out on a piece of paper.'

She placed a single sheet of blank A4 paper on top of the coffee table and started to sketch out the tables with a biro.

'Top table is sorted,' she said. 'Front row has to be any family and close friends.'

Una switched off until the bingo crowd were mentioned.

'We can sit Jean and John, Cassie and Raj all together on one table,' said Mum. 'We'd better put Arthur there too, I suppose. And your Uncle Len can make up the numbers.'

Una's preydar was alerted. 'Frankly, Mum, I don't think you're thinking through the risk profile for this group. You'll be doing well if they all make it alive to the wedding, never mind putting them together when they're there.'

'Una, that's a terrible thing to say!'

On the plus side, it would be easier for her to monitor them if they were co-located.

At this point, Ken and Anton arrived. Ken flung his car keys onto the coffee table and sprawled across the couch, leaving a just-about-Anton-sized space at the end. Anton squeezed into it and gave Una a small nod and no smile whatsoever.

'You look much better,' said Una, glancing at Ken.

'Never felt better, thanks,' said Ken, slapping his tummy.

'Una's helping me with the table plan,' said Mum. 'Want to make sure we've not forgotten anyone. Shout if you see something that will cause ructions.'

Anton picked up the draft plan. 'Just checking where Auntie Jess is . . . Fine. And I think you should leave a spare place.'

'Good idea,' said Ken.

There was going to be a spare place anyway if Una couldn't work out the number connection in time.

'The tricky bit,' said Mum, 'is allocating people to the tables at the outer flanks, suggesting a lower importance. I could put my friend Bev over there with Kath and Roger. They all get on. And my second cousin Steve is single. He's a bit older than Rosa, but I could move her next to him.'

Anton sat up. 'What's this Steve like? Is he really suitable for Rosa?'

So Anton knew Rosa too. Una wondered how he would react to finding out about Ken's secret visits to her house. With everything else going on, she hadn't made any progress on that line of investigation, and time was running out before the wedding.

167

'He's a total gentleman, thank you very much,' said Mum. 'I used to put five pounds in a birthday card for him every year and I always got a thank-you card back.'

'Put my second cousins there,' said Ken, dabbing his finger on the plan, 'as overspill from the first table, although our Sheena will read into things if she's right at the back.'

'I'll put her at the front of her table,' said Mum, 'so her chair is grazing the chairs at the back of the front table. That way it seems like she's close to the rest of your family.'

'She is on a different table, though,' said Ken.

'Well, we could move these two and swap them over.'

'No, they're all closely related, they see each other a lot. It makes sense for them to sit by each other.'

Una stood up. 'For goodness' sake, it's only a meal. Can't they just turn up and eat it?'

Mum raised her eyebrows. 'Have you got anything more constructive to add?'

'As I said, I could create an algorithm.'

'Let her do one,' said Ken. 'That's the future. In twenty years' time, there'll be robots planning weddings. You probably won't even go to a venue; you'll just stick on one of those virtual-reality hats and there you go. Isn't that right, Anton?'

'Marriage won't exist,' said Anton, 'but yeah, I go with the gist of your point.'

'I think marriage will last many more years, Anton,' said Mum. 'It's a public declaration of two people's love for each other.'

'Hear, hear,' said Ken, squeezing her hand. 'It will still be here, but perhaps it will be less popular.'

'And it will be easier to dissolve,' said Anton, 'because

people will live much longer and they won't want to stay with the same person for a whole lifetime. Some people don't want to stay with the same person for even a fairly small amount of their lifetime.'

'Now, now, Anton,' said Ken, 'I'm sure you'll meet someone you want to spend the rest of your life with.'

Una did a rough calculation in her head on how long that was based on current data, but kept it to herself. Then she concentrated on devising the perfect seating plan. She worked on this for about thirty minutes while the debate continued nearby. It was actually quite a tricky problem and she wasn't sure she could find a solution. She made a few working assumptions to help things along.

'Got it!' she said eventually, and connected her laptop to Mum's printer to print it out.

She placed her plan on the coffee table next to the hand-written diagram for the group to review. Mum swooped it up and brought it close to her face, examining it table by table.

'Interesting,' she said. 'A reasonable amount of overlap with my plan, but missing the following points. There needs to be an even distribution of men and women around each table. Also, let's not put Raj next to Jean, as they'll argue too much following the book club incident.'

'Okay, that's it,' said Una. 'What happened at the book club? I hear about it all the time. Now I want to know. It's not for me, it's for the algorithm.'

'Calm down, Una,' said Mum.

'It was a storm in a teacup,' said Ken, lurching forward. 'Here's the thing, we took it in turns to choose a book for the group to read each month. That way, we'd get a good mix. But when it came to Harry, he picked a book he'd written himself and was going to self-publish.'

'What sort of book?' said Una.

'*Harry's Life Hacks: two hundred ways to live longer by expanding your time.*'

'It was very interesting,' said Mum. 'I've never stacked the dishwasher in the same way again.'

'That sounds brilliant,' said Una. If only she'd got a chance to meet Harry; he sounded the most switched on of all Ken's friends.

'But Jean said it wasn't allowed,' said Ken. 'She said it was effectively self-promotion.'

'It is a bit narcissistic,' said Anton. 'And I'm not into this life hack scene. Why not take the time to do tasks properly?'

'Like table planning,' said Mum, nodding.

'There was a big hoo-hah about it,' said Ken, ploughing through this interruption. 'Raj stood up and said there was nothing in the rules to say we couldn't pick books we'd written and so Jean's position was untenable. Untenable.'

Despite his sinister behaviour on the cliff, Una was with Raj on this. Rules were rules and no rules were no rules.

'Jean got on her high horse and said that if he really believed they should pick Harry's book, then she was excommunicating him from the book club. Raj walked, closely followed by Harry, Eileen and a couple of the others. And with so few members left, the book club folded.'

Una wondered how this fed back into her investigation. Could this incident have provoked a mission of vengeance by one of the former club members? Jean, in particular, seemed pretty uncompromising.

She battled on with her next attempt at the table plan and compared it to the original.

'This is nearly perfect,' said Mum, 'except that Aunt Ida and Aunt Edith don't talk to each other any more since Ida's daughter's wedding, when Edith was put on a different table from the rest of the family. You see how these things can go wrong.'

'But all I'm doing is using the same rules as you were,' said Una. 'I was trying to automatically generate the best plan.' Her professional research at work was being questioned, and now she couldn't even organise the tables at a wedding.

'I'm very impressed with your algorithm, and it's good to have something electronic checking what I've put down,' said Mum, looking round at the others.

'So this is the sort of thing you do all day,' said Anton. 'Shame you can't generate a speech for me as well.' He gave her a half-smile and she took this as a sign that he was thawing towards her.

'I'll tell you something for nothing,' said Ken, 'you could make a fortune if you put it into an app. This is probably how Facebook started.'

Una didn't actually hate this suggestion. Perhaps an app was possible. Ken was growing on her. A bit.

'Anyhow, that's another job done,' said Mum. 'Thanks for the group effort. I'm sure it'll all run like clockwork. It's going to be a wonderful day.'

Except for the 99 per cent chance of one of the guests being murdered. A statistic that would be brought into sharp focus tomorrow.

## 21

## *Numb and Number*

Funerals were depressing, and it was best to avoid them. Una was keen to avoid her own.

Yesterday, she had packed the black jacket from a trouser suit bought over ten years ago, when people still wore suits to work. The suit, from Jigsaw, had been quite an investment, but she'd worn it until shiny patches had emerged on the elbows. It was a little tight now. Even tighter than when she'd worn it to Dad's funeral. This time, she'd jettisoned the trousers to preserve the integrity of her major organs. But she could still stuff herself into the jacket, and she'd leave it unbuttoned. There was a faint trace of CK One from its last outing, and she found a receipt in one of the pockets for a medium latte from Costa Coffee.

At 12.30, Ken arrived in his Prius to take them to Eastbourne cemetery, where Tommo's service was being held. Rain speckled the windscreen, and the dense grey clouds set a sombre mood. Despite the drizzle, the streets were busy with shoppers, who occasionally stepped into the road, causing Ken to brake and swear under his breath. Una sat in the back with Anton, who was wearing his usual boots with a black suit and what looked like one of Ken's ties. They were both browsing their phones.

'Anything interesting?' said Una.

Anton paused whatever he was streaming. 'I'm listening to a podcast about how to create a good podcast,' he said. 'I'm thinking of trying my hand at it. I just need to settle on a topic. What's that you're watching?'

'I'm watching the rocket launch from last night,' she said, holding her phone screen up to him. 'It's amazing seeing those little boosters land back down.'

'It is, though all that money could be spent on solving issues with the current planet.'

'But having a space station on Mars would mean we'd have somewhere to go if earth became uninhabitable.'

'I hope that's a big if,' said Anton.

'Well, I bought a reusable water bottle,' she said, taking it out from her bag as proof, 'thanks to Ken's advice to me the other day.'

'Every bit helps, I suppose,' said Anton, and glanced sideways at her with a not-quite-full-beam smile.

The funeral chapel was a low-rise red-brick building nestled amongst the grassy slopes and grey gravestones. There were many familiar faces inside: John, Jean, Raj, Cassie, even Rosa, Eileen's neighbour. Una sat down next to Mum and Ken, with Anton at the other end. Ken was wearing a formal suit today, which Una assumed he would also wear at the wedding. Hopefully without the Def Leppard tie. Mum was rummaging in her bag, her hand scrunched around a tissue.

It hit Una like a wave. The room. Sitting in this chapel again. The sombre organ music. It took her straight back to that day. She started to shudder.

'Una,' said Ken, leaning across and clamping her hand vigorously. 'You're cold, sit by the radiator here.'

Mum looked worried. 'Are you all right, Una?'

'I'm fine,' she said, forcing herself to sit upright.

'If you need to step out for some fresh air, then just go.'

'I'm completely fine. Okay?'

Actually, she *was* cold. She put her hands in her pockets, finding the notepad she'd brought to capture any useful information. She'd come to the funeral to try to solve the riddle of the mysterious deaths; that was the goal for today. But now that she was here, a cloud of invisible grief gathered in the ceiling above her.

Before she registered what she was doing, she was on her feet.

Outside, she felt like she could breathe again. Funeral-goers were still making their way inside the chapel, and she headed away from the entrance and the sound of their polite whispers.

She sat down on a nearby bench, and moments later Mum sat beside her, their breath rising and mingling in the cold February air.

'Do you want my scarf?' said Mum.

Una shook her head.

'I wasn't sure if you'd come today,' said Mum. 'I know it's difficult.'

The cold was setting in. Una crossed her arms. 'I'm supposed to be supporting you, but now you're out here with me.'

'Just take a moment. I needed a breather myself.'

They sat in silence, apart from the murmurs from the chapel entrance.

Mum turned towards her. 'Do you want to sit in the car?'

'No, I'm okay. You should head in, it's freezing out here. I'll only be a minute.'

Mum paused, stroked Una's arm, then got up and left.

Una knew she'd missed an opportunity to talk about Dad's funeral, but even sitting with Mum, thinking about it, was a small relief. She waited motionless for ten deep breaths, preparing to pay her respects to Tommo, then rose from the bench to follow Mum back inside. As she approached the entrance, she felt a hand on her shoulder. It was John, looming over her in a dark grey suit, smoking, the tobacco scent steeped in the past.

'You all right there, Una? Don't tell Jean,' he said, waggling the cigarette. 'It's just the one. Must have been a bit of a shock for you finding him like that.'

'Yes, it wasn't exactly what I'd expected.'

'Nothing you could do by then.'

'I don't think so, no. See you inside.'

She could have got to Tommo sooner if she hadn't been so fixated on catching Ken out, although what would she have done if the attacker had still been there?

She wove her way back to the pew. The chatter in the hall died down.

'Right, looks like it's starting now,' whispered Ken. 'They've got a humanist minister to do the service. That's what I want as well.'

175

Proceedings started with a solemn welcome from the minister. Tommo's daughter, Karen, stood up to read out a poem by Seamus Heaney, but her voice kept cracking and she had to repeat bits. Una gasped at intervals. It was difficult breathing when the air was heavy with sighs.

'Tommo was a well-loved member of our community,' said the minister.

Una could see from the turnout that this was true, but it was very likely that someone sitting close by was involved with his death. She studied each of the main suspects. Jean and John were sitting as still as snow globes; not a flake of movement drifted between them. Cassie was scrutinising the order of service. Raj was looking around the room as well, and their eyes met. He smiled at Una like someone had pointed a camera at him for a snap. She gave him a small nod before returning her gaze to the coffin.

'We never know when we need to be ready for our final journey,' said the minister. 'At least we can take comfort that Tommo was doing something he loved when he was called. Picking out seeds for his container pots. The cycle of life. We'll now hear a few words from his friend Ken McNamara.'

Mum squeezed Ken's arm as he stood up. He walked slowly to the podium and looked out at the mourners.

'What can I say about my friend Tommo? I used to joke that he'd turn up late to his own funeral, but he proved me wrong today, I'm sad to say. We worked together for donkey's years. I remember we'd be on a job and he'd be playing "Smoke on the Water" at full blast while telling us how to grow potatoes. He was a man of many talents, many interests, and he had many friends. I'm proud to say I was one of them. But his main interest, the main thing he cared about, was Karen and Mike . . .'

After his speech, Ken bowed his head and returned to the bench. Having heard so much about Tommo's life during the service, Una was struggling to maintain a professional distance. She'd returned to Eastbourne in a last-ditch attempt to uncover more information about those closely linked to him. But she was getting too much data. Tommo's personality had so many aspects that she hadn't captured in her spreadsheets.

In two weeks' time, someone sitting here might be dead, and despite Tim's doubts and the lack of numbers at the DIY store, she still had that hunch. But what to do about it? She'd failed to save Tommo. She'd been lucky not to get hurt herself. And she'd nearly hurt Ken. Her efforts were just causing risk to other people and her investigation had stalled.

After the service, the congregation moved outside, and most of them filed into the graveyard for the burial service.

'He's got one of those eco-coffins,' said Ken to Mum. 'Tommo was always up on what was new. I think I'll choose one of them as well. You have to do your bit for the environment.'

'I want something traditional,' said Mum. 'Oak with gold trimmings.'

'Fair do's,' said Ken. 'I would never peer-pressure someone about their choice of coffin.'

Una stayed silent, relying on Ken's natural conversation cadence to change the subject soon. But the delay as the crowd assembled for the burial service put her on edge. She hung back, and could barely see the minister's lips moving as he gave a brief blessing at the graveside. Then the crowd dispersed into groups as they organised themselves to get to the drinks that Tommo's family had laid on.

'Hey, Una.' It was Ken. 'You okay there?'

'All good, Ken. Is Mum up ahead?'

'She's just over by your dad's grave, she won't be long. You can go join her if you like.'

Una dithered. She knew she should go over there, but her daily emotional capacity had been emptied by the service, and so she stood swaying slightly. She expected Ken to start babbling away, but for once he remained calm, looking out into the distance.

After a while, he turned towards her. 'Why don't we head to the car and wait for your mum?' he said gently, offering his arm.

Una still had her reservations about him, but she had to admit he was being pretty thoughtful. She took his arm.

'I might just go back to the flat, Ken,' she said as they wound down the path to the road. 'I'm feeling tired and I don't think I'm going to be much company at the drinks. But I'm glad I came to the service after what happened.'

'Fair enough,' he said. 'We'll drop you off on the way. Take the keys and wait inside,' he said, gesturing to the Prius. 'I'm just going to nip over to Tommo's grave to say one last goodbye, as I was quite far back and I have something I want to leave there.'

He moved away, and somehow, because Una was curious about what he was going to do, she found herself edging towards the grave behind him. After a few steps, she stopped. She avoided graveyards in general, and this one in particular. Besides, Cassie had explicitly warned her not to come here. That was ridiculous; she was not going to get drawn in by superstitious nonsense. Her need to find out whatever she could about Ken before the wedding outweighed her fears, and she continued forward.

At the graveside, she stood just behind Ken and glanced down at the coffin. A man nearby was already starting to fill the grave. Poor Tommo. Ken's head was bowed, his eyes closed. After a moment, he opened them and straightened up. He put his hand in his pocket and took out a ticket for a rock festival, which he carefully dropped into the grave.

'Hang on, what's that?' he said, pointing downwards.

Una bent over and peered down. Something glinted on top of the coffin. Two numbers had been thrown into the grave. They were black on a gold background. Together they spelt out 43.

# 22

## *Clutching at Cheese Straws*

'What does it mean?' said Una. 'There must be some reason for putting those numbers there. Who did it?'

'Someone's remembrance gesture,' said Ken. 'That was his lucky number.'

Una quickly took a photo with her phone. Tommo's lucky number, the number next to Harry's and Eileen's on the scrap of paper in his wallet that she'd never followed up on.

'I don't think now is the time or place for social media,' said Ken, pointing to her phone. 'And I speak as someone who is no stranger to a selfie.'

'Sorry, Ken,' said Una. 'You know, I think I will come to the drinks after all.'

Her hunch had been correct. There really was someone behind this. She hated to admit it, but Tim must have been right: she'd disturbed the killer at the DIY store before they were able to drop the numbers. But they were still bold enough to complete their number sequence, even at the last possible opportunity. It also meant that they'd been at the service, and perhaps they would be at the drinks.

She got into the back of Ken's car with Anton for their trip to the pub where the drinks were being held. The Frog and Ferret was in a part of Eastbourne that she'd not been to before, far back from the sea, and they drove up and around the hills. She felt the nag of car sickness and wound the window down slightly.

'That was a great speech,' said Anton. 'Really moving.'

'Thanks,' said Ken.

'I hope I can do as good a job at the wedding. I'd just got into the mindset to do that reading, and now I've got a whole speech to do instead.'

'Don't sweat it,' said Ken. 'I've read tons of books on this stuff. Here's what you do. Just look out at everyone and imagine they're naked.'

'Honestly, Ken, not at a funeral,' said Mum, squirming in the passenger seat. She and Ken started to discuss which radio station to put on.

'By the way, Una,' said Anton in a quiet voice, 'I've made a start on putting all the photos together, so I'll let you know when I've got something to run through with you. I hope you'll like it.'

'Sounds good,' said Una. 'And let me know if you want me to be a guinea pig for your speech.'

'That would be great. I feel extra pressure after today.'

What could she say to reassure him? And then it came to her. 'Do you know that a significant percentage of people fear public speaking more than they fear death?' she said.

Anton frowned. 'Okay,' he said.

'Just to be clear, I personally fear death more. But the point is, it's really normal to feel scared in your position.'

181

Having helped Anton out, it was time to refocus on the case.

The pub was noisy, with a Friday-afternoon crowd half watching a snooker match on the enormous TV screen in the main room.

'We're upstairs,' said Ken, clearly familiar with the layout and shepherding them towards a narrow staircase.

The upstairs room was only slightly less rowdy than the sports crowd below, with around forty people closely gathered in clumps across the noisy patterned carpet. There was a bar on the right and a row of tables with platters of food on the left. Una could smell furniture polish off the wooden bar, and the distinctive scent of a dry-stone wall of sausage rolls.

She tried a slow breathing technique, repeating a positive mantra and standing in a power pose, but interrogating a grieving crowd about random numbers presented a massive challenge, especially since one of them might be a dangerous murderer. She was putting herself in danger by revealing what she knew. This wasn't a time to mess about with new-fangled stress management techniques. She grabbed a glass of red wine from one of the trays along the side, slugged it down and looked around for a familiar face.

She headed first to John, who was arranging a trio of mini pasties on a paper plate, having placed himself in a choice spot next to a loaded trestle table.

'John, how are you?'

'I'm good, thanks,' said John. 'It was a lovely service, wasn't it?'

Una hesitated about discussing the service. If she did that with all the people she was planning to question, that was going to waste time. Today's service was evidence that life was fleeting, and in two weeks' time, it could be very fleeting indeed for someone in this room.

'I was wondering,' she said, grabbing a paper plate to fit in, 'does the number 37 mean anything to you?'

'Thirty-seven? Well, it's a prime,' he said. 'I'm sure you already know that. But I think that's about it, why?'

'What about the numbers 43, 41, 37? Does that sequence sound familiar?'

'I mean, they could be in a pattern,' said John, crunching into a samosa. 'Nothing obvious strikes me. Is this some sort of quiz in the newspaper? What's your angle?'

After DIY City, Una needed to be wary around John. 'Just something I'm looking into at work. You know how it is when you're trying to get a link, see how the numbers connect.'

'I do, Una, I do,' said John. 'If anything occurs to me, I'll let you know. I just have a few other things on my mind at the moment. Anyhow, I'll see you tomorrow.' He plunged into one of his mini pasties.

'Sure. Thanks.'

Una looked around for someone else she knew. Raj was standing apart from the group in the corner. He'd chosen the sort of spot she herself would like – relatively quiet but with extensive surveillance opportunities. As she walked towards him, her steps slowed, a delayed response to the terrifying clifftop encounter, even though he was in full view of everyone. She was about to veer away when he looked up and peered at her as if she was an unusual sparrow. She forced herself forward.

'Hi, Raj. How are you?'

'I'm extremely healthy, thank you. I've already had five of my five a day,' he said, nodding at the broccoli florets and red pepper slices on his paper plate. 'I'll probably get to seven by day close.'

Una stood at arm-plus-pencil-length's distance from him. 'Talking of numbers and whether they're good for you, do you know of any links between the numbers 37, 41 and 43?'

'Is this a joke?' said Raj. 'I don't like jokes.'

'I'm totally with you on that. I'm not a big fan of them myself.'

'So why are you asking about those numbers in particular?'

'Just making conversation, really.'

'Well, I've no idea what they mean. The grebes were calling from the pier.'

'What? Is that a code?'

'No,' said Raj. 'I literally saw them this morning. The grebes. Got up early. Thought you'd appreciate the latest bird news.'

'Thanks. So, Tommo, was he one of your patients? Was he in good health?'

Raj picked up a broccoli floret. 'It's not appropriate for me to tell you about his hypertension; what I will say is that a better diet would have helped.' He crunched into the floret.

'I see,' said Una.

'And you've fully recovered from our birdwatching trip? Your little fainting fit?'

184

She glanced at his hands, fully occupied with supporting the plate and a beaker of cloudy apple juice; no writing implements in sight.

'Yes thanks,' she said. 'I took it easy for the rest of the day. Perhaps it was being so high up that caused it.'

'Perhaps. It certainly must have gone to your head, as you were making some very bold statements.'

'Sorry about that,' she said.

'All I will say on the matter is that no more messages will be forthcoming on the website we discussed, okay? Let's draw a line under it. Now, I'm just going to pop over to update John on the grebe situation while he's away from Jean's clutches.'

Una grabbed a cheese straw – surely you couldn't get food poisoning from a cheese straw? She noticed that Anton was talking to Rosa. They must be about the same age. He seemed relaxed and they obviously knew each other well, so different from the stilted conversations she'd attempted today. She wanted to have a relaxed conversation as well, but she needed to find out more. She could ask Rosa about her neighbour and perhaps move the conversation on to Ken.

But then she saw Karen and Mike nearby. Their children and spouses swarmed around them as they stood silent, side by side, propped against the wall.

Una had been at an insurance conference when Dad had died two years ago. His treatment had been going well and there was a high percentage of recovery. She'd decided that going to the conference was important; she wanted to present the project she'd been working on, and the numbers about his treatment suggested that this was the rational thing to do. But then came that phone call from Mum and she'd arrived back just in time. At least she'd been there at the end. Karen and Mike hadn't even had a chance to be with Tommo. She wanted to speak to them and let them know she'd been there when he'd died.

'Hello,' she said. 'I'm sorry for your loss.'

'Thanks,' said Karen.

'I was at the DIY store. I found Tommo. I'm Una.' She was struggling to link her words in the right order to deliver such an important message.

'That must have been terrible,' said Mike.

'It was. I just wanted to tell you that he wasn't in any pain when I saw him. It must have been really quick. I just wanted to tell you, that's all.'

'Appreciate that,' said Karen, taking Una's hand in both of hers and squeezing it.

Una backed away from them, giddy from her outburst, and bumped into Cassie, who was standing on her own by the table where people had stacked their empty glasses and plates. She was draped in a long black dress and carrying a bag with a fringe and tiny mirrors stuck to it, and was sipping from a large glass of red wine.

For all her faults, Cassie believed there was a connection between the deaths, and Una did too, even after all Tim's doubts.

'Hi, Cassie.'

'Hello there, Una. Nice to see you again, despite the circumstances.'

'Looking forward to the wedding?'

She knew that Cassie wasn't looking forward to the

wedding, but she'd just blurted that out. She tried to settle her face to look as if she'd asked something neutral.

'Yes. I'm still planning what to wear,' Cassie said. 'I guess you already have an outfit decided.'

'I just get told what to wear, as I'm a bridesmaid.'

Una was struggling to keep the conversation going. That hastily slugged wine was starting to make her a little woozy.

'And what about all your investigations, how are they getting along?' said Cassie. 'When we spoke, you were going to look for connections among us, see if there was anything to explain all this bad luck.'

'I'm on the case, don't worry,' said Una. 'In fact, I made a bit of a breakthrough today and spotted another connection – a set of numbers. But what would really help is if you had any visions of more danger coming up.'

Cassie raised her eyebrows. 'I can't just switch it on, you know. I'm not a tap.'

'Fair enough,' said Una. 'But please keep me in the loop if any gruesome visions do pop up.'

Cassie put down her wine glass and shuffled closer. 'Give me your hand, your right hand; perhaps that will help me channel my energies.'

Reluctantly Una offered up her hand. Cassie bent her head close to her palm.

'Yes,' she said. 'It's forming . . .'

Una could see Mum and Ken waving at her from the bar. Ken glared at Cassie, then set off across the room, battling against the tightly packed crowd chatting and eating.

'I see another time of danger in the offing,' Cassie said. 'This time I see the graveyard and I also see a spike.'

187

Una was wide-eyed. 'But what spike? Where? Who is going to die?'

Cassie suddenly shuddered as Ken appeared at Una's shoulder. 'Hold on.' She looked up in terror. 'I can see the town falling in, crashing down – like I told you, the awful vision. What does it mean?'

'Perhaps you're the next person in danger?' said Una.

'How is that possible?' Cassie asked, gripping her hand tighter. 'It's not safe for either of us. You must stay away from the graveyard.'

'Yes, you already told me that, but I was okay when I went there today, and in fact going there helped me get some really useful information.'

'Last time was a warning,' said Cassie. 'Now I see only darkness for you.'

Ken gently tugged Una's hand free. 'Stop it, Cassie! Stop with all your cock-eyed mumbo-jumbo. This is Tommo's funeral. Have some decency. Una, come and stand with us.'

Una followed Ken to where Mum was now chatting with Jean. Her right hand was tingling. She was no longer predicting other people's end of life; someone had just predicted hers. She'd been blurting out the numbers to everyone, drawing attention to what she'd uncovered – that was a mistake.

Mum gave her a questioning look.

'Cassie's been winding her up,' said Ken.

'I think I need to eat something,' said Una, starting to tremble again.

'Come here,' said Mum. 'Funerals are emotional. Just let it all out.' And she drew Una in tightly for a hug.

# 23

## *Looking Rocky at the Oche*

Una had never expected to attend a stag do, but here she was on a crisp Saturday morning, at a corner table in the Eagle and Snowdrop, surrounded by Ken's friends and Tim. After finding the third number at the funeral yesterday, she had woken up remotivated to discover the connection between the deaths. Today was a prime opportunity to grill the attendees for information, with help from Tim providing he stuck to their deal. It was also an opportunity to distract her thoughts from Cassie's ominous words.

As Anton was now organising today's event, she felt reassured that it wouldn't get out of hand.

'So, Anton,' said John, 'what have we got lined up for this afternoon?'

'Well, we're going to have a few rounds of drinks in here.'

'And . . .?'

'And some snacks as well.'

'Oh, right,' said John. 'That sounds a bit tame compared to my stag do.'

'Look,' said Ken, 'I'm under orders from her indoors not to go mad.'

'Fair enough.' John nodded.

'Fine by me,' said Raj. 'At least it's not paintballing. These trousers are new on.'

'Shall we get the pints in, then?' said Ken.

'Not with my tablets,' said John, rattling a plastic freezer bag full of pills. 'Just a sparkling mineral water for me. I'll pace myself.'

'I'll have half a Guinness,' said Raj. 'If I must drink, I'd like to have something I enjoy.'

'Yes,' said Tim, 'I'm going for a single malt.' He was in business casual today, which Una took as a sign he was going to take his interrogation duties seriously.

'Have a large,' said Ken, 'after all your efforts looking after me last weekend. Me and Una, we'll have pints, right?' He looked at her for permission. A twinge of guilt from the DIY store ambush meant that she nodded at him.

'I'll have a pint just this once,' said Anton. He was wearing a heavy-metal band T-shirt. Perhaps this was his tribute to Tommo.

Ken took his smartphone out. 'Super. Just making a voice memo for my assistant to remember – three pints, half a Guinness, a large single malt and a water. Reminder – weekly alcohol limit?'

'Reminder – your weekly alcohol consumption limit is seventeen units,' said the phone assistant.

'But it's a stag do,' said Ken, keen to form a double act with his deadpan electronic sidekick.

'Assistant, assistant,' said John in his booming town crier voice, leaning towards Ken's phone, 'not just water, sparkling water.'

Ken headed to the bar and Anton followed to help him. Una could see that Tim was deep in conversation with Raj, hopefully getting useful background. She turned towards John.

'So, John, was it you I saw outside the wedding shop the other week?'

'Wedding shop?'

'It's on a small lane of shops just off the high street,' said Una. 'Not much down there.'

'Could have been.' John was fidgeting with his bag of pills. 'I was probably trying to get my ten thousand steps in for the day.'

'Do you recommend any of the shops along there?'

'Didn't even notice them,' he said. 'You're better off asking Ken for shopping advice.'

'Will do, thanks.' There was no need to ask Ken; based on that enigmatic response, she'd return to the street where Bridal Dreams was located and investigate the charity shop herself.

Ken and Anton returned with the drinks.

'Our first toast,' said Anton, standing up and raising his pint. 'The sign on the table says "Reserved", but we're going to be anything but this afternoon. To the stags!'

Una laughed at his joke. It was terrible, but his confidence needed boosting ahead of his wedding speech.

'Thanks, Anton,' said Ken, also standing up. He was wearing a Burberry polo shirt with a good heft of aftershave. 'But let's also raise our glasses to our dear friend Tommo. He was my partner in crime for many years and I don't know what I'll do without him.' His eyes were shining and his mouth set firm.

191

Una scanned the pub for a quick risk assessment. There was a rug by the wood fire that was lying on a polished floor – plenty of opportunity for skidding into the flames. A large golden Labrador panted next to its owner – potentially could go feral. Brass hangings on the rough white walls gave a rustic feel but could drop on a customer from a sudden draught. Having completed her initial review, she sat back and relaxed, taking a few sips of the lager that Ken had chosen. She looked up to see Tim scanning the room, and she wondered what sort of risks he could see and whether he'd made a better job of it.

'Perhaps we could play cards,' said Raj.

'Not with you,' said John. 'I lost my lawnmower fund to you at poker.'

'What about darts?' said Tim. 'Board over there, I notice.'

Una hadn't spotted the dartboard. Darts would make a great weapon when used by drunken players. Even worse, this was the sort of extreme pub sport that Tim would enjoy; he'd probably ask to get sponsored for playing it.

'I love darts,' said Ken. 'I was a junior champion, not wanting to blow my own trumpet.'

'I'd be up for that,' said John. 'Perhaps I can win some money back from you, Raj.'

'It's not my usual pursuit, but I think my hand-to-eye coordination is in a better state than you two old-timers.'

'But you're only a few years younger than us,' said John.

'Leave it,' said Ken, 'let the arrows do the talking.'

Una stared at the table, hoping not to have to join in. She'd tried darts once before, at a holiday camp as a teenager. It had been stressful launching hand-held missiles at a board as

192

people oohed and aahed behind her. In her head, the trajectory of the dart and its target were clear, but her hand trembled and she couldn't execute the line she wanted. After she'd finished her go, Dad had patted her on the back and she'd asked him if there had ever been any casualties from darts. He'd assured her there hadn't, and in fact darts was probably safer than dominoes. But then a barman who was scrubbing beer rings off the Formica tables with a dishrag mentioned a staff budgerigar that had had its wing clipped. 'Flew in a circle for ever after that,' he'd said. Una had never played again.

'Let's split into teams,' said John.

'You and Ken should be a team,' said Raj, swiping off his Guinness moustache with a practised flick, 'as the more senior representatives.'

'Happy to do so,' said Ken. 'Raj, it's your go to pick as you're the next oldest.'

Raj summoned a surprised expression. 'I'd like to pick Una. I'd be delighted to have another younger player and a fellow birdwatcher to boot.' He clinked her pint glass.

'I guess we're a team then,' said Tim, looking at Anton.

'I'm really not that good at darts,' said Anton.

'Do we have to play as teams?' asked Tim.

'Yes,' said Ken. 'It adds dramatic tension.'

Being on a team with Tim was no fun and Una had plenty of advice for Anton on that topic, but she guessed he would soon find out for himself.

Ken wheedled some darts from the barman and then stood in front of a small blackboard that had been put up next to the dartboard.

'Team names?'

'The Outright Winners,' said Tim. Anton scowled at him.

'We'll be the All Stag Wonders,' said John.

'Brilliant,' said Ken. 'Look out, Tim, I've got a maths teacher here. We'll be all over you. Raj, Una?'

'Ladies' choice,' said Raj, making a small bow.

'That's a funny team name,' said Ken, chuckling.

'I simply meant that Una should choose for us,' said Raj.

The well-intended chivalry made her sigh. She'd have to think of some tedious pun name like when they had the sixth-floor Christmas pub quiz. This was tantamount to brainstorming!

'The Darts Slayers?' she said.

Raj clapped his hands. Anton laughed and put his head in his hands. Ken chalked up their name on the board.

'Let's start,' said Ken. 'Best of three.'

He walked towards the faded line on the lino floor.

'Hold on,' said Tim. 'We've not talked prizes yet.'

'Isn't the spirit of taking part enough in itself?' said Anton. 'This is just a friendly game in a local pub, after all.'

Tim's brow furrowed.

'No,' said Ken, 'he's right, we need prizes. What about the losers pay for dinner for the winners?'

'I should mention,' said Anton, 'that I've already ordered an assortment of bar snacks for this afternoon so that we don't all get too drunk.'

'Dinner sounds good,' said Tim. 'Three courses, right? Plus coffee and petit fours.'

'As much as you can eat,' said Ken.

'Wow,' said Tim.

'We're going to an all-you-can-eat buffet later. Amazing place. Curries, pasta, chow mein – it's like going on a trip around the world.'

'I see,' said Tim. 'I have quite a restricted diet, to be honest, with my training. Can't we have a cash prize?'

'Sixty-quid pot for the winners,' said Ken. 'So that's a tenner in each.'

Raj, Ken and John each put in £10, but Anton, Tim and Una only had cards.

'What about the losers have to donate to my charity triathlon?' said Tim. 'Happy to post you the link.'

'Hang on,' said Raj. 'What sort of charity is it?'

'It's for young people who—'

'Young people.' Raj beamed. 'That's where we should be investing our time and money.'

'Of course,' said Tim.

'Count me in.'

The game began. Una stood behind the other players in case a dart flew backwards. There was still the chance of one rebounding off the wall next to her, but her experiences in Eastbourne were helping her gain a better sense of perspective. A ricochet off the brass horseshoe onto the jukebox and into one of her major organs was pretty unlikely.

Tim, John and Raj took the first turns for their respective teams and racked up similar scores. Una wasn't that sure what to do except that it was probably best to aim at the central bullseye.

'Do we have a strategy?' she asked Raj.

'Just try and hit the board, let's start there,' he said, taking out a packet of chewing gum and offering her a stick. She declined. Chewing gum reduced the risk of gum disease, but could easily get lodged in the throat.

'Did you get that from Trunnocks?' She remembered the brand being on offer by the till.

'I occasionally go there in an emergency if I need supplies.'

'The lady doth protest. He loves Trunnocks,' said John, circling nearby. 'Although you did find poor Harry in there.'

'Yes, there was nothing I could do,' said Raj. 'He barely had a pulse by the time I got to him, so I removed the fish fingers that he was gripping on to and made him comfortable. What's more, I tried to keep the scene clear and calm, although Trunnocks shoppers are a little on the rowdy side.'

Ken made a loud *pfft* sound.

'Anyhow, it's your go, Una,' said John. 'I've just got a solid fifty, so no pressure.'

Ken took his place by the blackboard to record her score.

Una's focus on the centre of the board was wavering after the revelation that Raj had been at Trunnocks. Her first dart clipped the metal frame and hit the floor. She gripped the second dart and rocked her hand back and forth to find the right angle. She wondered if Raj had ever visited Eileen and perhaps shared his ageist views. The dart hit the wall and plunged to the floor.

'Concentrate,' said Raj. 'And a bit more force this time. Really attack it.'

She rotated her shoulders back and forth and shook out her right hand to release any tension. As the only female attendee at the do, there was pressure not to look weak or uncoordinated. And she was probably the youngest too, though not by much. She imagined the board was the work

196

promotion she yearned for. She wanted to hit that in the middle. Her arm drew back, and as it came forward, she suddenly thought about whether Raj knew about the trip to the DIY store. Had he been there? She couldn't remember seeing him.

The dart moved with pace to the board. It hit the central metal frame and bounced back into Ken's face.

'What!' He looked up from browsing his phone and then down at the dart at his feet. 'No, not the face!'

'Sorry, Ken,' said Una. 'I put too much force into that last one.'

'Could have had my eye out.'

'Let me see,' said Raj, peering at Ken's face. 'No mark there. And no marks for our team either, Una.'

'You did your best,' said Anton.

'I mean, if that was your best . . .' said Tim, with the same smile he wore in the prize-winner photo on his desk at work.

'First you give me a shock at the DIY store and now you're pelting me with darts!' Ken was smiling, but he'd paled – he was still wary of her after her recent ambush.

'It was an accident,' said Anton. 'It bounced off the board. I saw it myself.'

'Only teasing,' said Ken, picking up the darts from the floor. 'You're up next, Anton.'

Anton stood a little behind the line.

'No, on the line,' said Tim. 'You can go right up to it, you know.'

Anton shuffled forward. He raised the dart and started to rock it back and forth, the arm of his moth-eaten tweed jacket tight at the elbow. The first dart hit the edge of the board, but outside any scores.

'Terrible,' said Tim.

'At least he hit the board,' said Raj, 'and not one of us.'

'Aim higher this time,' said Tim. With Una's insider knowledge, she could see that his team-building skills were stretched.

The second dart pinged off the top of the board. Ken covered his face with his arms.

'You need to concentrate,' said Tim. 'At least get some kind of score.'

'Perhaps I should just default or something,' said Anton, his shoulders slumped beneath the stiff shoulders of his jacket. 'You could have my turn instead, Tim, as you're the expert at this.'

'We're playing teams,' said Ken. He swivelled towards Tim. 'But perhaps age and experience are needed to win the game.'

Anton threw his third dart and scored a two.

'Are you deliberately trying to lose this game for us?' said Tim. 'Are you just letting Ken and John win, because if so, that is really patronising to old people.'

'That's it,' said Anton. 'This was supposed to be a fun afternoon for all of us. Well, I'm not having fun. I'm going back to our table.'

He handed the darts to Ken and retook his seat, dabbing at his phone with angry stabs.

'Perhaps we should play singles instead,' said Tim, and the others all nodded.

'I might join Anton,' said Una.

'Good idea,' said Raj. 'We won't be long.'

She shuffled to the table and sipped her almost-full pint.

'Don't take it personally,' she said to Anton. 'Tim finds it difficult working in a team.'

'So I noticed. I find him an odd choice of friend, if that's what he is to you.'

'He's not my friend,' she said. 'In fact, we're in competition for a promotion at work, but I need his help on a particular piece of analysis, so I have to try to work with him.'

'I think it's great that you're trying to push yourself at work, but do you really want someone like Tim as the benchmark to aim for?'

Una decided it would be safer to change the subject. 'How's the wedding film going?' she asked.

'I've made a first cut,' he said, becoming animated, 'and now I'm looking for music to set against the photos based on the era they were taken in. I'll also intercut news footage from that time. I mean, I realise it's for a wedding, but why not add a layer of social commentary.'

Anton had been abruptly dumped from Team Tim. This wasn't the time to point out that people stuffing themselves with chicken chasseur weren't going to appreciate his film.

'Let me know if there's anything else I can do to help,' Una said. 'And I'll make sure Tim doesn't come to Eastbourne again.'

'Sounds good,' he said. 'Let me get your opinion. I'm thinking of starting the film with this special photo of the happy couple.'

He grabbed Ken's phone from the table and unlocked it. The calendar app was open, and she could see that Ken was due to meet Rosa at his house, 11 a.m. tomorrow. Anton swiped the calendar away and showed her a photo of Ken and Mum at Dino's, in front of a mound of ice cream with a sparkler in it. The sparkler was clearly inedible and simply added an unnecessary fire hazard. Ken was smiling full beam into the camera. She'd see if he was still smiling tomorrow, after she'd staked out Rosa's visit to his house.

'I won!' said Tim, bounding back to the table.

'Good game,' said Ken. 'Nice to have a bit of competition for a change. Another round, lads?'

'I guess that means you won't have to donate to your own fundraiser?' said Una.

'As a gesture,' said Tim. 'I'll also donate an additional ten pounds once I've worked out the most tax-efficient way to do so. And speaking of the Ironman, I might have to give the all-you-can-eat buffet a miss. I've got to start cycling back now. But thanks for inviting me, Ken.'

'It was a pleasure,' said Ken. 'Thank you for helping me at the store and coming all the way out here to see us. You know it's my wedding in a couple of weeks.'

'There's no room for anyone else,' Una said, glancing over at Anton. 'I did the table plan.'

'Are you sure?' said Ken.

'Completely.'

'Never mind. Nice to meet you all,' said Tim, buckling his cycling helmet on. 'See you Monday, Una.'

'Yes, safe cycling,' said Una. 'I'll get the next round in, then.'

'I don't normally let women buy rounds,' said Ken, 'but as I'm a feminist, I'll have another lager, ta.'

# 24

## *Kentrapment*

Sunday morning, 8 a.m. The gentle sound of joggers huffing, electric wheelchairs whirring and industrial coffee-makers shuddering through their cleaning cycle wafted through the window of the guest bedroom. Una swung out of bed and went into the kitchen. Mum was already in there, slicing avocado to put on top of a potato waffle.

'This is Ken's favourite,' she said. 'He calls it his hipster breakfast.'

Ken came into the kitchen, his damp hair unquiffed. He was a picture of lethargy as he leant against the fridge.

'Avocado? Very fancy,' he said. 'That should help with the hangover.'

'Any plans this morning?' asked Una. 'Are you going straight back to your house or making any detours?'

'Straight back today,' said Ken. 'Need to get there before eleven as I've got a delivery coming, and then I'll pick you up later, my angel, for the tastings with the caterers. Perhaps we could suggest avocado on waffle to them?'

Mum giggled. 'Not for a wedding, Ken! Here, your breakfast is ready.'

'Champion,' said Ken. 'I might just have a couple of paracetamol before I make a start on it.' He headed towards the bathroom.

Una needed to engineer the meeting with Rosa to take place with Mum present – make her aware that Ken was hiding something. She'd have to use all her recently improved fieldwork skills for the plan to succeed.

'Why don't we go with Ken when he leaves,' she suggested, 'get a spot of fresh air. We can pick up those extra confetti boxes you were after at the party shop on the way to his house.'

'You'll be quite safe walking around there at this time,' Mum said, 'if that's what you're worried about. I looked at the local BBC news and there's been no escaped zoo animals today.'

Una was going to have to think on her feet. 'I want things to be perfect for you,' she said, 'and I want to make sure I pick the exact brand that you like.'

Mum stopped fanning the avocado over the waffle and looked up. 'We don't have to have that extra confetti. I'm just making a fuss over nothing. Anyhow, I've got another two weeks to sort that out, you just relax.'

'I'd like to go for a walk with you this morning,' said Una. 'I just want to spend some quality time with you before the wedding.'

It was a low move to manipulate Mum like this, but as she said the words, they no longer seemed so disingenuous. She did want to spend some time with her before the wedding. She hadn't exactly been that regular in visiting these last few months, even after all her intentions to do better.

'Of course we can go together,' said Mum. 'But I'm not going to disappear after the wedding, you know.'

'We could pop by Ken's after. I've never been inside his house.'

'We won't have time for that,' said Mum. 'I've got choir practice at eleven-thirty, so we can go to the party shop together and I'll head off from there.'

Ken arrived back, quiff now in place, and picked up the potato waffle like a slice of toast.

'We're going to come with you when you leave,' said Mum. 'Walk to the party shop.'

'The more the merrier,' said Ken. 'Although it isn't a party shop unless I'm in it.'

After breakfast, they strolled towards Ken's house, stopping at the corner of his road near the party shop. Ken and Mum hugged and gazed at each other on the uneven paving slabs, unaware of the precarious foundation beneath them, before Ken strolled off down his street. Una scanned the area to see if she could spot Rosa hiding somewhere and point her out to Mum. She just needed to keep Mum here until Rosa appeared. If only she had her binoculars to zoom in on those leylandii.

'Hi, Rosa,' said Mum. 'How are you? This is my daughter Una, by the way. Don't know if you two have met yet?'

Una turned back. Rosa was right in front of her, hugging Mum. She was wearing pastel green dungarees with a dark green mohair scarf draped round her shoulders, and her hair was tied up with a brightly coloured piece of cloth. She looked like the sort of person who would hang out with Anton rather than Ken.

Rosa beamed. 'Hi, Sheila. Hi there, Una. I'm good, thanks, looking forward to the wedding.'

'We're just getting some more confetti – it never ends. Shame you can't make the hen do,' said Mum.

'I know,' said Rosa. 'Hope you have a great night.'

'Well, we don't want to be keeping you out in the cold. Take care now and we'll see you on the morning of the big day, if not before.'

'I've got my kit ready,' said Rosa.

'And do you live round here?' said Una. She needed to prolong this conversation while she worked out a new approach.

'Yes, just a few streets across from here,' said Rosa, wrapping her scarf tighter and pointing in the vague direction of Chamberlayne Road.

'So what are you doing in this neck of the woods?' asked Una.

'Una,' said Mum, 'I don't think Rosa needs to share her business with us. We'll be on our way now.'

Rosa waved and strode off towards Ken's house, leaving Una defeated. Her plan had failed – Ken was safely ensconced in his house, Rosa about to meet him, and she and Mum were standing on a corner, shivering.

'What was all that about the big day?' she asked.

'Rosa's coming round the morning of the wedding to do our hair and make-up,' said Mum.

'Is she any good?'

It was bad enough having to wear a peplum dress, but she didn't want to look like a clown in a peplum dress.

'She's a very creative person,' said Mum. 'She's been doing hair for years and she's studying on top of that. Look

204

at the time! I need to push on and get to the hall. I don't want to give the choir leader any cause for complaint – she's scary enough as it is.'

Una couldn't think of a way to bring Mum with her to catch Ken out. 'That's fine,' she said. 'I think I'll have a bit of a stroll while I'm out anyway, and I can pick up the confetti on my way back.'

'Okay,' said Mum, striding off before turning back to face her. 'But make sure to pull your fleece up around your neck, I don't want you catching a cold before the wedding. See you later.'

As Una started to walk down Ken's road, she considered her next strategy. Back at her desk on the sixth floor, data presented itself in spreadsheets in comma-separated files or through tidy tables output from data queries. She was in the wild now, hunting down raw data. She hadn't realised how much boldness it required.

She pulled her fleece collar up to hide the lower part of her face and advanced with quiet footsteps. Her new plan was to stake out Ken's house and peer through the windows to see what was going on with her own eyes. She could take photographic evidence.

Ken's house was a semi-detached with large lead-light windows at the front and a dark grey front door. The pointing on the brickwork was immaculate and the frames of the double-glazed windows were a gleaming silver. It was a solid house that felt safe and well maintained. She crept along the gravel driveway of tiny orange stones, making the low-level crunch of a bowl of cornflakes. Despite Ken's exuberant personality, the house blended well with its neighbours and she didn't notice anything with the stamp of Ken about it until she was close up and spotted the small, glistening disco ball above the front door. Eye-catching, unnecessary, but light enough to cause no serious damage if it dropped on someone's head.

She stood flat against the side of the house where it met the front, her shoulder nestled into the drainpipe. What next? She had reached her target destination, but as she wasn't usually spontaneous and had no skills at making stuff up on the spot, she was now at an impasse. She sneaked a glance at the front of the house from around the edge of the wall and noticed a security camera over the door frame, just inside the small porch. She might already be under surveillance.

This was no time to be a wallflower. She wiggled round to the large window at the front, with its pink velvet drapes, and dropped down low. She was now squatting under the window frame. Thankfully, the wall at the front of the house would hide her from any passers-by. She just needed to slowly come up enough to peek in through the window. Only hard evidence would slake her thirst for the truth.

She took three deep breaths, struggling to fully inflate her lungs as she hung onto the window frame in her squatting position, which was now burning her calves. Time to come up. She edged her head upwards, past the window frame, and looked inside. A large white living room ran all the way to the garden at the back. Ken stood in the centre with his back to her, and in front of him was Rosa. She seemed to be concentrating on his tummy area.

Una took her phone out, ready to snap. This didn't look good.

'Gotcha,' a voice said behind her, softly into her right ear, strong hands pressing down on both her shoulders.

Was it that nosy parker Arthur? He always seemed to be hovering about. Or was it the police? The security camera might have triggered some sort of hotline because of her suspicious movements. She was never going to get promoted if she had a record of snooping in quiet residential streets. She slowly turned her head.

'What on earth are you doing?' It was Anton. He was wearing a black leather jacket today, and she had to admit it went well with his scowl.

'I can explain,' she said.

He stood up and gestured for her to follow him inside the house. She was mortified. She didn't want Anton to find Ken and Rosa together, but he'd already opened the front door.

The living room smelt of expensive scented candles.

'Hello there,' said Ken. 'Been to your Hells Angel meeting today? Got your chapter outside, head out on the highway and all that?'

'Just a new jacket,' said Anton. 'Bumped into Una nearby, so I thought I'd invite her in for a coffee. You can carry on with your fitting. Hi, Rosa.'

Fitting? Ken turned to his side and looked into a mirror on the wall. Rosa took a few steps back. She must have come here to adjust this waistcoat he was admiring. It was in a similar style to the one that Tommo had worn at his last bingo-calling event. Ken was turning from side to side, assessing his reflection. Rosa darted forward to pick a thread off the waistcoat. It was mainly gold, with the same lavender colour as Una's bridesmaid dress on the buttons and trim.

'I'm keeping my special wedding waistcoat secret from your mum,' said Ken. 'I'm making it match the dresses you were trying on at the wedding shop. She'd only go on at me about keeping costs down. Get the confetti all right? That was quick.'

'I can't believe it. I've only just met you, Una,' said Rosa, 'and five minutes later we meet again. It's a small world.'

Una smiled. Eastbourne felt very small as she stood in the room with her fleece still covering her mouth. She rolled it down.

'Don't want to disturb you,' she said. 'Lovely house, Ken. Yes, I'll take you up on that coffee, Anton.'

She followed him out into the kitchen. It looked like a showroom kitchen – gleaming with chrome and subtle grey and white tiles.

'I don't know why Mum doesn't move in here instead,' she said.

Anton opened one of the matching storage jars to put some coffee on. He'd shuffled off his jacket and carefully placed it over the back of a chair, just like Ken did.

'Dad wants to cash in and spend some money on holidays,' he said. 'He's also planning to give a good chunk to Chrissie and me. Anyway, that's not what we're here to discuss, is it?'

He was looking at Una directly. She couldn't think of an excuse, so she decided to come out with something resembling the truth.

'I happened to see Rosa coming into the house,' she said, 'and I just wanted to see why she was here. I have to be curious about things in my job, you see, and perhaps I got a bit carried away.'

'I was at school with Rosa,' said Anton, handing her a coffee, 'and ever since her mum died a long time back, Dad likes to keep an eye on her. We used to live next door to them. He even put some money towards the fashion degree she's doing. I'm very fond of Rosa as well. But I'm even fonder of Dad, and I don't like the way you're acting towards him. Suspicious, like. You could do him some serious damage sneaking up on him like that. I know he can be a bit much at times, but he's a really good guy if you take the time to get to know him. Trust me.'

Una almost hoped for a freak sinkhole to open up and swallow her into the earth's core. 'I'm sorry, Anton.' She winced as she gulped some coffee without waiting for it to cool. 'I got the wrong end of the stick. I'll make it up to Ken. And you.'

'We'll see,' said Anton, scowling again. 'Is there anything else you have to tell me? I feel like there's more to come. You're clearly up to something . . .'

Una looked at him. He was pouring coffee from a cafetière into three brightly coloured mugs that he'd banged down onto the marble worksurface. It didn't seem a good time to tell him she'd seen a series of black and gold numbers that had brought doom to Ken's friends.

'From a professional point of view, statistically speaking, everything should be fine,' she said. 'Thanks for the coffee.'

# 25

## *Holmes in the Home*

Una packed her backpack ready to head back to London and slumped onto the sofa. She'd made progress this weekend – she'd confirmed that there was a series of numbers and that it was very likely someone was planning these deaths. But that was the limit of what she'd achieved. She'd managed to irritate Anton by stalking Ken as an assumed philanderer when his only crime was a penchant for richly patterned waistcoats. And she still didn't know who was behind it all, who the next victim was, and after Cassie's doom-laden words at the funeral, how to deal with the possibility that the next victim might be her.

She stood up and wandered across to the mirror that hung over the mantelpiece. The face that looked back was fearful, not the face of someone who was going to stop a murder. It didn't even look like the face of someone who was going to achieve a minor promotion in a top-flight insurance corporation. Why those numbers?

There was a scrabble of keys at the front door.

'Hi, Una,' said Ken. He tiptoed towards her in a highly ineffective way given he was wearing tap shoes. 'Just been to over-sixties Jazzercise. Got some proper French croissants on the way back for a little afternoon treat. They sell them off cheap after three.' He patted himself on the head. Putting the bag down on the kitchen table, he then tippy-tapped towards the armchair next to her and nestled into it.

Una was growing more used to Ken, and under normal circumstances his ability to hold a complete conversation with himself would have been quite relaxing. 'Mum's having a nap,' she said.

'Good idea,' said Ken. 'That final *42nd Street* number got me out of puff with all the step ball changes. Where's 42nd Street, Jeanette?'

'42nd Street is between 41st and 43rd Street.'

Ken chuckled, 'Makes better jokes than I do.'

Una had no doubt of that.

'42nd Street,' Jeanette continued, 'is in the New York City borough of Manhattan.'

'Ta,' said Ken. 'Knew it.'

Una had overlooked Jeanette as a data source, and yet it had answered a question concerning a number. It was sitting there on the mantelpiece in front of her, in silence, accumulating more and more data about them all without them even knowing. It probably had a better idea of what was going on than . . .

'Ken, do you think Jeanette knows much about numbers?'

Ken sat forward. 'Let me show you. Jeanette, what are Ken's numbers?'

'Ken's numbers are 17, 23, 37, 41, 43, 45,' Jeanette replied.

Una picked Jeanette up and twirled it in the air. She now knew the series that the black and gold numbers came from.

But if they were Ken's numbers, that must mean he was involved.

'You okay, Una?' said Ken, giving her a wary look. 'Just excited, right? I knew I'd get you into these assistants. I'll buy you one for your birthday.'

'What are those numbers?'

'Just the lottery numbers.'

'You do the lottery, Ken?'

'Every week.'

Una's heart raced. 'And what is your view about the lottery? Ever make you feel angry? Homicidally angry?'

'Angry? No way! Not after our win last year.'

'Win!' she repeated. 'You won the lottery? Nobody's mentioned that before.'

'Not just me,' said Ken. 'We do it as a group and so we split the money six ways. We didn't get the top prize as we only matched on five, but we all did all right out of it.'

Suddenly it all fell into place. This was why Ken was so extravagant – the makeover, the wedding party, and of course Jeanette, who had turned out to be a very sound investment.

'But who came up with the numbers?' said Una.

'We have one each. We all put one in.'

'Who's we? And who chose which number?' asked Una, putting Jeanette back and sitting on the edge of the sofa.

'Hold on, let me think,' said Ken, staring at the coffee table in front of him. 'Seventeen is Jean and John, their anniversary; 23 is Arthur; 37 was Harry, 41 Eileen, and 43 for Tommo, his lucky number. Last but not least is 45 for me, my house number.'

The numbers matched the victims, and if that was the sequence, then Ken was in danger. She'd wasted time trying to prove he was behind the killings when in fact he was the next intended victim. But why had the killings started midway through the sequence?

'And when did you win, when exactly?'

'I'll never forget it,' said Ken. 'I ran outside into the back garden. It was night-time and it was cold – I hadn't even bothered to put on my limited-edition North Face fleece. And when I looked up at the sky, there was a full moon and I punched my fist in the air.'

'Just the date,' said Una.

'It was a Wednesday, 1 November,' said Ken.

The first! Every one of the deaths had happened on the first of the month. This was it, this was the link.

She paused, wondering what to ask next. Her mind was buzzing with questions. 'And was there anyone unhappy about splitting the money six ways?'

'No, not at all,' he said. 'I mean, we all did well out of it. But perhaps don't mention it too much in front of anyone else; it's not really the done thing to go on about winning like that when not everyone took part.'

Una leant further forward. 'I would like to know more about your syndicate. How did it get set up? How do you pay for the tickets?'

Ken perked up. 'Sure, if you're interested. Well, we set it up last year after one of the book club meetings. What was it now? John's choice – it was *Casino Royale*. Jean was chuntering on about how she enjoyed the glamour and the senseless killings but she didn't approve of gambling, and then I chipped in to say that I did the lottery once a week and it was harmless. Raj said the lottery was a tax on the poor, he wasn't having any of it, but by the end of my speech, six of us had decided to form a lottery syndicate, including John, on the provision he'd share any winnings with Jean.' He paused, glanced at Una. 'Am I waffling?'

'No, not this time. Go on!' she said.

Ken beamed. 'So, we each chose a number and then every month one of us takes our turn to buy the tickets, in order of the numbers. Harry set up a WhatsApp group so that we can remind whoever's on duty to confirm they've bought the ticket before the draw. I'm up next month, but when I next see everyone, I'm going to tell them that I'll tie up any loose ends and we should call it a day after that. It's getting to be a right faff.'

There was something she was missing; it was nagging away at her. Something she'd already seen that didn't fit.

'But were there any arguments? Someone unhappy with the process?'

'Why do you want to know that?' asked Ken, making circles with his ankles. 'I mean, there was a bit of a to-do at the Halloween party because Cassie hadn't paid her subs two months running. I offered to cover her, but she refused, and then Harry had a go at her because, well, it was her turn coming up to buy the tickets and he said he'd done a full audit of the whole year and she'd missed a small win on her last go – three matching numbers. It was only a tenner each, but Harry had picked up on it, being very thorough, and of course she didn't have the ticket any more. Cup of tea before you go?'

'No! Go on. What happened next?'

Ken leant back in the armchair. 'Cassie lost her temper, said she didn't want to be in the syndicate any more. And Harry said that was fine because if she had special powers she should be able to pick the winning numbers herself anyway. And as no one else wanted to step in – Raj said he didn't think large sums of money should be won by a group of old people – we asked Arthur to make up the numbers and take Cassie's slot and he was delighted. He's very diligent, I'll give him that.'

Una would have to tread carefully and find out more about the repercussions of Cassie's argument with Harry. Having seen Arthur's lonely house, it was cheering to hear that he'd been included, no longer the outsider, a bit of luck. She slammed her right fist on the arm of the sofa – she mustn't say 'luck'.

'Nothing went wrong with the numbers?'

'No. Not with Harry at the helm. After Cassie mucked up, Harry said that whoever was buying the tickets had to check the ones for the last month and confirm they were okay to make sure we didn't miss any more wins. Foolproof.'

The attitude to governance, the book of life hacks – Una was sorry not to have met Harry.

'And nothing else strange occurred with any of the others?'

'Nope, can't think of anything,' said Ken. 'The only thing I can think about is that I'm a little bit peckish. I'll put the kettle on and warm the oven for these croissants.'

Una watched Ken choke on a corner of croissant he'd ripped off and tossed into his mouth, and then unblock himself by carrying out a surprisingly efficient self-initiated Heimlich manoeuvre. And as she observed this ludicrous man who had insinuated his way into her family with his banter and gadgetry, she knew that she had a duty to protect him. The right thing to do was to actively prevent him from suffering an unpredictable statistical outlier of a death, lying in the wedding hall with the numbers 4 and 5 strewn across his fancy waistcoat. That was what both Mum and Dad would expect her to do. And that meant taking on a significant personal risk if the killer twigged what she was up to.

She didn't want to face her increased life insurance payout risk alone. She could ask Tim to help, but he had been so dismissive at the stag do, plus she would have to negotiate with him to get him here and she didn't have anything left to bargain with. She couldn't worry Mum or Ken about it – Mum would dismiss her concerns as overthinking and she had to avoid giving Ken any more shocks. That left Anton. He'd want to protect Ken even if he didn't fully believe her theory. But she knew she'd lost his trust this morning. He might think she was making all this up to postpone the wedding because of her reservations about Ken. She didn't want to annoy him any further.

She needed a way to prolong Ken's life without causing any danger to her own.

'Don't you think it would be better to put off the wedding for a bit after all these unfortunate deaths?' she said, in a pleading tone. 'Give you and Mum time to recover.'

'There's no time like the present. I've learnt that.'

Ken seemed intent on dicing with death. And it was difficult to concentrate on murder with the smell of warm fresh croissants wafting through the flat.

'Or perhaps have a wedding with fewer guests to make it more intimate and less stressful for you both.'

'The more the merrier,' said Ken.

'Surely it's the fewer the truer.'

'I appreciate you looking out for us, but I love your mother and want to spend whatever time I've got left with her. We're getting married on the first, come hell or high water. Let me wake the sleeping beauty,' said Ken, at which point he tippy-tapped towards Mum's bedroom before turning to give Una some jazz hands.

# 26

## *The Favour Swap*

Back in the office on Monday morning, Una had successfully aligned two rectangles on a PowerPoint presentation – and it was only 10.30 a.m. Time to exhale. The sun was beaming full force through the toughened glass window. It was pinballing off her colleagues' screens, causing them to squint, its intrusive rays highlighting the dust particles swarming around the room. She stood up and shimmied the vertical blinds across to block the natural light. The office had perfectly good overhead lighting, lighting she was confident would remain firmly attached to the ceiling.

After this good deed, she was ready to talk to Tim and see if he'd learnt anything at the stag do. She'd kept her side of the bargain, after all. As her first task that morning, she'd gone down to the fifth floor and handed out some flyers about Tim's fundraiser. When she'd stepped out of the lift, she'd felt nervous about having to speak to these strangers, but the people in the pet insurance team were unnervingly friendly. Every time she reached a new row, they frantically bobbed up and down and said things like 'Can I help you?', 'Are you looking for someone?' It was an interesting contrast to her own floor, where a new presence would trigger a response along the lines of 'Can I see your pass? Just need to check you have the correct access to be on this floor.' Thanks to the onslaught of goodwill, she'd generated a reasonable amount of interest in Tim's race, even though none of them knew him.

And then she got to Gareth. On his desk were two photos: a picture of him with his parents and sister, and one of the pet team at a fancy dress party. She couldn't leave him out, so she explained that one of her colleagues was doing an event for charity.

Gareth gave a patient smile. 'I'd be happy to sponsor Tim, he only had to ask.'

And so, there were no debts in the favour bank to Tim. Instead, he owed her the information he'd collected. She hoped this might close some of the missing gaps in her investigation. It would be Tim's last contribution. Thanks to her bold and innovative approach, an approach that had caused a great deal of personal distress, she'd discovered who the intended next victim was, and the connection between the numbers.

*Are you free?* she typed. *Kitchen? We have a great deal to discuss.*

She sat and watched the *Tim is typing* message stay up for longer than she'd expect, given his claim to be the fastest touch typist in the office. Eventually his reply appeared on her screen.

*Have you spoken to Ajay yet?*

*No. Why?*

*Go and see him. Let's speak after that.*

*Okay. Will ping you in a bit.*

Tim's message set off a flurry of worries. As she tried to catch one, many more accumulated behind it. What was important was to identify the worst-case scenario. She was good at that, and knowing the worst case would be comforting. What could Ajay's news be? Further humiliation by the internal audit team? Demotion? Manning the firm's stall at a graduate jobs fair? Redundancy? Yes, redundancy. Perhaps being cast out into the harsh, cold world, forced to break into the emergency fund that she'd squirrelled away. A fund set aside for rainy days. Three months' worth of rainy days, to be exact. But not enough for her projected life expectancy – she hoped to have many more rainy days ahead of her.

She stood up to see if Ajay was free. He was pacing around his desk, looking like he was giving himself a tough talking-to through his headset. She returned to her presentation. The top rectangle had somehow moved right of its companion without her bidding.

Her phone bleeped with a text from Mum asking her to source some novelty sashes for the hen do on Saturday, and to put a message on them, but nothing too crude. Perhaps she could put *Someone's about to murder the bridegroom*? That might force a nervous cluck from one of the hens.

She looked up again to check if Ajay was free and caught him standing without his headset on. She hurried over.

'Hi. Have you got a minute?'

'Una! Come in. Just the person I wanted to see.'

She stood opposite him. There was a half-eaten croissant on a napkin on his desk. Should she warn him about the risk of inhaled croissant, having seen Ken's incident yesterday? She decided to keep silent; Ajay had a PhD in Maths and a PADI diving certificate – he could calculate his own risks. She looked up to find he was giving her his fullest attention. Normally it operated at about 80 per cent, and she would occasionally see competing work thoughts stream across his face. Full attention meant he was about to deliver either particularly good or particularly bad news.

'How are the preparations for your mother's wedding going?' he asked.

'Just a few final pieces to put in place.'

'Great stuff. You know, if you need to take any more time off, just give me a bit of notice and we can get it booked in.'

'No, I don't think that will be necessary,' she said. 'I might work from Eastbourne for the odd day coming up, if that's okay? I'll make sure to set myself up in a confined space so that my mum can't hear anything confidential.'

'Flexible working? Of course,' said Ajay. 'Hybrid working arrangements are something we're actively encouraging as part of our people pillar.'

'Okay. So was what you just said a yes?' she asked.

'It's a big yes.'

'Great. But what was it you wanted to speak to me about?'

'Yes, so, as you know,' said Ajay, 'we're undertaking some restructuring within the department to realign our best people with the strategic goals of the group so that we can remain on the front foot. And that means reviewing the team structure for opportunities to synergise our departmental skillset. Any questions so far?'

Una sat down.

'With the vacancy coming up after Kelly's departure,' he continued, 'we've decided to appoint a new team lead for the special projects team.'

'Okay.'

She wanted to press her hands over her ears because she was so eager to hear what he would say next and so eager not to.

'And we've asked Tim to take on that role.'

Una stood up again. 'What?'

'Well, as you know,' he said, 'Tim is an outstanding member of our team and we think his vision and innovation will help us move to the next level.'

'But you know that I'm doing some really cutting-edge analysis too. I just need a little more time to complete it.'

'I completely appreciate all the terrific work you've been doing and I recognise your dedication to your role here. In fact, Tim said how much he'd enjoyed working with you on the seaside trend analysis and what a great team you made together.'

Una sat down again. Tim had only helped out when it had suited him.

'What will happen to me, though?' she asked.

'As you know,' said Ajay, 'you were reporting to me on a temporary basis while we were reviewing our path forward, but now you will be transitioning to work for Tim.'

'What?'

'I know how much Tim respects your work and I'm sure he will look for opportunities to grow your current role.'

She hadn't brought her comfort biro – that was a mistake. 'I'll have to think it over,' she said.

'Completely understandable. My office is always open to you. I do have a call coming up now.'

Una stormed back to her desk, heedless of the potential for spontaneous combustion from vigorous friction with the nylon-blend carpet below. She pulled back the blinds and let the golden sunshine blast into the office – that was how annoyed she was. She unlocked her screen and was greeted with a new message from Tim.

*Saw you come out of Ajay's office – want to talk? Kitchen?*

She typed her response, aggressively depressing the keys – *OMW!* – then grabbed her comfort biro and headed to the kitchenette.

This time Tim wasn't doing exercises. He was standing motionless by the fridge, looking at her with a grave expression.

'I'm just making a tea if you'd like one,' he said.

'I'm going to have a Coke. A full fat Coke.'

She'd never ordered a Coke before and had to look up its code. Then she slapped the vending machine until the can donked into the release tray.

'There's no way I'm going to work for you, by the way,' she said.

'You don't need to decide straight away,' he said. 'Sleep on it. That's how I learnt to distance myself from anger. I've read quite a few articles in *Men's Health* about—'

'I'm not angry,' said Una, her throat blasted by necking the Coke.

'We worked together so well recently. You've been much bolder than I expected.'

'Well, let me tell you how bold I am,' she said. 'I've worked out the number series. I found a third number at

Tommo's funeral and now I've got the link between them. They're lottery numbers, a syndicate, in fact. And I know who the next intended victim is.'

'Why didn't you tell me this before?'

'Now that I've had a taste of using my own methods, I decided to just go ahead. No more negotiating for help from you and having to be in your debt.'

Tim took a protein bar out of his pocket and slowly parted the wrapper, the smell of chopped cashew filling the kitchenette. 'So you're not interested in what I found out at the stag do?'

'I can't imagine it was very much, since you were so focused on winning the darts match.'

'Actually, I took copious notes on all the information I extracted, and it was interesting stuff. In fact, I'm wondering if there is something in your rather maverick approach. Perhaps I should formalise it into an actual methodology.'

'Don't you dare steal my ideas,' she said. 'And you've still not said what you found out.'

'I'll send you the notes once you've been round the pet team, as we agreed,' said Tim.

She swigged down the rest of the Coke and slung the can into the correct bin. 'Oh, is that how it is? Well, I did that this morning. You're the one in favour debt. So tell me.'

'I think you should check out more about the doctor, Raj. I got him talking about his recent movements and it turns out he was going to the DIY store the day that guy died but he said he arrived after it happened. Was after a dado rail. Probably a coincidence, but still. And look, I'm happy to help you going forward without any strings attached – send

224

me through what you've found out,' he added. 'It could be dangerous. And no one else will get what you're trying to do except me. I mean, you can hardly rely on that drippy Anton. He couldn't even throw a dart.'

'He is not drippy,' she said. 'It hardly takes much strength to play darts. But you do have a point. I'd rather not tell him about what's going on.'

'And in return, you can give the new team structure a go,' Tim said. 'There's some new regulatory policies that need a safe pair of hands to work out how to implement them, and that's got you written all over it.'

'I don't need your help. I don't need anyone's help,' she said, the bubbles coursing through her veins now. 'And you'll have to find someone else to do your regulatory policy grunt work.'

She went back to her desk and, fuelled by caffeine, annihilated the dozen emails that had arrived during her short absence. She didn't need Team Tim; she was the Una Unit.

# 27

## Eyes Down

On Friday evening, Una was back in the same community hall in Eastbourne where she'd started her investigation only a few weeks ago. That evening, Tommo had called the bingo, but tonight there was a substitute for his specially convened memorial game.

'Good evening, everyone. My name is Anton and I'll be filling in as your bingo compère,' said Anton, in his slow, ponderous voice, a little too close to the hand-held microphone. 'We'll be starting in a few minutes.'

The hall was packed out tonight, and his announcement barely caused a dent in the din, which sounded like seagulls fighting to get their fair share of a dropped ice cream.

Una was sitting at a table with Mum and Ken, cards at the ready. Jean and John were on the next table along with Cassie and Arthur. She'd spent the day working in the small spare bedroom at Mum's after getting a painfully early train. The room had no window and she had to contend with a wobbly table to perch her laptop on. But without the intrusive sound of her colleagues on calls or their low-level coughs and movements, it provided a better place to concentrate than her usual open-plan floor. Working away from the office also meant she could avoid Tim. She'd logged off promptly at 5.30 p.m. and girded herself for more bingo, a prime opportunity to observe any unusual behaviour among the suspects.

Raj arrived and sat next to her, having carefully robed the chair with his wax jacket and laid out a blue biro and a yellow pencil in parallel on the table.

'How are you, Una?' he said. 'You know, I think we must be the youngest people in here. It's really not my scene.'

'I'm well, thanks,' she said, placing a silver ballpoint pen on the table as part of her own stationery arsenal.

'Hold on. Why is Anton up there at the front?'

'We were short of a bingo caller tonight,' said Ken, 'so I mentioned it to Anton and he volunteered to step in. Works out well for us all, to be honest, as the caller can't be a player, right? This way, we can all play as normal to honour Tommo.'

'I see,' said Raj. 'Well, that is quite good of him.'

During the drive over, Anton had confided in Una that he was undertaking this challenge to build his confidence for his wedding speech. She could see how calling out numbers was less emotionally taxing than having to spout heartfelt words, but it was still a tough gig. That had been the extent of their conversation. She'd wanted to tell him not to be angry with her after the stake-out last Sunday, and that she had discovered Ken was in danger rather than posing one, but she hadn't known how to word it.

Anton was wearing an elaborate waistcoat tonight similar to Tommo's, but with some kind of birdlife embroidered on it. Una speculated that Rosa had made it – another indicator of how close their families were. And a reminder of how much she'd got wrong.

'I thought you didn't like the bingo,' said Ken, nudging Raj's arm with his elbow.

'I had a ticket to see a local chamber orchestra at St Swithin's, but unfortunately it was cancelled at the last minute, so I thought, why not join you all here, as it's for charity and in honour of our friend.'

'You're very welcome,' said Ken. 'What with all the funny goings-on and the excitement of the bingo, we may need to call on your professional services this evening.'

Raj nodded, then carefully took the top off his biro, impaled it on the other end and smoothed out his bingo card.

'Tonight's event is a memorial for Tommo, who served as the bingo caller here for the past few months,' said Anton.

The crowd were still chatting.

Ken's chair rasped against the floor as he stood up and bellowed, 'Will you lot shut it, please. Anton's trying to start the bingo. Okay?'

The sound died down.

'Thanks, Dad,' said Anton. 'Where was I? All funds raised tonight will be donated to a local charity, Tread Softly.'

'What!' said Raj.

'Have you got a problem with that?' asked Jean.

'I would have preferred it to be a charity whose aims I support.'

'Let's start the numbers,' said Anton, his tone high-pitched with nerves.

He leant forward and pushed the button to make the

228

number dispenser mix up the balls. Then he took out the first one, showed it to the room and announced: 'Thirty-four. A quiet number with the smell of lightly burnt toast.'

The crowd stirred.

'What was that?' said a lady at a table near the stage.

'I repeat: 34. A quiet number with the smell of lightly burnt toast.'

The atmosphere in the room was certainly charged as the crowd absorbed this new and highly idiosyncratic bingo style. Una hoped a riot would not ensue.

'I've got 34,' said Mum.

'What was all that other stuff he said?' asked John.

'He's got synaesthesia,' said Ken. 'He experiences things with different senses. He associates words and numbers with colours, sounds.'

There was an eerie tapping noise. It was John, thumping his hand on the table.

'But that's what it's like for me too,' he said. 'There's a name for it?'

'Yes, it's been documented for ages,' said Ken.

'Wow,' said John, now chopping the table with excitement. 'I'm special.'

'It's not a competition, John,' said Raj. 'And it's more common than you think.'

'Perhaps I should see a doctor about it,' said John.

'It's not dangerous or anything, not if you have it mildly,' said Ken. 'It simply means you have a different way of seeing the world.'

'Whatever it is, he's certainly providing a very different style for bingo,' said Jean. 'I'm not one for unnecessary change, and let's face it, no change is necessary. Can't he just do the normal stuff, the standard phrases that we're used to? It's going to slow us down.'

Raj started to twirl his yellow pencil cheerleader-style. 'You know,' he said, 'I'm actually finding playing bingo rather soothing – my resting heart rate is lower than normal.'

'You're really getting into this now,' said Ken. 'Knew it.'

'It's hardly the Bank Holiday jumbo crossword in the *Telegraph*,' said Raj, 'but it gets one out of the house.'

'Next number,' said Anton, '27. A rich purple with a spiked outline.'

'No, it's more like a claret,' shouted John from the audience.

Anton looked up, frowning. Clearly he wasn't expecting hecklers this evening. He paused for a few seconds. 'A claret *is* a rich purple, so I don't see that we are in any way disagreeing,' he said.

John grumbled, then looked back down at his card.

Anton continued announcing the numbers until Raj shouted, 'Line!'

'It's always the crowd at that table who win,' said the woman near the front. 'I bet they've brought some ringer in to call the numbers. It's a fix. Fix! Fix!'

Everyone in the hall was now looking at Anton. He was radiating humiliation.

'Fix, fix,' continued the woman, on her feet, chanting.

'I'm just pulling out the numbers from this machine,' said Anton, 'and then saying them.'

Una's ears pounded. This was basically a call from the cockpit enquiring, 'Is there a statistician on board?' and yes, there was. She strode to the front of the room and asked Anton to step aside while she addressed the baying mob. She had let him down last weekend, snooping about Ken's house, and now she had an opportunity to show her support.

'Let me assure you all,' she said, 'this apparatus generates a sufficiently random number given the rules of this game. And if you take into account the number of people per table and the number of lines across the games, the probability of two people on the same table getting a line across all the games in one evening is much higher than you would think. I'd be happy to prove that to you.'

The crowd went quiet as Raj went up to collect his prize, and Una returned to her seat. Of course, she hadn't actually calculated the odds, but she knew she was in the right ballpark.

Ken saluted her. 'That told them,' he said. 'I knew you'd take to bingo with your skills.'

Raj was at the front table, grimacing at a bottle of wine that Anton had handed to him. He continued studying the label as he returned to his seat, bringing the bottle close to his eyes. But this meant he failed to see a walking stick that protruded out onto the floor from underneath a nearby table.

'Urrrggh!' he said, as he tripped over the stick. He fell gracefully forward, the bottle rolling away, still intact.

Ken sprang up to go over to him.

Raj slowly gathered himself into a sitting position. 'My ankle. I think I've sprained it.'

Ken helped him hop back to the table and lowered him into a chair, panting with the effort.

231

'Perhaps you should go to hospital, get it checked out,' said Jean. 'Could be a broken bone. You have to be careful about that at your age.'

'I don't require your medical advice, thank you,' said Raj, swinging his right leg onto his backpack. 'It's very likely to be a simple sprain that a few days' rest will resolve.'

A lady from a nearby table placed the winning bottle of wine in front of him. 'Lucky for you it didn't break,' she said, and retreated.

'That blasted bottle,' said Raj. 'I was trying to read about the vineyard and grape varieties on the back and then some oldie left their stick sticking out like a hooligan. Unbelievable.'

Jean picked up the bottle and scrutinised the label. 'I can read it easily. Spellings are all correct. You need your eyes testing.'

'Now, now,' said John.

'I hope I can still make our birding tomorrow,' said Raj.

The games continued until someone from another table had got the next line, then a short break was called and Anton joined the group.

'That was great, Anton,' said John. 'I also experience numbers the way you do.'

'Were you the one who kept interrupting me?' asked Anton.

'Yes, that was me. I've never met anyone else who sees things like that. It's exciting.'

'I appreciate you stepping in, Anton, but really you should be using the traditional phrases,' said Jean. 'I've brought them up on my iPad so you can have it next to you if you're unfamiliar with them. Please use them for the final games.'

'I'll take a look,' said Anton.

There was a short silence; the only sound was Cassie's needles clacking to and fro.

'Making good progress there,' said Ken. 'What is it?'

'You'll find out soon enough, Kenneth.'

'I see, so no predictions from you this evening, thank God.'

The needles stopped, and Cassie sighed and then resumed her knitting. 'No, I've said enough. You've all had plenty of warnings.'

Una pushed her chair back so that she could have a word with Cassie without the others hearing. She thought it was time to follow up on Tim's tip-off. Fortunately, Ken had launched into an anecdote about meeting Judi Dench at a motorway service station.

'I wondered if you had any thoughts on Raj,' she said.

'Thoughts?' said Cassie.

'From an astrological point of view, any insights? Or anything else at all really.'

'Well, Raj is an interesting individual,' said Cassie mistily. 'A Virgo, of course, with his well-ordered ways. But his obsession with youth is dangerous, don't you think?'

Una thought about this for a moment. 'He is a bit ageist, I suppose. But dangerous?'

'I just worry about his single-mindedness. I can't tell you what to do, but I think you're right to be wary of him, that's all.'

'Una, another drink for you?' said Ken, interrupting.

'I'll just have a fizzy water, thanks.' She needed to keep a clear head to watch everyone. She chewed over Cassie's words about Raj and thought about her recent clifftop encounter.

'I'll start the final game,' said Anton.

He took his place at the front and picked the first number. He stared at Jean's iPad before addressing the bingo players.

'Eleven. Also known as "legs eleven", a phrase that draws attention to the shape of the numbers being like a pair of legs – I'd say there's a strong suggestion that the phrase coiner had a biped in mind. And if this is the case, one hopes this isn't an objectification of the legs, especially if they are female legs seen through the male gaze.'

'He's very articulate, isn't he?' said Raj. 'No surprise that he's involved in the creative world.'

'That's my Anton. He doesn't want to be a cog in someone else's wheel,' said Ken. 'He's an independent thinker.'

'I can't understand a bloody word he's saying,' said Arthur from the next-door table, looking like a sad clown who'd run out of custard pies. 'I think we need your leadership to sort it out, Ken.'

Ken stood up and beckoned Anton over.

'A few seconds, please,' said Anton to the room. The crowd tutted, paused and re-tutted.

'I'll give him some constructive feedback,' said Ken as Anton arrived at the table. 'You're doing well, Anton, but just read out the numbers.'

'There's no point in me just reading out the numbers,' said Anton. 'You could get a computer to do that. In fact, you could get a computer to mark off randomly generated bingo cards online so you wouldn't even have to tick the boxes. You'd simply wait to be alerted by the computer to find out if you've won something. Is that what you want?'

'Just the numbers, Anton,' said Ken. 'We haven't got a computer like that anyway; we've only got Jean's iPad.'

Anton returned to the front and set the machine going again, then picked out the next ball. 'Eighty-eight. I repeat, 88.'

The two fat ladies at the front of the room looked stoic, but slightly melancholy, as if they were no longer needed there.

'House!'

It was Cassie. Throwing down her knitting, she ran to the front and took the box of mint choc sticks and the bottle of Prosecco from Anton before hurrying back to the table.

'Finally, my luck has turned!' she said.

'Good one, Cassie,' said Ken. 'Two wins for our tables. Let's hope that marks the end of the run of bad luck our little group has had.'

'I don't believe it is bad luck,' muttered Una.

'Sorry?' said Arthur, leaning across.

'It's nothing, Arthur,' said Mum. 'She's got a bee in her bonnet about some numbers.'

'Have you now?' said Arthur. 'And have you got any money tips? Bought any of these NSFWs I've been reading about?'

'I think you mean NFTs,' said Una, 'and no, I prefer less risky investments.'

'Gotcha,' said Arthur, tapping his nose.

With the games complete, the group started to put on their coats.

'That leg doesn't look good,' said Ken, pointing to Raj's ankle. 'Looks more like legs ten than legs eleven – get it? Anyhow, it's all puffed up.'

'We'll take you to hospital to get it checked,' said Jean.

'The morning will be fine. May not even be necessary by then,' said Raj.

'Let's do it now,' said John. 'Only just gone half eight. Then I can still go out birding tomorrow morning. I'll take some pictures for you.'

'And if you're in pain, I can drop by to check you're doing okay,' said Jean. 'We pensioners have to look after each other, don't we?'

'I can look in on you as well,' said Mum.

'I've got that foot spa at the shop – still in its box. That might help,' said Jean. 'Of course, there will be a modest cost involved. But it will help Tread Softly and therefore other elderly people.'

Raj glared at her. 'No thanks.' He swung his leg off the backpack and zipped the bottle of wine inside. 'Let's go, then. I'm not a big fan of supermarket Californian Chardonnay, but perhaps I will have to acquire a taste for it.'

'See you at the hen do tomorrow, Sheila,' said Jean.

'Hen do?' said Cassie.

If a pin had dropped, it would have been heard.

'Didn't you get your invite?' asked Mum. 'It must have got lost in the post, it's been very on and off recently.'

'My Chrissie will be there,' said Ken, his tense expression betraying that he was complicit in Cassie's snub.

Cassie looked smaller than usual. Sometimes Una got left off invites for work drinks, and she knew that feeling of being the outsider even if those social events looked awful.

'I'll be there too,' she said.

'That's okay,' said Cassie. 'I might have plans for tomorrow night anyhow.'

'Raj, we'd better get going,' said Jean. She scuttled off, dragging John behind her. Raj hopped along in their wake.

Anton handed Una her coat.

'That was a good preparation for your speech,' she said. 'I mean, it should be much easier than dealing with that lot.'

'Thanks. Yes, in theory it should be easier, but it will be really emotional at the wedding compared to just calling out some numbers.'

Una nodded.

'But thanks for handling the hecklers with your statistical knowledge.'

'I just made it up, to be honest with you. But the spirit of it was true – I mean, the machine isn't biased, so now and then people from the same table will win on the same night.'

'Whatever you did, it worked,' said Anton, smiling at her. 'But I never want to see another number again.'

Una was growing less keen on them herself.

# 28

## *Age Against the Machine*

Saturday afternoon had been designated for a final clear-out at the flat. Mum had asked Una to sort through two large cardboard boxes in the storage cupboard by the front door. The cupboard was filled with bric-a-brac that had survived the move from their old home. Una hovered around the hallway while Mum and Ken got ready to leave to meet the wedding caterers for a final tasting. Mum was leaning into the hall mirror, putting on lipstick, and Ken was taking a selfie.

'There you go,' he said, 'hashtag foodie.'

'Anything suitable for the charity shop, take to Jean,' said Mum.

'I'm still doing my own clear-out,' said Ken. 'Anton's on the case for that; likes to make himself useful while he's staying with me. He thinks he's going to uncover something that could go on the *Antiques Roadshow*, but it's just a load of old tat. Speaking of which . . .'

He picked up an onyx-effect ashtray from the hall table. The ashtray that everyone had used at the smoky, spirit-fuelled parties Mum and Dad had held when Una was a small child. Then it became the loose change pot. And now it was empty.

'You can't throw that out without my express permission!' said Una.

'Sorry, Una love, don't get upset – of course, if there's anything you want to keep, no problem,' said Ken.

'What are the three Post-it notes on the floor over there for?' said Mum.

'I'm going to do Keep, Throw and Give Away piles,' she said. 'See you later.'

She scooped out the first tier of objects and sat on the couch ready to sift. The Spice Girls posters carefully unpicked from a magazine with only the barest of staple marks marring Mel C's midriff and Geri's armpit were going straight on the Throw pile. They were followed by some of her old school books. No charity shop customer would want to see her Class 2C English language essay, 'The Highwayman and the Duchess'. Glittery fingerless gloves that she used to wear at school when it was cold – Throw. She examined a box of Monopoly to make sure all its pieces were present – Keep. The game had provided early lessons in risk management. Mum, the Racing Car, would always try to get Park Lane or Mayfair, whereas Dad, the Wheelbarrow, built up a balanced portfolio of mid-range properties that didn't yield as much as the higher-end properties but provided a healthy income whatever the roll of the die. Una, the Thimble, took a prudent approach and concentrated on the utilities and railway stations. She rarely won.

The final item was a 1,000-piece jigsaw of Worcester Cathedral that seemed to be complete with some approximation – Give Away.

After forty minutes, she had two relatively small piles of Keep and Throw and a larger pile of Give Away, which she stuffed into her backpack to take to Tread Softly.

She no longer needed to check the map on her phone. Instead, she strode forward with purpose, the pieces of puzzles rattling in her backpack like a giant maraca. It was Saturday afternoon and the streets were busier than during the week; mainly locals, with the occasional clump of tourists who'd braved the February chill. She made her way to the small parade of shops. When she got there, she walked past Tread Softly and looked into the window of Youth Fountain, Jean's charity shop rival. The display showed mannequins in various sorts of leisurewear; at their feet were jigsaws of brutalist architecture in stark urban settings. She leant in to further examine a stack of books in the window – they were Harry's book of life hacks. Jean must have donated them en masse.

She retraced her steps and entered Tread Softly. She knew the shop bell would ring, so she had no palpitations this time when it did so.

'Hello, Jean,' she said.

Jean beamed. The shop was fuller than ever. Una noticed that the foot spa was missing. Had someone actually bought it?

'You managed to sell the foot spa?'

Jean nodded. 'My Saturday girl, Louise, was in this morning. She said someone took it when she wasn't looking but left the money on the counter. She was probably on the TikTok.'

'And is Pedro around today?'

'No,' said Jean. 'You just missed him, I'm afraid.'

240

Una dumped the jigsaws and other knick-knacks on the counter.

'You're giving away that jigsaw?' said Jean. 'A cathedral jigsaw?'

'I'm not the sort of person to do a jigsaw twice, Worcester Cathedral or not,' Una said.

'That'll go quickly,' said Jean. 'It's a very attractive one. Feel free to have a look round. Got lots of great books in today. Prize-winners – I'm going to do a prize-winner display. Just the sort of books I used to pick out for the book club.'

'Thanks, but I'd better be off,' said Una. 'I have to collect some things for the hen do.'

'Looking forward to that,' said Jean. 'I'm going to get my hair done for it in a bit. I've been waiting for John to turn up so I can have a lift, but never mind, I can get the bus. He's been in his own little world the last few weeks.'

Una swung her backpack on, now jigsaw-free, and opened the door. As she stepped out, she saw a swirl of waterproof poncho. It was John, walking with purpose down the street, heading away from Tread Softly.

She had never followed anyone before. She stuck on her sunglasses and took out a baseball cap from her backpack, putting it on so that the peak was low over her face. She looked like any other February pedestrian in Eastbourne. John was striding at quite a speed. According to the fitness app on her watch, she was now walking at a Fast pace to keep up with him, and she was getting out of breath. Luckily, he was a man on a mission, and didn't check behind him at any point.

As he turned off the road parallel to the railway station, Una realised he was heading towards Bridal Dreams. A few minutes later, he turned into the dead-end street and went right to the end of it, entering the charity shop, Age Against the Machine.

Una dashed past the wedding shop to avoid any chance of Lilah seeing her and entered a few seconds behind him. He was standing at the single till at the back of the store, swirling his rain poncho. If she was quick, she could head out and hide – but no, she was fed up of hanging back and observing at a distance. This time she was going to get a result. She picked up an old copy of the *Guinness Book of Records* from a nearby bookshelf in case things got ugly, and approached the till.

'John,' she said. 'Fancy seeing you here. I think I spotted you the other week when I was at the wedding shop. Do you come here often?'

John turned round. His face was ashen. Una looked down at the counter, where a snow globe sat, its contents mid drift. She waited a few seconds while more of the flakes settled.

'I can explain,' said John.

Why would someone look guilty about a snow globe?

'Why don't we go for a coffee?' he added.

'I know a café nearby that's pretty unpopular,' Una said.

'Okay. Yes, let's go there.'

John swept the snow globe into the furls of his poncho. Una led him out of the charity shop and they walked in silence to the café. This was helped by her having offloaded the 1,000-piece jigsaw from her backpack. The

242

café was as sparsely populated as on her last visit with Tim and Anton.

'I'll get the coffees, John, what would you like?'

'Just a small Americano, thanks.' The coffee choice of someone who was trapped in a corner with no way out.

'Take a seat,' said Una.

She collected the coffees and joined John at an empty table at the back.

'Here's what happened, Una,' he started before she had even sat down. 'Jean and I put our heads together about what to get your mother and Ken as a wedding present. We wanted it to be something personal. I mean, we had a look at the wedding list, but how fondly can you remember someone when you're using a stainless-steel colander they gave you?'

Una didn't reply. She sipped her coffee – only three and a half minutes since pouring, but she was absorbed in John's tale.

'And so we decided on a snow globe of Eastbourne. It was where they met, after all. Thanks to our previous purchases, we're top of the list when it comes to limited editions, which of course this was. It came through no problem and I went to collect it from the post office when they left a little card. But then disaster.'

He stopped and glugged some Americano.

'I stopped by at Tread Softly on the way back,' he went on. 'Jean wanted me to get some stuff down from the top shelves in the storage cupboard. Suddenly there was an almighty shriek, and I could sense a blur of orange and sharp teeth approaching at speed – I'd stood on some aspect of Pedro. I panicked and dropped the parcel. I heard the tinkle of delicate snow globe smashing on the floor, then looked down and saw a puddle of glittery glycerine water. There was no way to repair the dome, and parts of Eastbourne had fractured too. I was welling up, I don't mind telling you.'

'I also had a bad experience with Pedro – it dug its claws into me,' Una said.

'That cat has become completely out of control. Anyhow, I didn't want to tell Jean about the broken snow globe, so I picked it up and put it in the bin outside, then started looking for a replacement. Sold out online, of course, so I tried to track one down at likely retail outlets around town. I knew I wouldn't bump into Jean in any of the other charity shops. And today – triumph! I have a replacement.' John had swigged down all of his Americano and was slightly giddy.

His odd behaviour now made sense. Pedro was clearly a general menace, but at least the cat didn't have a personal vendetta against Una, which was a sort of consolation.

'I hope they like it,' he said. He removed the replacement snow globe from his bag and shook it. 'Perhaps it will kick off a collection like our own. Hours of pleasure.'

Una had to concede that the snow globe had a sort of calming quality, as the flakes settled on the seafront. That said, she knew Mum would see it as a dust trap.

'It's very thoughtful,' she said.

John smiled and stood up.

'Better get home before Jean. We're going round to see Raj later as his ankle's still painful, and then I've got to drop her off for this hen do.'

'I just saw her, actually,' said Una. 'She was saying something about a hair appointment.'

His eyes flashed as he remembered. 'Thanks for the coffee. And you'll keep this as our secret, won't you?'

'Okay,' said Una.

John got halfway across the café, then turned back. 'By the way, what happened about our photos? I'm looking forward to seeing the old crowd together.'

'Anton's already made a first cut; it's all taking shape.'

He gave her a thumbs-up, then headed out of the café. He'd made a good point about the photos. Perhaps it was worth taking another look at them in case there was something she'd missed about the victims. She would ask Anton if he had a rough draft of his film yet. Taking an interest in whatever he'd put together could be a way to show she was making an effort to support the wedding. She knocked back her flat white, girding herself for the mandatory fun of the evening ahead.

# 29

# Hen Do or Hen Don't

'Which bar is it we're going to, Sheila?' asked Chrissie, carefully placing a silver sash over her fulsome bust. 'Shame I didn't get here earlier, I could have helped with the planning. We want to give you a proper night out. I bet after a few drinks you're a saucy little minx.'

Una sensed that Chrissie found the factual sash slogan she'd chosen at the party shop, *Sheila's Hen Do*, disappointing. On first impression, all the Ken-ness that Anton lacked was present in a concentrated form in Chrissie. Even though she'd just flown in from Dallas for the wedding with her husband and two daughters, she'd insisted on coming to Morningview Mansions for a pre-do drink. There was no sign of jet lag.

'We're going to the Taxidermist, Trafford Street,' said Mum, putting her own *Bride To Be* sash over the black dress that she'd got in a sale after a tussle with another shopper.

'Never heard of it. I wonder if it's the old Tainted Shrew?' said Chrissie. 'I used to go there when I was a teenager for a pint of snakebite and a snog behind the Trivial Pursuit machine.'

Una's ears pricked at the mention of snakebite.

'We need to push off soon,' said Chrissie, necking her Pinot Grigio. 'Are you going to get changed, Una?'

Una was wearing a striped top, paired with jeans. She'd considered adding a necklace but if someone tripped and grabbed it, it might garrotte her. She'd settled for a close-fitting bracelet instead. The evening ahead, with its potential for squeamish revelations and enforced hilarity, was gruesome enough; she could at least dress comfortably.

'This is what I'm wearing tonight.'

'Oh, I see, it's like a day-to-night outfit.'

It was very much a day-to-day outfit.

The three hens got a taxi to the bar. Lilah from the wedding shop was already at their reserved booth, supping from a champagne flute, with a silver ice bucket in front of her. She was wearing a sequinned top that acted as a proxy glitterball under the spotlights.

'Got some fizz in, girls. You all look lovely.'

She poured a glass for each of them and started talking about the wedding. Jean arrived with Cassie. Jean's top had an appliqued anchor, and Cassie was carrying her trusty velvet bag with tiny mirrors.

'Cassie,' said Mum. 'I wasn't expecting you.'

'That's right,' said Cassie. 'I thought I'd better show my face.'

'The more the merrier, they say,' said Mum, glaring at Jean.

'I haven't got enough sashes, sorry,' said Una, dangling the last one at the new arrivals. 'But you can have mine.'

'I'll be okay, thanks,' said Cassie, smiling at her, 'but appreciate the thought.'

The group was silent. The bar was not. It was Saturday night, and even Maroon 5 were struggling to make themselves heard over the shouts and whoops from the young crowd who'd appropriated the snooker table. Una made a mental note that in the unlikely event that she ever got married, she'd have a hen do with at most one guest in a sparsely populated, music-free venue with no traditional paraphernalia or antics. In fact, she'd probably disguise it as 'just a quick drink'.

'A toast,' said Chrissie. 'To Sheila and Dad and a wonderful wedding day.'

They all clinked glasses. Una had become quite adept at air clinking these past few weeks.

'What about a drinking game?' said Chrissie. A sentence that struck a chill into Una's marrow. No way was she going to provide risqué revelations to this crew.

'Let's just get ourselves settled first,' said Mum. 'We'll order some nibbles from the bar.'

'Mini cheeseburgers, whoo whoo,' said Chrissie, looking at the bar menu. 'Anton only had vegan food stocked up when we arrived. Bloody typical.'

'He seems lovely, Anton,' said Mum. 'Such a gentle soul.'

'He's all right. He's been a bit of a wet weekend since he split up with Marcella.'

'I said I'd look out for someone for him at the wedding,' said Mum.

'I was thinking about Rosa,' said Chrissie. 'If only they could see what a good couple they'd make.'

'She's lovely,' said Mum.

For some reason, the idea of Anton and Rosa together nettled Una. Perhaps it was because no one was trying to fix her up with anyone at the wedding, like she was a lost cause. She finished her champagne in one chug. It didn't help.

'The problem with our Anton,' said Chrissie, 'is that he puts women on a pedestal.'

'Nothing wrong with that,' said Jean. 'That's how John is with me after forty years of marriage. Puts me on a pedestal.'

'Well, you are rather on the short side,' said Mum, revelling in the reaction to her joke. This was payback for Jean bringing Cassie along. Mum had clearly had too much to drink already.

'Ladies,' said Lilah, 'have you all decided on your wedding outfits yet?'

Una could tell that a discussion on statistical methods versus machine learning techniques was not on the cards tonight. She was not averse to buying clothes, updating her wardrobe once a quarter with similar items, but she felt no need to spend valuable time discussing it.

'I've got to decide between two outfits,' said Jean.

'I predict you'll be wearing pink,' said Cassie, who was taking tiny sips of Baileys and licking her lips after each mouthful. Una had to look away.

'One of the outfits *is* pink,' said Jean. 'Yes, I should wear that one. I'll keep the other one for when John and I go on our luxury Baltic cruise with complimentary lectures.'

Cassie was pretty good at these predictions, but was this just sideshow flummery, knowing that Jean would likely have a lot of pink clothes in her wardrobe? Una decided to test her further.

'What about you, Cassie? What are you going to be wearing, given that you think there'll be trouble at the wedding? A suit of armour?'

She was quite pleased with this joke, given that it was actually quite a good idea, but the table went silent.

'I'm sorry that you're not taking my gift seriously, Una,' said Cassie. 'I was only trying to help.'

'Help or not,' said Jean, 'I don't think Sheila wants to hear about any trouble, thank you. We just want a quiet evening. A bit of fun.'

'Yeah, girls just want to have fun,' said Chrissie.

'Let's top up your glasses,' said Lilah.

'You know what I'm seeing in our future, ladies?' said Chrissie, making mystical movements with her hands. 'A tray of shots coming up. That's right.'

Everyone seemed to find that funny except Cassie. Chrissie swaggered towards the bar.

'Anything you want to get off your chest, Una?' said Cassie in a low voice, still sipping her Baileys. She gave her a knowing look.

'There is something,' said Una, leaning in closer. Cassie signalled for her to continue. 'I've worked out a connection between all the deaths. In fact, I'm pretty sure I know who the next target is going to be. Although I'd rather not say.'

Cassie slowly put her glass back on the table. 'That's impressive,' she said. 'At least someone's taking what I say seriously.'

'I just don't know what to do next.'

'Perhaps you can't do anything – it's fate. Have you mentioned this to anyone else?'

'No. No one.'

'That's probably a good idea. You don't know if it might put you in harm's way. You should take care. I know I am.'

Ken had asked her not to mention the lottery win in front of his friends, and now Cassie was giving her similar advice.

'Thanks, Cassie. And I'm sorry, I didn't mean to make fun of you earlier. It just came out wrong.'

'Don't you worry,' said Cassie, smiling up at her. 'I'm used to it.'

'We should play a drinking game now,' said Chrissie. 'What about "Would you Rather" or "Have you Ever"?'

Una gulped a large sip of warm, fizzled wine. This was the type of hideous game involving embarrassing revelations combined with spontaneous thinking on your feet that did not play to her strengths.

'Let's start with you, Una,' said Chrissie.

Una girded herself as Chrissie leant forward.

'Have you ever—'

'Hello, ladies!'

She opened her eyes and turned around. There was Ken, and she was actually pleased to see him. And lurking behind Ken was Anton.

'Ken, what are you doing here?' said Mum, beaming up at him. 'You're not supposed to be at the hen do!'

'I was bored, wasn't I? Anyhow, I had Una at my stag do, so fair dos I should gatecrash your party. Isn't that right, Anton?'

Anton looked even less keen to be at the hen do than Una, which simultaneously made her warm to him as well as feel slightly irritated at him for taking away her self-appointed role.

'New jacket?' said Chrissie, clutching his motorbike jacket. 'Who are you trying to impress? Rosa couldn't make it, by the way.'

'Just decided to treat myself, that's all. Can I get anyone a drink?' asked Anton.

'Let me sort out some more champagne for these lovely ladies,' said Ken, giving Mum a kiss on the cheek. 'Ken's here – the party has officially started.'

Anton squeezed onto the table next to Una. 'How are you?' he said. 'That's a nice bracelet. I like that minimal style.'

'Thanks,' she said. 'I'm glad you turned up. Chrissie was about to start us off on drinking games.'

Anton grimaced. 'Nightmare. Anyhow, I'm nearly there with putting the photos together, so perhaps you want to attend a VIP premiere.'

'Sounds good,' she said. 'I'm going back to London tomorrow, but I'll be back here on Thursday, ahead of the wedding. You could run through your speech as well. I could time it.'

'Deal. Probably best not to come to our place, as it's a madhouse now that Chrissie and Duncan have arrived. We could go to that café again?'

'It's a plan.'

Ken returned with a bottle of champagne. 'Let me open this like a professional,' he said, shoving the bottle between his thighs and gripping the cork.

'Actually,' said Jean, 'you're supposed to open champagne with a sword. John and I saw an expert do it on our last cruise. Spectacular.'

Death by champagne cork was a no-no. Una adopted an airline-style brace position. There was a loud plop and she looked up to find everyone alive and cheering.

After pouring the champagne, Ken proceeded to entertain the group with his anecdotes. She was relieved that this had pushed out the drinking games. Her attention occasionally wandered back to Cassie's warning – perhaps someone at this table had picked up on her investigation and she was now in their sights. But at least nothing would happen until the wedding, and she was going back to London tomorrow, back to the safety of the office. She lifted her champagne glass for the next toast and secretly congratulated herself on how far she'd got with her new bold approach.

# 30

## *Red Signal*

The next morning, Una waited on Platform 1 for the train to London. She stood far back from the edge, evenly distributing her weight on both feet, placed hip distance apart, at the end of the platform away from everyone else. She'd left a few inches between her back and the railings behind her that separated the platform from a small car park.

She did a quick once-over for hazards at the station. Further along the platform was an abandoned paper coffee cup and a half-eaten packet of French fries – either could cause someone to slip and hit the hard platform floor. There might be last-minute travellers who hadn't left sufficient time to get to the station, suddenly launching themselves onto the platform to get to their designated carriage. Seagulls, always the seagulls, though there was no sign of wildlife on the platform at this time. She sipped her coffee – everything was under control.

There were about twenty other people waiting to board on the platform. No one she recognised, although she'd bumped into Raj on the way, outside the shopping centre. He'd been vague about his plans; only that he was searching for a present for someone. His injured leg was hidden in a rigid grey plastic

254

boot that clunked on the pavement. She'd told him that she was in a rush to get to the train – which was true, although she'd built in a lot of contingency time – and said she'd see him at the wedding next weekend. 'The wedding,' he'd replied, rolling his eyes and stomping his boot.

She had already bought a snack bar and coffee at a stall on the concourse, and with only a few minutes to go until the train was due, she started planning tasks for work tomorrow, beginning with a full risk assessment of the wedding venue and how to protect Ken without endangering herself. She glanced along the platform. The couple next to her had started bickering about whether they had booked forward- or backward-facing seats. And then they bickered about whether the seats were in fact facing each other, and how to resolve that.

Two minutes to go. A shadow passed over her, and movement. It was a seagull swooping in to start on the chips. It had quite a swagger and she was glad that she had her sunglasses on. Someone ran forward to shoo it away. The seagull picked up another chip, then lifted and lowered its enormous wings, and the person retreated. This was the sort of birdwatching observation that would appeal to John and Raj. She put her snack bar in her backpack in case any gulls got ideas about swiping it.

One minute to go. Two teenage boys had arrived on the platform and were trying to grab each other's sweatshirts at the back. They were diving round and round in a spiral along the platform. They were quite far from Una, but she could see that they were moving closer and closer to the platform edge. She looked at the other passengers to see if

255

they were going to intervene. They looked about as indifferent as the gull.

The two boys were near her now; she could hear the squeal of their trainers on the platform as they wrestled near the edge. In the distance, she could see the train sweeping round the bend, approaching the station, but her focus was on the two boys shouting and darting about. Now the squatter one was leaning his friend's head over the edge of the platform.

'Be careful!' Una shouted.

They carried on scuffling.

'The train's coming. Be careful!'

The squatter one looked back at her. 'What? Are you talking to me?'

'Yes,' she said, 'the train's coming. Look!'

He stopped, and this allowed his friend to flip him over onto the ground.

'It's miles away,' he said, looking up at her from the ground and rolling his eyes. Then he got up and they both strolled back down the platform towards the benches.

A few seconds later, the train was at the far end of the platform, where the signals were. Una was on edge after speaking out in public, but she also felt a tinge of professional pride – not only had she placed herself in the safest spot in the station, she'd actually tried to help other people with her risk assessment skills. That was what she'd learnt from her time in Eastbourne: she may not have got the promotion, but she was still excellent at finding the worst-case scenario. That was why she'd be the best person to help Ken.

The train was slowly crawling along the platform. People were throwing away bits of food packaging and rolling their luggage towards the train. Just a few seconds and she'd be safe to move forward without the risk of falling onto the tracks. She put her reusable coffee cup into her backpack, twisting round to fully buckle the left clip and then the right.

The clip fell from her fingers as there was a huge crash and something heavy burst apart on her right side. Pieces hit her, and the ground wobbled under her feet. Or was *she* wobbling? She could see people moving around her, the train even slower now.

'Are you okay?' asked the seagull.

'I think so,' she said. Then she turned her head slightly.

'Are you sure?' It was actually a woman in a red leather jacket and lots of make-up. The seagull was next to the woman, at her feet, studiously indifferent to Una but delighted at the chaos.

'I think so,' she said again. 'What was that noise? Was it an asteroid?'

'I really need to get this train, sorry,' said the woman as she let go of Una's arm. 'I don't think you're hurt. Drink lots of water.'

Doors were whooshing open and shut along the length of the train.

Una looked down at her feet. There was a mess of splintered plastic and pieces of cardboard. It had been a box of something. Then she saw the picture on the front of the box. It was the foot spa from Tread Softly! How had that got here? She looked at the railings behind her, expecting to see one of the familiar Eastbourne crowd staring back through the slats, but no one was there. There was no movement in the car park either; her initial state of shock had allowed her attacker to get away.

Someone had tried to drop that foot spa on her. One of Ken's friends. Someone who knew she was leaving today. Someone who knew that she would stay well back from the platform. She'd been intent on collecting data about them, but she'd given out a lot of information about herself.

'That yours? Did you drop it?' said a station attendant, who'd appeared with a broom and dustpan. 'I suppose I'll have to clear that up now. Don't think you can fix it, although you might want to take a picture for insurance purposes.'

Insurance purposes were not her main concern today. Una waggled her extremities: all good. At least the foot spa hadn't clipped her head. She shook off some plastic shards from her jeans.

'No, that's not mine,' she said. 'Someone must have dropped it from behind these railings.'

'Really? You should go to the police about that,' he said. 'If you think it was thrown by someone. Why can't people take things to the tip?'

The train would be leaving soon. She could see a guard walking towards the front of the train, holding up a whistle.

'Perhaps it was an accident,' she said, taking slow moon strides towards the nearest door, her legs trembling. She wasn't going to dilly-dally around Eastbourne any longer. Although how safe was the train?

She got on, but instead of finding a seat, she hovered by the door and looked back at where she'd been standing. The station attendant was brushing the debris away, the seagull supervising him. The impact of what had just happened hit her harder than the foot spa. Someone had yoiked that box over the railings, targeting Una. Either someone wanted her gone, or someone wanted to make her think twice about coming back.

She knew she was losing valuable information by escaping like this. She should be back there at the station, looking round the car park for clues. But she didn't want any more data; she just wanted to get back home in one piece, unlike the foot spa.

She couldn't see any way that the box-dropper could have scaled the railings and got onto the train, but she decided to be cautious. She looked for a crowded carriage instead of the quiet spot she normally liked, and found an empty seat on a noisy table of three students. Safety in numbers – except when you were in Eastbourne.

Back at her flat, Una sat on the couch and stared at the wall for some time. She could have faced her final moment today. She'd not made a will. She'd not tidied up for those who would sort through her affairs. She looked at her bookshelf. What would they make of all those numerical romance books that she enjoyed reading? At least they were in ascending order.

Acting as a team of one was a lonely business. The best-placed person to bring in on her plans was Anton, as he was going to be close to Ken on Friday, but he would either be sceptical of her number theory or think she was making it up to derail the wedding. There was one other person she could speak to. She texted Amara to see if she was free, and an hour later they had started up a video chat.

'What's up?' said Amara. 'You look like shit. Are you okay?'

'I had a bad thing happen to me today.'

'Why? What happened?'

Una gave a condensed version of the falling foot spa, leaving out the details about how she'd been personally targeted by a deranged killer.

'You should report it to someone,' said Amara. 'You might be entitled to compensation. And anyway, the cleaner is right, it's fly-tipping, middle-class fly-tipping. People on our road are always sticking random bits of furniture outside their houses.'

'I just wanted to get back to the flat.'

'You're in shock, of course. Well, just rest yourself, as you've got the wedding next weekend. It sounds like you're warming to Ken as well.'

'He's okay really,' said Una. 'I misjudged him, but now it might be too late to make it up with him.'

'Oh, I'm sure he understands it's going to be difficult at first – you're all new to each other, right? Why not just tell him what you're telling me?'

'I suppose so,' she said. 'I'll wait until the wedding's out of the way.'

'I mean, you can, but don't put it off too long. You never know when you'll miss the chance.'

Although this sounded like a phrase from one of Amara's fridge magnets, she had a point. Ken was in danger and Una wasn't even brave enough to tell him that she no longer detested him. She needed to step up, get over the foot spa incident and keep him safe on Friday. What she really

260

needed to do was recruit Anton, but how and what to tell him?

'Let me ask you this,' said Una. 'Say you knew something bad might happen to someone . . .'

'Okay.'

'. . . and you didn't want to worry them about it, but you could tell someone close to them about it so they could help do something about it as you can't do much on your own, except they might be really angry with you for having told them because you could have told them a bit earlier . . . would you tell them?'

Amara was silent for a few seconds. 'I've absolutely no idea what you're talking about,' she said. 'And I can see I won't be getting any useful details. But my advice on telling people stuff is to think about how they would react if they found out too late that you hadn't told them when it would have made a difference.'

'Thank you! That is excellent advice. I just don't know how I'm going to tell this person.'

'Get it over with,' she said. 'Be bold. And then let's set a date for you to come and visit us in sunny Leeds.'

'I'd love that. I miss being there. I just need to get this wedding out of the way first.'

As Una ended the call, she reached the irrational conclusion that being the intended victim of a foot spa attack didn't seem as scary as telling Anton that she thought Ken was in danger next Friday due to a theory she had about a bunch of lottery numbers. But she didn't want her team of one becoming a team of none.

# 31

## *Spilling the Coffee Beans*

The following Thursday morning, Una arrived back at Eastbourne station just before eight o'clock. There was no trace of the foot spa on the platform, but she thought she recognised the seagull that was standing near that spot. She kept focus as she made her way into the concourse and towards Mum's flat. It was a grey day, the sky matt and gritty like the pavement, and that meant there were none of the annoying shadows a sunny day could bring.

The last day of February had crept up like a dentist's appointment. Tomorrow would be Mum and Ken's wedding, combined with a highly probable life insurance event for Ken. Nearly getting brained by a second-hand foot spa last Sunday had dented Una's confidence. She'd mechanically carried out her meetings and tasks during the week, but inside something had shifted. Like Cassie losing her gift, she found that she could no longer step back and assess the worst case because she could see worst cases everywhere. And when everything was the worst case, then nothing stood out as the worst of the worst.

Even if she did spot something or someone acting dangerously towards Ken tomorrow, there was nothing she

262

could do to stop it. The incident at the station had been a warning, and it had worked. She was now focused on her own safety and she wasn't sure if she had anything left over to protect Ken.

She made slow progress to Morningview Mansions as she avoided pedestrians and cracks in the pavement.

'Hello, love,' said Mum, smothering her, her hair newly highlighted and bouncy. 'You look tired. Did you have an okay week at work?'

As the team changes hadn't been formally announced, Una had gone for her normal one-to-one with Ajay, who spent the time assuring her that her role still had potential to grow. Tim had pinged her a few times, but she'd made excuses about being too busy to meet him. He'd pleaded with her to allow him to help on the investigation, and she'd sent him her notes to shut him up. It was good of him to make an effort, but there was no way she was going to accept him as her new manager. Thank goodness she'd arranged to work from home today, well, Mum's home.

'Is Ken okay?' she asked, removing a cushion and sitting in the armchair. If he had a cold or an injury, then perhaps the wedding would be postponed. Perhaps she could injure him herself? Just enough, of course.

Mum's face lit up. 'He's full of beans. He's going to have a quiet night in tonight with Anton. Chrissie and Duncan are taking the girls to see one of her old school friends, so he'll have a bit of peace. We're not supposed to see each other, of course, being traditional. But he's under orders to rest this evening. And no jumping out at him tomorrow, right?'

'No. No jumping out.'

'We can have an evening in together as well,' she said. 'I've got a bottle of white wine in the fridge. And some chocolate-coated cashews. There's a new *Inspector Montalbano* on.'

'Sure, Mum. I'd better get on with some work now, I'm already late starting.'

'Oh, and Anton says he'll see you this afternoon about some last-minute wedding prep. You'll need to ask him about it.'

Una slung her backpack in the spare room and texted Anton. He texted back and they agreed to meet in the café at 5.30. He wanted to run through the final cut of the photos before the premiere at the wedding lunch. She wanted to tell him about the dangers Ken faced tomorrow. It would be a difficult conversation.

She set up her laptop on the dressing table in the spare room and started downloading various mail attachments to review. She draped a T-shirt over the mirror in front of her. It was bad enough having to see her face onscreen during meetings.

She fired up a video chat for the daily catch-up with her team and unmuted herself. 'Morning,' she said. 'I'm working from home today.'

'What's that on the wall behind you?' said Rachida, IT Program Manager, looming towards Una, her face fully filling the small square in the top left corner of the screen.

Una hadn't done a corporate appropriateness sweep before starting the call. But there was nothing Mum would have put up in the flat that would cause any concern. Before she had a chance to turn round to check, Tim's face shimmered onto a small box onscreen. He was already installed in his new office on the sixth floor, a stack of statistics books on the bookshelf behind him next to his trophy.

'Hi, guys, just want to listen in to your daily catch-up, so I can start learning what you're all working on.'

'Really looking forward to working with you,' said Niall from the graduate programme, who'd been given a desk next to the toilets.

'Thanks, Niall.' Tim unleashed a dazzling remember-you're-only-a-graduate smile. 'But please carry on as if I'm not . . . Hold on, I didn't know you liked cats, Una?'

She looked round. There, announcing its presence against the floral wallpaper, was a calendar of cats in costumes. She'd not paid any attention to it before; it was just another generic thing cluttering up the room. But now it was all she could see when she looked back at her own square onscreen. February's cat was dressed in spats and a bow tie.

She hadn't even been able to spot this anomaly in a tiny room, and she was supposed to monitor a venue packed with people tomorrow.

'I don't like cats,' she said emphatically, her leg starting to itch. 'I don't like cats at all.'

'Why not?' asked Rachida. 'Cats are brilliant. I love my Suki. Although I'm not sure about putting them in little outfits like that.'

'It's my mum's calendar, okay? I'm logging in from her flat. Now let's carry on.'

'Sure,' said Tim. 'No one's judging you. It's all purrfectly fine.'

She would normally chuckle at such a great joke, even if it was Tim who made it, but she couldn't muster the slightest smile; she just kept churning over the potential wedding risks.

The rest of the day passed safely. Mum brought her hot drinks on an hourly basis, oblivious of how this might look to her colleagues on the video chat. At 5.15, Una logged out and set off for the café.

Inside KeenBeanz, Anton was sitting at a table by the window, laptop open. He was beaming at the screen and slowly rocking his head to whatever was playing on his outsized silver headphones.

'Hi,' she said. 'Can I get you a drink?'

'Go on, I'll let you buy,' he said, 'as I've done so much work on the film. Double espresso, please.'

She got the coffees and sat opposite him. He spun the laptop round and then moved his chair to sit beside her. She connected her earphones and pressed play.

The video started off with the photos in chronological order. There were ones of Ken as a boy in the fifties, with an Elvis track playing over them; the photos had been cut to appear in time to the music and sometimes segued from black and white into colour. There were also photos of Eastbourne from that time – people on the beach on deckchairs, openly soaking up the sun.

'I've curated a specific Spotify list to go with Dad's pictures,' said Anton, looking at her for encouragement. She nodded to look interested, but it was difficult to suppress what she knew about the danger Ken was in.

There were some photos of Mum as a girl, next to her two sisters. Then a picture of Una, Mum and Dad at a caravan site in the nineties, standing under a grey sky with a rainbow in it. Una was wearing a baseball cap in case the sun suddenly came out and Mum was leaning into Dad; she could almost hear the squelch of their plastic pac-a-macs rubbing together. Amara was right. Mum was moving on with her life, not moving away from her old one.

Now the video focused on Mum and Ken with the bingo crowd at various group events. These were the photos that Una had collected in person, hoping to find the final clue. Something bothered her about one of the images she'd just seen, but what was it? The montage continued. She watched Harry, Eileen and Tommo laughing and joking with their friends; somehow all the people in the photos she'd collected had come back to life.

'What do you think?' said Anton when the video finished.

Una's eyes were tearing up, but she sipped her coffee until she'd blinked them back. 'You've done a great job. Really.'

'I can't wait to play it tomorrow,' said Anton. 'I just hope Dad enjoys it.'

'Yes,' she said. 'I hope he will too.' She took her earphones out and sighed – there was a high probability that Ken would never see the film.

'So . . .' Anton looked at her, 'I can't read your reaction. Honestly, did you like it?'

'Ken! Ken's going to die tomorrow!' blurted Una. 'I'm sorry, I can't keep it in any longer. I don't know what to do!'

Anton sat back, looking confused. 'What do you mean by that?'

'It's a long story,' she said.

He remained seated, but moved his chair back to its original position, opposite her. 'Go for it,' he said.

She gave a brief summary of everything she'd uncovered in Eastbourne – the numbers at each scene, the link with the lottery syndicate and the dates of the deaths. She left out the foot spa incident, as she'd temporarily put that into mental storage.

'You've been sitting on this for over a week about the lottery numbers,' said Anton. 'Why haven't you gone to the police?'

'No one's made any threat. All I've got to show is some numbers that have turned up in different locations, and all the deaths look like accidents.'

He scowled. 'But you think there's something going on? Why didn't you tell me earlier?'

'I thought you'd be really angry,' she said.

'I am really angry,' he said. 'If there's any truth in what you're saying, we could have had more time to look into it. The wedding is tomorrow!'

Una had no response to Anton's completely correct observations.

'I have to get back now.' He stood up and slammed the laptop into his bag. 'I'm going to ask Dad about the lottery and if there was any fallout, but honestly, Una ... I'll see you tomorrow.'

She stood up to face him. 'I was looking out for Ken,' she said. 'Surely you can see that now? I'm trying to protect him.'

'I don't know what to believe,' said Anton. 'Perhaps because you see risks all over the place, you've got this all mixed up. Don't mention it to him – he needs to stay calm, not have you telling him about his impending doom.'

'That's a good point,' she said, 'and it's probably better if you don't tell anyone about what I've told you, in case you put yourself in danger.'

'Don't worry,' he said. 'I won't be telling anyone the story you've just come out with.' He picked up his jacket.

'But what about the speech?' she said. 'The dress rehearsal?'

'Look, Una, forget about the speech. I have to go. I need to get my head around all this.'

Once he'd left, Una sat back down and finished her coffee, then pushed the cup away. She had thought telling him would make her feel less anxious. Mum always said that a problem shared was a problem halved, but she had somehow made the problem bigger.

'Bye,' she said to the guy at the counter as she stood up to go.

'See you soon,' he said. 'Do you want to start a loyalty card? I notice you've been in here quite a bit recently. You can have two stamps to kick it off.'

'Thanks,' she said. 'But I don't feel I deserve a loyalty card at the moment.'

# 32

## *Licensed to Peel*

Una woke up two minutes before her alarm call and waited
for it to ring. It was a long and annoying two minutes and
she was on edge as she lay staring at her phone, knowing it
would come menacingly to life at any second. When it rang
its electronic trill, she picked it up and swiped it silent. Then
she went into the lounge.

Rosa had already started on Mum's wedding
beautifications. The sickening scent of heavy hairspray
hung in the air. Una opened a window, as she didn't want
her lungs to be in a firm hold, thank you. Their dresses were
on coat hangers draped over the curtain rail.

'Good morning, sleepyhead,' said Rosa, brandishing a
palette of rainbow-hued eyeshadows (would those make-up
brushes be sterilised between uses?). 'We'll do your make-up,
and then you just need to be careful when you put your
dress on.'

Una sat in the armchair, eyes shut, and let Rosa carry out
her make-up skills. While Rosa pulled at and etched on her
face, she mentally prepared herself for the day ahead, listing
the tasks she needed to do to maximise Ken's security, and
her own. She'd do what she could to keep all the guests

alive today, but the attack at the station last weekend was playing on her mind. As a precaution, she'd do a quick scan of the cutlery drawer for something she could use in self-defence that would fit into her tiny frilled bridesmaid's purse.

Rosa had now worked her way up to Una's hair, which she was scooping with gusto.

'You can leave the hair,' said Una. 'Look, I've got a scrunchie I can stuff it into.'

She held it up. In the bright morning light, it looked like a roadkill scrunchie.

'What do you think, Sheila?' said Rosa.

'That scrunchie's seen better days,' said Mum. 'I think you've had your money's worth out of it. Today you're having your hair done properly, thank you.'

'I'll get to work,' said Rosa.

'You'll thank her for it, Una,' said Mum. 'You'll see.'

'Okay,' Una said in defeat. She knew she had to pick her battles today, so she put the scrunchie back around her wrist.

Rosa started backcombing sections of her hair. It was uncomfortable seeing her dark wavy locks sticking up in matted fur balls all over her head. Fumes invaded her nostrils and burnt her throat. She closed her eyes again. Then she felt Rosa's hands sweeping and clipping her hair into submission.

'All done,' said Rosa. 'You look amazing. Do you want to take a look in the mirror?'

Una slowly opened her eyes. What was this before her? Rosa had made her look like a heroine from the cover of one of her numerical romance novels. Her face had a doll-like appearance from the exaggerated lines that had been drawn on and her hair had been whipped up into a mousse-like blob sitting on top of her head. A mousse that looked light and fluffy, but in fact was a rigid helmet that even emitted a slightly hollow noise when she gently rapped it. But this wasn't Regency London, and she wouldn't be spending the day looking for love at a ball with help from her best friend Ada Lovelace and a set of Bernoulli numbers hidden in her crinoline. No, she was going to be on display at a municipal registry office in front of fifty of Mum and Ken's friends.

Assisted by Mum, she negotiated herself into the peplum bridesmaid dress and they set off for the ceremony in a beribboned Jaguar that Ken had hired. Una's hairdo tickled the ceiling of the car and that put her on edge, even though she knew that in a fight between the hairdo and the ceiling, the hairdo would win. Mum sat next to her wearing a pristine cream-coloured dress with a matching jacket. Una could feel the excitement radiating off her.

'I can't believe it's finally happening,' said Mum, grabbing her hand. 'I've been so wrapped up in the planning. I'm sure it will all go fine.'

Una gave what she hoped was a reassuring squeeze and opened the car window to let in some fresh air.

At the registry office, they found the reception room that had been booked for the ceremony. The tall wooden doors at the front were flung back, and beside them there were enormous flower displays that threatened to play havoc with Una's hay fever. She hadn't packed any antihistamines in her handbag, as she'd had to keep space for her phone and a potato peeler that she'd squeezed in as a makeshift weapon.

'Can you pop your head in and check that Ken's there?' asked Mum. 'I can't look. It's tradition.'

Una looked inside and spotted Ken in the front row, his quiff extra tufted. She looked for Anton and found him in the corner setting up a video camera. There were already thirty people huddled into the chairs that had been tightly packed together either side of the aisle that she and Mum would soon walk down.

'He's there, don't worry.'

'Great,' said Mum, beaming. Perhaps she'd been worried about being jilted – Una was so distracted, she hadn't even thought about that scenario. 'Can you do some greeting while I sort out these blister pads for my shoes? We've got some time before everyone's here.'

Una stood by the entrance side-on to reduce how much the guests could see of her while Mum headed to the cloakroom. The stress of the threat to Ken was throwing her off her game. She needed to focus and perform a solid risk assessment of each guest.

Jean arrived five seconds after the heavy floral scent she was wearing. There was a huge pin in her hat that was skewering a curled beige rattan ribbon – almost an insulting load for a pin that had clearly been meant for greater things. But in the right hands, Una was sure it could puncture through the ribs into vital organs or be calmly introduced into someone's back. Jean was literally dressed to kill.

'Hello, Una, you look beautiful,' she said. 'Like you've just stepped out of a Jane Austen novel. Doesn't she, John?'

John was wearing a navy suit and paisley tie and was bowling along with a walking stick. Una assessed its potential for physical harm. That chunky grey plastic handle at the top could deal a smart blow to the back of the neck or knees. It was chilling to think about the array of murderous tools that well-meaning local health authorities were doling out to the older generation.

'Looking forward to the photo montage, Una,' said John. 'And thanks for our chat the other day.'

Una ushered them through to the reception room.

Cassie arrived next, wearing a matching jacket and dress, a fluttering fascinator and a handbag over her arm. This outfit was challenging – what trouble could she cause? Who knew what lay in that handbag of hers, not large enough to accommodate a sandbag or cosh, but still roomy enough for a lady pistol, a poison dart, or a ball of twine that could be strung low at the top of a staircase, causing someone to topple and plunge step by step on their last flight.

'Big day today,' said Cassie. 'I hope it all goes as planned.'

'I'm going to do what I can,' said Una. 'I just hope that will be enough.'

'What I've learnt in life,' Cassie said, sighing so hard that the feathery affair on her fascinator trembled, 'is that fortune favours the bold. See you later.'

Una dismissed this well-intentioned advice – as a professional actuary, she was pretty sure that fortune favoured the cautious. She was hoping for a few minutes' rest from her kitten-heeled shoes, which were pinching and were certainly not the comfy all-day slippers that Lilah had claimed. However, Raj appeared, hobbling towards her wearing a sheeny grey suit with a deep gold tie. No obvious weaponry, but she assumed there'd be a couple of freshly sharpened pencils tucked into his jacket pocket. If they were 4H or above, she'd have to watch out.

'Aha,' he said, 'I nearly didn't recognise you all glammed up like this. No drab plumage for the female of the species today.'

Una briefly considered attacking him with the potato peeler, but she had to channel her energies into Project Ken today. And it was draining enough having to deal with all this bridesmaid chit-chat.

Chrissie, Duncan and their two daughters arrived among the last guests. Chrissie had clearly asked for some alterations from Lilah, as her dress had less peplum and more room to move around in. But it was still a lilac bridesmaid dress. They both made the most of it and complimented each other before Chrissie and her family went inside to take their seats.

Now that everyone had assembled, there was just Mum and Una, standing in the entrance hall waiting for Ken's great-niece to start the music on her MP3 player, which had been rigged up to some speakers. People inside the room were turning round to look at them. In the lull of anticipation of the ceremony starting, Una's anxiety mushroomed.

'I don't know if I can do this, Mum,' she whispered.

'Stop worrying, Una, you can sit down once you get to the end of the aisle. It will only take a couple of minutes and then you can relax.'

The music began.

'Is this . . .?'

'I've no idea,' Mum said. 'Ken did the music.'

It was 'The Scientist' by Coldplay.

Una started the walk down the aisle, Mum's frail left arm resting on her right arm. It was terrible; her eyes were stinging. Halfway along, she had to wipe her eyes, and the pressure shifted so that it was Mum pulling her towards the front of the room. She felt Mum's arm drop from the crook of her elbow, then Ken was patting her on the shoulder. With relief, she took her seat next to Auntie Val.

Ken was wearing the heavily embroidered waistcoat that Rosa had made. There were beads of sweat on his newly spray-tanned forehead. He no doubt had nerves about the day ahead, and from Una's point of view they were completely justified.

The service began with a few words from the celebrant, Pauline, to welcome everyone. Then a small teenage girl, Ken's other great-niece, got up and read out the lyrics to Adele's 'Make You Feel My Love'. One of Mum's friends from school read a Shakespeare sonnet. Mum had picked her because of her speaking voice. The verse made no sense to Una, but the rhythm and the old language made it sound meaningful.

It was time for the exchanging of rings, and Anton stepped forward wearing a dark grey morning suit with one of Rosa's brocaded waistcoats. His beard had been neatened. He handed the rings to Ken. The ring that Ken had bought for Mum looked expensive, based on its dramatic sparkle. Despite the limited success of her investigation in Eastbourne, at least Una now knew how he could afford to be so generous.

Pauline asked if anyone knew of any lawful impediment why the couple should not be married. Una had a quick glance back and could see hints of sniffles and sobbing. She gripped the edge of the chair in front of her with determination – there would be no more tears from her. She was going to stay alert to the possibility of danger. Luckily Ken wasn't actually a bigamist and no one said anything. The service continued until the kiss between bride and groom, then Ken and Mum walked back out of the room to the strains of 'Heaven Is a Place on Earth'.

There was a transition period between the end of the ceremony and the start of the wedding lunch at the hotel. Ken had booked a grand reception room for the meal and disco. The guests shuffled out of the registry office and arranged lifts with each other. Una went with Auntie Val, whose car reeked of the tiny tree air freshener that hung from the driver's mirror.

The hotel had been converted from an old manor house and had its own extensive garden. Una noticed on the drive over that it was only a short walk from the cemetery, and Cassie's warning returned to her.

When they arrived, Una and Chrissie were put in charge of collecting any presents from the guests and stowing them in the cloakroom. Then Mum ushered them outside into the garden for the wedding photos. There followed a photo session that lasted forty minutes and yet seemed to take four hours as the photographer put the guests into different combinations. Once that was over, Una checked on Ken and found him standing right foot forward, left arm resting on the branch of a willow tree, his jacket thrown over his shoulder.

'Just trying out a new pose,' he said. 'What do you think? I often thought I could be a model. I bet the catalogues have to cater for the mature man these days. The silver pound and all that.'

'You know, I could have done the photos without you having to pay someone,' said Anton, appearing from behind the tree. 'Although Gary is a good choice.'

'You've already done enough today with the video. Relax and enjoy yourself,' said Ken. 'Righty-oh, I'm going to start rounding people up for lunch. That means you two as well.'

'Shall we go in?' said Anton, gesturing for Una to go first.

'You're still speaking to me,' she said.

'Just about. As it happens, I have a bit of news from talking to Dad last night.'

'What news?' she said.

'Get a chivvy on,' said Ken, dropping back. 'You can gossip later.'

'We'd better go in,' said Anton, 'but I'll text you at the meal. I'm sure it's nothing to worry about . . .'

# 33

## *The Pattern Emerges*

As the guests took their seats in the reception room, conforming to the table plan that had so thoughtfully been constructed for their benefit, Una's phone went off. Ken was still in danger, so it was essential she find out what Anton had discovered, no matter how trivial. As she reached for the phone, a bedazzling hand shot forward and removed it from her grasp.

'You are not taking work calls during my wedding, thank you.'

'But Mum, this isn't a work call.'

'I know your job is important to you, but let's just have a nice meal.'

'I'll put it on silent.'

Mum wagged her finger at Una before confiscating the phone in her handbag. 'Just while we're eating,' she said.

The wedding lunch took place without any casualties. Una had a commanding view of all the suspects from the top table. Next in the schedule was the speeches. Anton opened his Moleskine notepad, forcibly tested its spine and then set it flat. He was only a few feet away from Una, and she could see he was trembling.

'Thank you everyone for coming to this happy occasion of Ken and Sheila's wedding.' His voice went croaky at the end of the sentence. 'As the best man, I would like to say a few words. First, about Dad, who many of you know. I've had my ups and downs over the years, but he's always supported me to follow what I wanted to do in life. In this family, he's the rock. And the roll.'

At this point, he stopped and took a sip of water while the audience murmured.

'He told me about his marriage plans to Sheila about eight weeks ago. I came down and met Sheila and Una, and they made me feel welcome right away. I could see how happy Dad was, especially about planning a big party.' Anton sped up to this humorous remark, but the audience were silent. He took a deep breath. 'I wasn't originally down to be best man, that was Tommo, and I'm sure he is somehow present with us to toast you all. Thank you to Sheila's friend Margaret for the beautiful flower displays today. I realise it's customary for the best man to tell a few humorous, risqué anecdotes about the bridegroom, but as I'm not interested in following convention, I'll simply say, I love you, Dad. Please raise your glasses to Ken and Sheila!'

There was now a crescendo of glass-clinking that sent chills down Una's spine. It had been a rather short speech, but well received by the audience, and Anton was now necking his champagne. Una was pleased for him.

Ken, still red-eyed from Anton's remarks, leant over to her. 'Do you want to say a few words, Una?' he asked. 'About your mum?'

She shuddered. There had been no mention of a speech from her. Was Ken trying to publicly humiliate her? He had some nerve given that she was looking out for him today, his fateful numbers already waiting in someone's pocket or handbag.

'You don't have to,' said Mum. 'It's not like a traditional wedding anyway.'

'When you say I don't have to, it sounds like I do have to,' said Una.

'Una's great with speeches,' said Anton, his cheeks still flushed with relief. 'She gave me so much help with my nerves today.'

Ken stood up and clinked his glass with a fork. 'And now a few words from the daughter of the bride.'

Una stood up. Her mind was blank. The crowd looked at her. Table nine had somehow shifted and was now topologically, but not topographically, correct, which was distracting. Her lips felt blubbery. Surely no one had ever actually died of embarrassment. She'd been so nonchalant with her advice to Anton, and now everyone was looking at her. Ken's suggestion had been to imagine the people in the audience were naked. It didn't help.

The room was silent. She felt the weight of everyone listening.

'Thanks to everyone for your massive effort in coming here today to celebrate this happy occasion,' she started. She wasn't sounding in control. 'What can I say about my mother? She grew up in the sixties and once met Keith Richards.'

She could hear people laughing. Which was good, even if that wasn't a joke.

'Six months ago, she met Ken, who I'm still getting to know. What I'd say about Ken so far is that he's the sort of person you have to get to know. But the important thing is that he has made my mother very happy. I didn't want her to be on her own for the rest of her life after . . . although living on your own is a valid life choice that should have no social stigma attached to it. But I don't think she would have been happy living alone.'

She needed some way to round off the speech – fortune favoured the cautious.

'Right. Well. Don't clink your glasses again, you've already done that once. Instead, just take a small sip as we toast Ken and Mum.'

She sat down. The crowd buzzed with confusion, but not so much as to miss an opportunity to drink some more champagne.

'Thanks, Una,' said Ken, clapping with vigour.

'Very thoughtful,' said Mum, putting an arm around her shoulders and giving her a squeeze. 'You can have your phone back now.'

'Thanks.'

'And one thing more,' said Mum, in a whisper. 'Can you keep an eye on Ken and make sure he doesn't get too excited today? I'm worried he's going to overdo things.'

Una doubted her ability to restrain Ken and his enthusiasms.

'I'll try my best,' she said.

With the speeches over, most people got up and started to mill about, and at that point, the photo montage started playing on a large screen behind the top table. Even though

Una had seen it yesterday, she watched it again. One of Tommo's photos appeared on the screen – a group meal where everyone was smiling into the camera. Eileen was at an awkward angle at the front of the table, sitting with her back to the photographer but twisting uncomfortably to show her face to the camera. Not helped by the bulky jumper she was wearing, a jumper that looked similar to the one Una had seen at Tread Softly a few weeks back, one of Harry's belongings. She peered at the pattern on it – a set of squiggles? No, a number: the number 22. The photo of Eileen's jumper was replaced by Ken dressed as a vampire holding a glo-stick.

Una focused on that number. The jumper and the number were the same as Harry's – she'd thought his had a pattern of tiny 2s, but it could easily have been 22. Not one of the lottery numbers, so what was the link?

She stood up and felt the unfamiliar wobble of walking on kitten heels instead of flat shoes. Looking round, she spotted Jean and John, who had established themselves in a couple of chairs looking out of the window at the hotel grounds.

'Jean, the jumper you had in your shop, Harry's jumper, was it anything to do with Cassie?'

'Yes,' said Jean. 'Cassie knitted it.'

'And what about the number on it? What does it mean?'

'Number? I've no idea,' said Jean. 'Did it have a number on it? I don't remember. Perhaps it has some astral meaning for Cassie. I'd prefer to have a word on a jumper myself, like "plush", that's a wonderful word.'

'What?' said Una.

'You didn't say what sort of number,' said John.

'Sorry?' said Una.

'An integer?'

'Yes. A whole number, 22.'

'I see,' said John. 'Well, I've absolutely no idea why she knits them. She's been doing it since before Christmas.'

'I hope I don't get the next one,' said Jean, her rattan ribbon quivering with indignation. 'They're bulky-looking things, I wouldn't be seen dead in one. Let's get you another low-alcohol beer, John. I'm going to help myself to another glass of Bucks Fizz if that's everything.'

Jean and John walked off, leaving Una unsatisfied. She spotted Anton taking some photos next to the chocolate fountain and headed over to speak to him.

'Anton, the montage! I think I've spotted some kind of number link.'

'You didn't reply to my text,' he said.

'Mum confiscated my phone during the meal. Tell me.'

'It's about Cassie,' he said.

'What about her?'

'I was chatting to Dad last night and I brought up the lottery win to see if there was any aggro about the numbers.'

'I already asked him all about that,' said Una, exasperated.

'Well, I thought it was worth me asking too. I wanted to dig into this syndicate business, as it all sounded a bit cobbled together. Although I'd probably not do much better.'

Una softened her frown. 'Sorry, what did you find out?'

'Dad said that when Arthur stepped in after the row with Cassie, they assumed he'd keep her number, but he picked

284

23. Which is bonkers. If he'd kept Cassie's number, they'd have won the jackpot! What are the odds?'

Una didn't want to speculate. 'Do you reckon the others were mad at Arthur for not keeping Cassie's number? And Cassie must have been furious to have left the syndicate, when a few more weeks would have won them the jackpot.'

'I suggested that to Dad,' said Anton. 'He just said what did a group of oldies like them need a million pounds for. But then he started listing what he'd spend it on. He also said that Cassie thought staying in the syndicate would bring bad luck, so she wasn't bothered about them winning. Although she might have felt differently if they'd got all six numbers.' He shrugged. 'Anyhow, not especially useful, but I thought I'd let you know. I still don't know what to make of all that stuff you dumped on me yesterday.'

'It's starting to fall into place,' said Una. 'Cassie's been knitting jumpers for people for the past few months. I saw Eileen wearing one on the film, number 22 on the front. Harry had one as well. If they had kept 22, they would have hit the jackpot. She thinks the win should have been hers. Perhaps this is her way of showing them all that they now have bad luck. It's like a curse . . .'

'Aren't you jumping to conclusions about this?' said Anton. 'She's probably just winding people up with those awful jumpers and coming up with dramatic visions.'

'Thinking about it, Cassie didn't say much to me when we got to the hotel earlier. She just thrust this enormous bulky present at me, wrapped in Christmas paper. A soft and fluffy present, like the parcel Tommo got the day before going to the DIY store.'

'I buy neutral, non-occasion-specific wrapping paper for that very reason,' said Anton.

'It could have been a jumper. Let's check.'

They went into the cloakroom and searched through the presents until Una found the one from Cassie. 'I feel bad opening it,' she said.

'They're going to be opened soon anyway,' said Anton. 'I'll do it.'

He tore the paper apart. Inside was a jumper, a plain white jumper with a red pattern that unfurled itself to be a number 22.

'You were right,' he said. 'She's knitted one of those jumpers for Dad.'

He took the glittery Christmas tree gift card off the present, and read: ' "Congratulations, Sheila and Ken. Here's one of my famed jumpers for you, Ken – please be careful." '

'There you go,' said Una, panicking. 'She's warning him.'

'Really?' said Anton. 'I don't know. I can see there's something going on with the jumpers. But she could just be causing a bit of aggro, like I said. She's pretty good at that. Seriously, Dad was adamant that she wasn't that bothered about the lottery win. Didn't want to be involved.'

'We can't take that chance,' Una said. 'If you care about Ken, you need to make sure he's safe at all times today.'

Anton faced her square-on. 'If there is even the remotest chance that something or someone might harm him today, then I'm in.'

'Great,' she said, relieved. 'So where is he?'

# 34

## *Don't Look Up*

'I'm trying his mobile,' said Anton, as Una refolded the jumper.

'He probably switched it off during the service,' she said. 'We were under orders.'

'Not getting through. I'll have a look round, he might have gone back to those gardens at the front of the hotel.'

'Okay,' she said. 'I'll check the main room. Meet you back here in five minutes.'

Una returned to the reception room, where the guests were milling about, unsure what to do during this hiatus in the day's schedule. She spied Arthur at the edge of a group who didn't seem to be including him in their conversation. No doubt he was listening for gossip that he could pass on elsewhere. But that was what made him an information hub.

'Hi, Arthur,' she said.

'Look who it is,' he said. 'My London property friend. All dolled up today. You should dress like that more often.'

'I'll be getting changed soon, thanks,' said Una. She scanned the room. 'Is Ken about?'

'He said he was popping over to the cemetery to visit his sister's grave. Wants to pay his respects. Ken's like that. He's a people person.'

The revelation hit her in the peplum. The graveyard was the only place she wasn't supposed to go today. She'd been warned by Cassie. Was that intentional? Maybe Cassie wanted to scare her off.

'What about Cassie?' she asked. 'Seen her recently?'

'She gives me the shivers, to be honest with you. I don't think people should dabble in the other world. What business do you have with her, then? Something I can help with?'

'No. It's fine. I just wanted to ask her about a number that's important to her. Number 22? From when she was doing the lottery.'

'My God,' said Arthur, spluttering pale ale over her. 'Do not mention anything about the lottery to that woman.'

'Why not?'

'I mean, she says she's okay about it. But if it were me, seeing a win that I could have shared in and not getting anything, I'd be spitting feathers.' He mimicked doing just that. 'Perhaps let the dust settle.'

'And were you happy about the lottery win?'

Arthur sighed. 'It's more of a burden than a boon in some ways. But your new family set-up will benefit from it, I'm sure. Ken's been talking about getting a hot tub. Very nice. Have you got a hot tub in London?'

'No,' she said. 'I don't have any outdoor space, there's nowhere to put a hot tub. Thanks for the info.'

'There's a lot more to me than people think,' said

Arthur, looking a little sadly into the cloudy heeltap of his pint.

In her day job, Una was supposed to find answers by looking at patterns of data about age, health, location. Now she was dealing with psychological motives, signs from the stars and gossip-mongering.

'Okay, I'd better circulate,' she said. 'If you see Ken, please tell him I'm looking for him.'

She searched for Anton. He was in the hotel foyer with Mum, listening to Chrissie's daughter, Scarlet, give her thoughts about Elsa from *Frozen*.

'I'm going upstairs to the suite to get changed,' said Mum. 'What about you?'

'Might stay like this for a while,' said Una. 'I'm getting used to this dress.'

Mum looked her up and down. 'Do you need blister pads for those shoes?'

She did, she really did. But she had to put aside thoughts of decent circulation to her feet and embrace the chafing silver straps in order to save Ken.

'Honestly, it's just like Lilah said. It's like I'm wearing slippers.'

Not that she ever wore slippers, with their inadequate grip on laminate flooring. Mum nodded in a way that Una knew meant she was unconvinced, then headed off up the stairs to the bridal suite.

'Ken's in the graveyard,' Una mouthed at Anton. 'We've got to go.'

Anton made his apologies to Scarlet, and they hurried out of the hotel and down the road. When they arrived at the main gates to the graveyard, Anton stopped.

'I can see where he is,' he said. 'You're right, he's at Auntie Sandra's grave, it's just a bit further in.' He set off across the grass.

'I don't think I should go on,' Una said. 'Cassie made a prediction that something bad would happen if I was in the graveyard. I've already had a close call at the station.'

Anton stopped. 'The station? You didn't say anything about a station.'

'You go on, make sure you look after Ken. Anyway, it's better if I stay back here. I can text you if I see anyone approaching.'

'Okay. I'll keep close to him. He looks fine to me – I'm sure you're worrying about nothing.'

Anton strode forward, slaloming through the graves towards Ken, who was up ahead in his wedding suit. Una spotted a small red-brick shed further up the path that ran along the edge of the graveyard, and she darted over, finding a spot of cover beside it. This way she could avoid being near the graves but still keep a lookout for anyone approaching. It was also near enough for her to hear what Ken and Anton were saying.

'Sheila said she wanted to pop down later to spend some time at Bob's grave before the disco starts up,' said Ken, 'so I thought I'd just check it was all looking good, and then I thought, why not say hello to Sandra and tell her my news.' Una watched as he removed the square diamanté cufflinks from his shirt cuffs and rolled up the sleeves.

'Good work, that's really thoughtful.'

'Great speech, by the way,' said Ken. 'Good pacing and delivery. Need to work on the timing for the jokes, but you have the makings of a decent bingo caller if things don't work out for you in London.'

Anton moved to stand beside him. 'I'll add it to my career plans.'

Ken put his arm around him, which was a bit of a stretch as Anton was much taller than him. 'I'm made up that you, Chrissie, Duncan and the girls are here today,' he said.

Anton smiled down at him. 'I'm happy to be here.'

Ken started wiping his eyes with his hands. Una's own eyes were tearing up – probably just mirror neurons in her brain reacting to Ken.

'Do you want my handkerchief?' said Anton.

'No, I don't want to get your lovely clean handkerchief messed up. I'm fine now. Deep breaths, Kenneth, deep breaths.'

Ken put his hands on his hips and stood silent for a few seconds.

'And Una, do you think she's coming round to things?' he asked. 'I can't make her out. I have tried, you know, to make an effort.'

'I know you have. But it's like what she said in her speech about you, she's someone it takes time to get to know, that's all. I can't always make her out myself. But I know for a fact that she's looking out for you today, even if it doesn't come across that way.'

Una's neck started to ache from peering around the side of the shed, but she hardly noticed it. This was what Ken and Anton really thought about her. Perhaps it had been challenging for them to get to know her because she'd been so focused on extracting information about them? She'd suspected Ken of killing his friends and having an affair with Rosa, but she'd followed up on that and now she knew she'd been mistaken.

It was possible that what they had said about her was right, and the more she thought about it, the more possible it became. How was she going to regain their trust? It wasn't something she could solve with numbers. And it wasn't something she could solve while she was shivering at the side of a shed in a graveyard in a flimsy peplum dress.

'I'll just put some fresh water in this vase,' said Ken, 'and stick the leaves in the bin, and then we'll do a quick once-over of Bob's grave to make sure it's shipshape before we head back.'

He started walking towards the shed. Una looked back and saw a tap on one of the walls, which she thought was odd. But then she realised it was there for visitors to the cemetery to fill vases for their flowers.

She didn't want Ken to discover that she'd been listening in on their conversation, so she stepped into the shed and hid behind the door. She heard him approach and turn on the tap with some effort. She'd have to hope that he wasn't going to look inside.

It was dark in the shed, and she could hear a scratching sound on the roof – no doubt a bird or small mammal. She tried not freak out, but it was making quite a clatter up there. The shed was gloomy and dank; she strained to make out the faint outline of a small tin pot with a poison warning on its label. How had she picked this house of horrors? It had looked innocuous from outside, but it was full of danger. She needed to leave. She pressed her ear against the door and heard footsteps retreat.

'Super,' she could hear Ken saying. 'Once I'm done here, we can head back for a boogie on the dance floor; they should have cleared the tables by now. It's a good spot here, isn't it? I wouldn't mind resting somewhere like this. There's a bit of a drop over there, though. Come on, I'll show you the pond at the bottom of it.'

She must have miscalculated again. Ken was clearly safe, and soon he'd be back among the wedding crowd. She edged towards the door, nudging it open and peering around. Anton and Ken were now standing on the edge of a high verge just up from Sandra's grave.

As she came out of the shed, she implemented her new personal safety policy of looking upwards outside any entrance, in order to avoid hanging basket or foot spa injuries. But instead of open sky, a pair of amber eyes bored down into hers. A very familiar pair of eyes.

# 35

## *Showdown in the Shed*

They were the eyes of Pedro. And Pedro wasn't purring.

Locked into his fierce gaze, Una generated a range of options for his presence. Perhaps Cassie had brought him along as her 'plus one' to the wedding. Sensibly, Pedro had decided to swerve the group photos and seek solace on top of the shed. But this innocuous situation brought back the scenario of the hanging basket that had fallen onto Eileen. Could a creature have nudged the basket to dislodge it? Could Pedro have landed on a supermarket trolley and triggered a terrifying and fatal last spin? Or disturbed a stack of scythes, escaping their deadly crescents with his agility and speed? Una had watched documentaries on serial killers, but here she was, face to face with a ferocious feline.

She didn't want to die due to a plummeting psychotic cat felling her in a graveyard. She'd be another statistic for someone else in her team to use, a number to be aggregated with all the other ones. As she continued to stare upwards at Pedro, ready for him to pounce, a light crunch on the gravel path to the shed grew louder – footsteps. Soft, slow footsteps. A figure appeared outside the shed window.

It was Cassie, her fascinator fluttering half a second behind its owner. She wore a look of pure focus. And she was focusing on Ken.

Cassie hadn't predicted what was going to happen in order to help her friends, to try to warn them about their fate. She'd known the predictions would come true because she was the one actioning them. And she also knew about Una's sensible attitude towards risk. She had warned Una to stay away from the graveyard so that she could get a clear shot at Ken.

Anton and Ken were still chatting on the ridge, oblivious to the situation. Una wanted to shout out, but her throat had constricted in fear. Cassie was getting nearer, and she might be armed.

She felt her gift of looking for the worst-case scenario returning. She would think through all the awful ways Ken could die here in order to save him. What would Cassie have planned at a graveyard? One of those metal pots that people put flowers in could be used as a missile. Or she could jump out at him from behind a gravestone – Una had seen the results of that herself at the DIY store.

To Una's horror, Cassie was moving towards the front of the shed. She scuttled back inside and hid in a corner. Who knew what insect life was also hiding there? She manoeuvred herself into a space among various sharp gardening implements – spades, trowels, dibbers. Cassie's plan might be to use something in the shed. And Una would be in the way.

Through the window she could see Cassie outside, near the door, looking up at the roof.

'Pedro,' said Cassie. 'Come down from there, we've got things to do . . .'

Cassie was hovering by the doorway. Una needed to somehow alert Ken and Anton to her presence without drawing attention to her own vulnerable position in the shed. She sent a *Help!* text to Anton, but there was no response. Ken was probably wittering away to him. She could try and run past Cassie, but what if she was carrying a weapon? Who knew what could be lurking in that handbag? Una had to do something, cause a diversion, catch Cassie off guard.

Spotting an empty flower pot near her feet, she shuffled over as silently as she could in her silver kitten heels and picked it up at arm's length between her right thumb and index finger. In the dim light of the shed there could be millions of unseen microbes wriggling onto her hand. She crept towards the door, swung her arm back and threw the pot as hard as she could. It arced forward, but instead of landing somewhere outside, it hit the edge of the door and dropped down, smashing into several pieces. Disaster. Without a Plan B, she shrank back inside the shed.

'Is someone in there?' Cassie called, and then her silhouette appeared in the shed entrance. To Una's horror, she opened the door wide and peered in. 'Una? You gave me a fright. What are you doing here? Aren't you supposed to be taking part in the photographs?'

'Hi, Cassie,' said Una, 'the photos are all done and dusted. Just sorting out some stuff for a visit to the grave. How are you? Did you enjoy the service?'

This was it. She'd developed her chit-chat skills over these last few weeks. She could do this.

'Really?' said Cassie, still in the doorway, only her fascinator twitching. 'What sort of stuff are you sorting out? You're not holding any flowers.'

'I'd just picked up that plant pot and I was going to wash it under the tap ready to stick in some of the flowers from the wedding, but I dropped it. What a clumsy clot. But look, I've found another one, so it's all fine.'

Una picked up another, larger plant pot from the floor. She tried to avoid looking down at the scurry of tiny ants that she'd disturbed and that were running frantically around her open-toed sandals.

'Didn't I warn you the graveyard was dangerous?' said Cassie, looking rather pleased with herself as she nudged the red shards from the broken pot away from the door with the toe of her shoe, making a grating scrape on the floor.

'You were really clear on that,' said Una. 'Super clear.'

She had to get out of the shed and away from the looming, shadowy presence in the doorway. Negotiation was not an option; she needed to use physical might to overcome Cassie. Inspiration struck. Gathering up her dress with her left hand, she strode towards the door. As she reached it, she shouted, 'Look! A leopard!' and pointed outside.

Cassie swung round. Una leapt forward and slam-dunked the upside-down plant pot onto her head, crushing the fascinator. She swerved past Cassie and pushed her into the shed, then shut the door and barred it with a nearby spade. All sorted.

Now to find Anton and Ken. She walked further along the path, looking across the jagged rows of gravestones.

'Una,' called a distant voice.

She looked round to see Anton waving at her from about twenty yards away, where he was standing next to Ken on a ridge of higher ground.

'Over here,' he said.

'I can't walk properly on the grass in these shoes,' said Una.

She could see him saying something to Ken, making him chuckle.

'I'll come over to you,' he said.

He jogged over to her and swerved towards Pedro, who was sitting in front of the shed, completely unconcerned about his missing owner. He approached Pedro from his right side and crouched down next to him.

'Careful!' said Una. 'Are your tetanus jabs up to date?'

'Snugglemonster,' said Anton, chucking Pedro under the chin. Pedro rolled onto his back and stretched his chin upwards. 'He's a cute little furry bundle, aren't you?'

'That cat is an accessory to murder,' said Una. 'Probably not a very helpful one, but even so.'

Anton put his hands gently over Pedro's ears. 'What are you talking about murder for?' he said. 'Dad's fine. You were worrying over nothing, like I said.'

Una edged towards him, keeping Pedro in sight. 'You don't understand,' she said. 'Cassie was out here looking for him. She's been behind all the deaths of Ken's friends, I'm sure of it. Putting aside that she had both the opportunity and the motive, how did her predictions mirror the accidents that subsequently happened? They were descriptions of what she planned to do. And she just blocked me in the shed and was very threatening.'

'How threatening?'

'The way she was standing there . . . but don't worry, I managed to lock her in. We should call the police.'

There was doubt in Anton's eyes, but once she got Cassie to spill the beans about how she'd targeted the lottery syndicate, he'd see how brave she'd been today. She had saved Ken from a permanent cemetery visit.

'That shed?' said Anton, drawing himself up. 'We should go and get her out, it will be really dark in there. I mean, I'm sure you must have had a good reason to do that. But either way . . .'

'It's fine,' said Una. 'I stuck a plant pot on her head, so she won't be able to see much anyway.'

They walked to the shed. Everything had become low-risk now that Cassie had been detained, and Una's shoulders were sinking back down until she noticed the shed door was slightly ajar.

'I shut it, I definitely shut it,' she said.

'I'll look inside.'

Anton pushed the door wide open with his shoulder and stepped onto the broken plant pot, which crunched under his tread.

'It's empty,' he said. 'Perhaps she got the message and headed off.'

'No way! Anton, I'm serious! All these "accidental" deaths. She's responsible! She's going to try to kill Ken, like all the others. We must keep watch over him.'

But Ken was no longer standing on top of the ridge.

Anton was swaying from side to side. He still didn't believe her. 'You're overthinking things. I'll get Dad and see you back here.'

Una stood by the shed, shivering in the March chill and staying alert for danger. After a few minutes, Anton returned with Ken and Cassie.

Cassie glared at Una. 'Why did you attack me like that?'

'I think you'd better stay with me, Cassie,' said Anton, 'while we sort all this out.'

'The police will sort it out,' said Una. 'They'll hear about your so-called predictions. The jumper threats you've been sending everyone.'

Ken looked between Una and Cassie, flummoxed.

'Police?' he said.

'This is all a misunderstanding, Ken,' said Cassie. 'I get very confused with all the tablets I'm on, and perhaps I shouldn't have taken them with Prosecco, but you know I don't get out much. Una's right. I feel so guilty about the predictions I've made. They keep coming true, and there's one for today.'

'We can all talk a bit of nonsense at our age,' said Ken. 'But not to worry, we've still got the disco, so let's get back to the reception. It cost me an arm and a leg, that room. We'll sort this out later – crossed wires, that's all.'

'Crossed or not,' said Cassie, 'there was no need for her to put a plant pot on my head. My hat's ruined.'

'A plant pot?' said Ken.

'A big clay one,' wailed Cassie.

'It was self-defence,' said Una. 'I was cornered.'

'Una, what were you thinking?' said Ken. 'I sometimes joke about Cassie seeing things that aren't there, but you really take the biscuit.'

'Once the police get here, I'm going to explain everything,' said Una, searching for her mobile phone but not finding it in her purse. It must have fallen out when she was lunging at Cassie in the shed. 'The predictions. The jumpers. The lottery. I've got pictures of the numbers, you know. I bet you have the number 45 in your bag.'

She grabbed Cassie's bag and unclasped it. She scrabbled under a layer of crumpled tissues, but there were no numbers.

'Okay,' she said, 'what that means is that she's already placed them at the scene of the next accident.'

Anton looked unconvinced, but continued to keep Cassie clutched firmly to him.

'I'm not following this at all,' said Ken. 'I just want to get to the disco and we can all make friends again. Chrissie has put a heavy set together.'

'Yes,' said Cassie, 'let's get to the disco.'

'Perhaps we should listen to what Una has to say,' said Anton.

'Yes,' said Una, turning around and facing Ken full-on. 'I've been telling you over and over. Cassie's trying to kill you.'

'Is that right?' said Ken. 'Because it seems to me that the only person round here who's tried to harm me over the last six weeks is you.'

Una fell behind them as they made their way back to the cloakroom. The noise of the disco in the main hall next door was pounding through the walls. The coat rack was rammed with coats and umbrellas. Next to it was the trestle table of presents. A safe space.

301

'Let's wait here until the police arrive,' said Una. 'Anton, please give me your phone so I can call them. I must have dropped mine. Just trust me.'

Anton looked at her. He looked at Ken. He looked at Cassie. And then he took out his phone.

'Stop!' said Ken. 'You will not ruin this wedding without a good explanation. No one calls anyone until Ken says so.'

'Fine,' said Una. 'This is what happened . . .'

# 36

## *The Case Against Cassie*

'If you're going to start accusing me of all sorts, then I'd like my friends around,' said Cassie, easing herself into a chair and holding her bag on her lap like a shield.

'Of course,' said Una, 'good idea. They'll be able to corroborate what I'm about to say.'

'I'll round them up,' said Anton.

Una looked at Ken's exasperated face and Cassie's worried one. Their expressions would change once she presented whatever it was she was going to present.

'I'll start at the beginning,' she said. 'Which was when I noticed that there had been some unusual accidents happening in Eastbourne. I didn't see any personal connection until examining the scenes of both Eileen's and Harry's demise.'

Anton reappeared, followed by Jean, John, Raj and Mum, who sat down on fold-up seats next to Cassie.

'It's fine,' said Una, 'you've not missed much.'

'She's accusing me of murder,' said Cassie. 'I need you to stop her.'

'Una,' said Mum, 'are you feeling okay?'

Anton sat in the corner, camera pointed. 'Think I'll record this.'

'Can I join in?' Arthur had poked his head round the door. There were no more chairs left, so he leant on a large suitcase at the back of the room.

Ken rolled his eyes. 'Let's get on with it. I'd better not be missing David Guetta for this.'

'As I was saying,' Una continued, 'at Eileen's house and at the supermarket I found that numbers had been put up – 41 and 37 respectively.'

Mum put her hand to her forehead. 'Numbers. I should have known this would be something to do with numbers. I think you need a proper break.'

Una straightened herself in the bridesmaid dress, 'What was the significance of these numbers and who put them there? This question continued with Tommo – Ken, you remember when we saw that number on his coffin?'

'I do,' said Ken. 'But so what? A few numbers, that doesn't mean anything.'

'It was a sequence,' said Una, 'but what did the numbers mean? Bingo numbers? Addresses? Birthdays? And what was the reason for leaving them there? A remembrance, or something more sinister? What if these accidents weren't accidents at all?'

'She's no Poirot,' said Jean. 'The David Suchet one, of course.'

Raj nodded. 'Inimitable.'

Una adopted a power pose. 'Why would any of you want to kill Eileen or Harry?' Una continued. 'John, for example.'

'What!' said John, nearly falling off his seat.

'Harry and Eileen voted against you being the new bingo

caller and appointed Tommo, who was the next victim. But I couldn't see how the numbers related to bingo unless they were random. And Jean . . .'

Jean stared at her full-on.

'. . . you had a row with Harry about picking his own book for the book club. Eileen and Raj supported him and walked out. Your beloved book club was over. That must have made you angry.'

Jean pursed her lips. 'This is making me angry, that's for sure.'

'But Tommo hadn't walked out and there was no link to the numbers, those numbers. Now I have to admit, my initial suspicions were centred on Ken.'

'Am I going to get a go?' said Arthur, in a loud whisper from the back of the room.

Una continued. 'You initiated the flash mob outside Trunnocks and suggested to Eileen that she invite you all round to look at the photos from her cruise. But then at DIY City, I was with you when Tommo had his accident. No, you were not involved, Ken.'

'I'm not impressed,' said Mum.

Ken patted her arm. 'I'm getting into this now.'

'Then there were the messages on the Tread Softly website, messages that were anti old-people, suggesting there were too many of them in the world.'

'Well,' said Raj, 'read the room. Oldie City.'

'Knew it!' said Jean, glaring at him.

'I might need the toilet soon,' said Cassie.

'I'm nearly there, I'm on a roll now,' said Una. 'But those messages have now stopped, and why would *you* target those particular individuals? No, it had to be about the numbers, and then Ken provided the breakthrough!'

'Did I?' said Ken, perking up.

'Yes, you told me about your lottery syndicate. How a group of you had each chosen one of the six numbers for the lottery. The chances of winning are tiny, not worth taking part in, so I find it quite annoying, but anyhow, last November, your syndicate won one of the main prizes. Not the top prize – you matched five out of the six numbers – but a significant sum to those concerned. Everything was paid out smoothly, everyone was happy, except for one person . . . Cassie!'

Una stopped and turned to Cassie.

'In October, you fell out with the syndicate. You were behind on your subs and you hadn't checked the numbers properly – a small win was overlooked. The more detail-oriented members of the syndicate like Harry and Eileen were unsympathetic, and from my own point of view, checking six numbers is pretty minimal.'

'It's not what was said, it was how it was said,' said Cassie. 'I was spoken to like I was a simpleton. And some very uncalled-for remarks were made about my gifts for seeing into the future.'

'How must you have felt,' said Una, 'when the very next month, the syndicate had a significant win. That should have been yours. And if they'd kept your number, 22, instead of changing to 23, you would have won the jackpot!'

'We did offer some of our share,' said Jean.

'It wasn't my money and that was that,' said Cassie, 'but I was sad about it because I wanted to visit Kevin and I didn't see how I was going to save enough.'

'You should have said,' said Ken. 'I would have seen you go out there, I would have seen you go premium economy.'

'Ken,' said Mum. 'You are not spending a penny of our money on that vindictive old witch.'

'Vindictive I may be,' said Cassie, pointing at Mum's shoes, 'but at least I don't have Sagittarian ankles.'

Mum's eyes flashed.

'The point is,' said Una, raising her voice, 'you were unhappy about the win and that was when you embarked on your plan to kill off each member of the group!'

'What!' said Ken. 'Una, that's a very bold statement.'

'It all fits,' said Una, addressing Cassie. 'To confuse people you made a vague warning about each death beforehand that looked sort of related to the death, as if your gift was coming back. No doubt you hoped to make people take you seriously again, like you told me. You started with the person with the number up from yours, Harry. On 1 December, exactly one month after the win, you attended the flash mob at Trunnocks and somehow found a way to push him into that shopping trolley, knowing that his health would be sensitive to any shocks . . .'

'No, I didn't go near him!' said Cassie.

'. . . and then you placed his lottery number on the wall nearby to mark off your successful revenge on your list. Go forward a month each time and you do the same to Eileen and Tommo. Today is also the first, and following the sequence of numbers, you were targeting Ken.'

'Wow,' said Raj, leaning forward in his chair, 'this is fascinating stuff.'

307

'I'm going to make mincemeat out of you,' said Mum, rising to her feet.

'Whoa,' said Ken, patting her chair to get her to sit down. 'How did you come up with all this, Una? Why would Cassie do it? It wasn't like we wouldn't have helped her.'

'Exactly,' said Cassie. 'The money was already won and divided up. There was nothing for me to gain from killing them. Why would I put myself in danger going round arranging accidents? For a start, if I was going to kill someone, I'd poison them with stuff from my herb garden. I wouldn't do all this rigmarole; too much could have gone wrong.' She was still holding onto her bag tightly.

Una paused. She hadn't been expecting such a well-thought-out counter.

'I forgot about the jumpers!' she said. 'Yes! Before each killing, Cassie sent the victim a jumper with the number 22 on it. I thought it was just a squiggle at first, but in fact it was Cassie's lucky number that she used in the lottery. I imagine it was one last attempt to get them to believe in her gift before she savagely executed them.'

'Steady on!' said John.

'And where is your evidence for all of this?' said Jean.

'Yes, empirical evidence that she's a murderer,' said Raj.

Una huffed. 'I'm not saying categorically that she is a murderer; I'm presenting the evidence that makes it probable. I've considered all the data I've collected, and based on the dates, the numbers at the scene, the predictions and the jumpers, as well as the accident rate for the local area, I think the most likely solution is that Cassie is behind all these deaths.'

'It's also possible they were just accidents,' said Mum. 'Terrible accidents that happened to fall on the same date.'

'That is possible,' said Una. 'But what about all the other patterns?'

'Well, if you must know, I did leave the numbers,' said Cassie. 'They were just a little gesture to my departed friends, when I had a chance to visit. And yes, I also made the jumpers, but they took about a month to knit so it just happened that they got sent out when they did. I'd been told that 22 was a lucky number for me by a visiting numerologist on the pier in the last summer season I was there, and I was simply spreading a bit of good fortune to my friends. They did win on the lottery, after all, and now you're making out those jumpers were to do with murder.'

'Well, they're certainly a crime against knitting,' said Mum.

Una's right thumb was twitching, biro-less. 'So you're claiming it's a coincidence that the jumpers and the predictions took place when they did?'

'That's what happened,' said Cassie.

'Sure,' said Una.

'So where is *my* jumper then?' said Ken. 'And my number?'

'The jumper was among your wedding presents,' said Una. 'Anton and I already opened it up to check.'

Ken was a mottled red. 'Bloody hell. You'd better not have broken anything. I love opening presents. While you're finishing off your shaggy dog story, I'm going to check out this jumper.' He glanced at Mum, and then got up and strode towards the trestle table in the corner.

'Anton,' said Una, 'keep close to him in case there's a trap!'

'Claptrap, more like it,' said Ken. Anton huffed and shuffled towards him.

'Well,' said Raj. 'This is eventful.'

Cassie took out one of the tissues from her bag and snuffled into it.

'So what have you lined up for Ken?' said Una. 'What have you rigged up around here?'

'Una,' said Mum, standing up quickly, her chair screeching on the wooden floor. 'We all know I'm not Cassie's biggest fan, but this has to stop. You're accusing this poor woman based on nothing. Some numbers, jumpers she's knitted. No evidence. If this is what you do at work, then I'm not very impressed.'

Una stopped. This was all she had; she'd hoped to wear Cassie down, get the others to help.

Cassie continued to sniffle. 'I haven't done anything. And I've dropped one of my knitting needles somewhere and I can't see it to get on with my next jumper.'

'It's basically bullying,' said Jean. 'Come on, John, give me my handbag, will you, it's under your chair.'

Everyone was starting to move about.

Anton's phone pinged. He looked at it and groaned. 'Una, there's a text for you from Tim about some numbers. As if we needed any more disruption today.'

Why would Tim text Anton? Probably to gloat about running a half-marathon up a 45-degree-angle hill, backwards.

'Thanks, and sorry,' said Una, taking the phone from him. She inhaled deeply and read the message:

*Hey Anton! Learned to play darts yet? It's Tim, from the stag do, in case you haven't saved me in your VIP list. Please pass this onto Una as it may be important and she's not responding to my messages.*

*Una – there's something odd about the lottery numbers. I checked the results, and the winning amount is just as you said, but neither of the two five-match winners were from Eastbourne – one in Hull and one in Cardiff. How can that be? Link below. You now owe me one favour.*

*P.S. Sorry not to be there, but taking part in a half-marathon, hopping.*

Una clicked on the link and looked through the winners for that date. Exactly as Tim had said, none of them came from Eastbourne. Only the jackpot was anonymous. She glanced at the line of winning numbers, and the realisation hit her like the excess on an uncompetitive car insurance policy.

'Ken!' she shouted over. 'Be very careful.'

'I'll have that back now,' said Anton, taking the phone off her.

'Don't go!' said Una.

Anton scowled, 'Fine but I'm going to start looking through what I've filmed today.'

'Well, I've had enough,' said Jean. 'Let's head back to the disco. Coming Sheila?'

'Yes,' said Mum, 'I'm ready to party.'

'You all need to help me!' said Una.

'I think you do need some help,' said Raj.

Una pushed past John to the back of the room. She now knew why Harry's last words had been 'Wrong number.'

# 37

# *Worst-case Scenario*

Ken was at the trestle table, feeling a present through its wrapping paper and then shaking it next to his right ear. Arthur was next to him, holding open a bag to collect Ken's chosen gifts. Anton was slumped in a corner, looking through video footage. Una glanced behind her. Her former suspects were heading to the disco – they'd lost faith in her. She no longer had any backup.

The only person left was Cassie, who was a few steps behind her. Still wary, Una took the potato peeler out of her bag and gripped it in her right hand, trying to put the pieces together. She needed to process Tim's text about the numbers, but she wasn't ready to let Ken out of her sight just yet.

'Ken,' she said, 'let's go into the disco. I'm sorry about all the stuff I said in there, I'll apologise to everyone.'

Ken didn't look up. 'I'll be there in a bit,' he said. 'Just having a look at this jumper from Cassie.'

'I'd be delighted if someone knitted me a jumper,' said Arthur, stooping over the table.

Una scoured the room for something that could cause an accident. What was the worst-case scenario in a ten-foot-square space? A fire extinguisher – that could go off in someone's face. The thick yellow tie-backs on the curtains might somehow end up around someone's neck. A shotput could come through that window. The metal coat racks were on castors, which could be a trip hazard. Paper cuts from the wrapping paper, stiletto ends to one of the umbrellas; the air-conditioning unit above them, was that stable?

'You okay?' said Anton, glancing up.

Una nodded, feeling anything but.

'You've seen something,' said Cassie, now beside her.

Una shrank away from Cassie and positioned herself as a barrier in front of Ken.

Ken held up the jumper. 'Here, this is it! Very nice, Cassie! I'll have to check it against my colour wheel, but I could break it up with one of my allowed colours if needed.'

Cassie pointed. 'And look, it has 22 on it, lucky for you.'

'Let's see,' said Una. She stepped towards Ken and stood to his left as he examined the red design on the jumper. Cassie was shuffling behind her.

'Look out, Ken!' said Arthur, grabbing Ken and spinning him round. 'She's got a knitting needle. I'll protect you.'

This was it. There was no need to look for the worst-case scenario. Una was in it.

She closed her eyes and launched herself at Ken, grabbing his embroidered waistcoat and pushing him to the ground. As they fell, she felt her shoulder hit the leg of the trestle table. She opened her eyes. It was Arthur, not Cassie, peering over her, needle in hand, ready to strike.

In a highly improbable sequence, the knock to the table had jolted one of the wedding gifts. This particular present had shrugged off its carefully sellotaped wrapping and curly

313

gold ribbon and was making its escape across the table. It rolled towards the edge, picking up momentum, and then launched itself into the abyss and straight onto something hard. *Crack.*

Una turned her head. She still had a head, so that was good news. There before her was a scenario she hadn't predicted. For a few seconds, all was silent in the little room – though if you listened very carefully, you could hear the gentle smattering of snow falling flake by flake onto the buildings of Eastbourne: the pier, the bandstand, the white stucco hotels.

And next to the snow globe was Arthur, unconscious, his mouth half open.

'What the . . .' Ken was stirring, face-down on the floor, his quiff all mussed up.

'The snow globe,' said Una. 'It saved me. It was just as Cassie predicted. Perhaps she does have a gift.'

'The town falling down,' said Cassie, leaning against the table for support.

'Una,' said Anton, his face looming at her from above, 'don't move. I'll call an ambulance.'

'I'm fine, I think,' she said.

His face had gone puce, clashing somewhat with his lavender waistcoat. 'You've got a head injury,' he said. 'Don't touch your head, just sit back. Deep breaths.'

He started talking into his phone in a panicked tone.

'What the hell?' Ken was sitting up now, bleary-eyed. 'Why did you jump on top of me like that, Una? Look at my suit, it's all dusty from the floor . . . and my waistcoat – you've ripped off one of the special covered buttons.'

Una didn't answer. She was still absorbing the news that she had some kind of head injury. She couldn't feel any pain, but that could be the shock.

'Relax,' said Anton, sitting next to Ken. 'Deep breaths.'

'What about Arthur?' said Ken. 'Is he alive?'

'He's alive,' said Una, checking Arthur's wrist.

'Did you know,' said Ken, looking up at Una's hair, 'you've got a knitting needle stuck in your head?'

# 38

# *Needle in a Hairstack*

Una's body was a solid lump of flesh that she could only stare at in shock. It was like she was experiencing a greater gravitational pull. How serious was this injury? She couldn't feel anything in her head, but that might be a bad sign. At least Ken was safe and the wedding had gone ahead.

Ken had now propped Arthur against the leg of the table. He was still unconscious but breathing. Ken shook him gently by the shoulders. 'Arthur, it's Ken, can you hear me?'

'Of course I can flaming hear you,' said Arthur. 'You're shouting down my ear.' He opened his eyes and flinched at the sight of an active Ken and an inactive snow globe of Eastbourne at his feet. Una wiggled herself round to watch them.

'You've had a bump to your head,' said Ken. 'I don't know what happened, but we fell over and that globe dropped on you.'

'It was only to be expected,' said Cassie, looking at the snow globe, her fascinator twitching with defiance. 'My gift has come back; the town fell down just as I saw.'

Anton moved towards Ken, avoiding looking at Una's head. 'He tried to stick a knitting needle in you, Dad. It wasn't an accident. And Una protected you.'

'Just get an ambulance, will you? He's clearly out of it,' said Ken, patting Arthur's head. 'Let's focus on getting everyone well again.'

Jean had appeared now, with John and Raj behind her. 'What's happened here?' she said. 'Did he fall over?'

Ken stood up. 'I'm sure this is just a misunderstanding we can clear up between us.'

Una was unable to tell them the full extent of Arthur's actions; it was taking all her energy to sit there and listen to them. But she could feel anger welling in her stomach and the flimsy lavender peplum of her dress was struggling to contain it. John crouched down and examined the snow globe.

'Don't check that for damage,' said Ken. 'We should be more worried about people being injured.'

'It's completely intact. Just as well,' said John. 'They aren't easy to replace, that's for sure. If you do have any problems, they have excellent customer service. 4.5 star average.'

Raj approached Una with clumsy, awkward steps in his grey plastic boot. He peered at her head and then burrowed his hand into her hair to reach her scalp. 'Let me just . . .' He removed the knitting needle.

'What are you doing?' said Una. 'What if my brain leaks out?'

'I think because of your rather rigid hairstyle today, the needle was unable to do any substantial damage.'

She put her hand to her head and immediately felt the huge, sticky, matted mound of hair. Rosa's enthusiasm with the hairspray this morning had protected Una and her skull.

'Thanks, Raj,' she said, looking at the vicious needle in his hand.

She'd survived! She had gone all in to save Ken and got through it safely. She could feel sensation spreading through her limbs. She wiggled her toes and fingers.

'Better not touch that needle,' said John, 'in case the police want to dust it for fingerprints. I've got a resealable freezer bag in my backpack I can dig out.'

Raj carefully placed the needle on the trestle table. 'Good observation. I'll leave it here.'

'Fancy trying to attack someone with this needle,' said Jean, shaking her head. 'If he wanted to do some real damage, he should have chosen a four millimetre, not a six – sharp, but still sturdy enough.'

'I had to find something at short notice,' said Arthur, groaning. 'Anyway, I wasn't attacking anyone; I was trying to protect Ken from Cassie.'

'No,' said Una, climbing to her feet. 'I got it all wrong. It was you who was behind all the so-called accidents.'

'Not this again,' said Ken, going back to the heap of presents.

Arthur dabbed at his scalp. 'Fancy going on at me when I've just been hit on the head,' he said. 'It seems to me that you're making some very big accusations here, with nothing to back them up.'

'It was because of the lottery,' said Una, steadying herself against the table. 'It has to be.'

Arthur was right, she didn't have anything significant to prove his involvement, just speculation. But finally it was all coming together.

'Here's what I think happened. You took over Cassie's place in the syndicate when she fell out with Harry. On 1 November, it was your turn to buy the tickets for that month. You kept 22, which was Cassie's number, but also the number of your house. So when the draw took place that day, you actually matched all six numbers and won the jackpot, but for some reason you'd previously told the others that you'd chosen 23 as your number.'

'That's right,' said John, nodding assertively.

'After the draw, you continued as if you'd chosen 23 and not the winning 22,' continued Una. 'That meant you could keep the big jackpot for yourself. I think you claimed the money, looked on the site for the amount for five numbers and paid everyone their share based on that smaller win. It was perfect – everyone was happy and you were 1.2 million pounds richer!'

'What!' said Jean. 'This is all rather far-fetched, Una.'

'Is it?' asked Una. 'If you followed the pattern, on 1 December, Harry took over. He was very precise and wanted to check the previous month's numbers. You, Arthur, probably said you'd had to hand the ticket in to claim the prize. But from what I've heard about Harry, I don't think he would have let that slide. He must have found out – perhaps he looked at the location of the other prize-winners, like Tim did. He must have questioned you, right? That's when you came up with the idea of an accident.'

'This is pure speculation,' said John.

'Okay,' said Una. 'What I'll say is that there is a regular coincidence of the person who has an accidental death on the first of the month also being the person in your syndicate who checks the past month's lottery tickets.'

'Better,' said John.

Ken's face was reddening. 'I've lost the plot here. Why did you mention Tim?'

'I might have known Tim would stick his oar in to help,' said Anton, still filming.

'Tim texted me. He checked through the lottery winnings for that day,' said Una. 'He could see the names and locations of the two winners who'd matched five numbers, and neither of them were from Eastbourne . . . but the jackpot was anonymous.'

'What's all this about, Arthur?' said Ken.

Arthur was holding his head. 'My head hurts. You know, I can't remember anything.'

'Pull the other one,' said Ken. 'You were compos mentis two seconds ago.'

'Did you really take our money?' asked Jean, bustling forward. 'A million pounds! We could cruise for the rest our lives, John. Like Jane McDonald.'

'I could get two Ferraris and a hot tub and still be nowhere near spending it all,' said Ken. 'I'd be like the Hugh Hefner of Eastbourne.'

'Kenneth!' said Mum.

'Obviously,' said Una, 'you would invest the sum in a diversified portfolio of investments and live off the interest payments. No! We're getting sidetracked. There's the money, but also the accidents.'

'Okay, Arthur,' said Ken. 'Did you speak to Harry about these numbers? Don't lie.'

Arthur whimpered. 'It really was an accident. All of it. It started with a typo. I told you on the WhatsApp that I'd

320

gone with 23, but I meant 22. None of you called me out on it. Or asked why I'd chosen that particular number. You just believed we had a five-number match. I couldn't believe it! Well, until Harry. I bumped into him after you did that flash mob and he said it was very odd about no one from Eastbourne winning. He was going to speak to the lottery people to check if I couldn't explain it. We had a bit of a disagreement, I pushed him gently, and he went flying, skidded across the floor. I panicked and left.'

He pulled himself up against the table leg. 'And I got away with it. Until I went round to Eileen's to see if you were still looking at her holiday pics. A holiday that I'd handed the money over for, just to remind you. Well, she collared me and asked about the same thing. Said that as Harry hadn't confirmed his checks, she'd redone them herself. She was watering her plants and I offered to help get the basket down for her to reach – it was like an accident. I called the ambulance that time and waited with her.'

'And Tommo?' said Ken.

'Well . . . that wasn't so much of an accident,' said Arthur. 'He found my bank statements when he was clearing some stuff out of my house and asked to see me.'

'It's unthinkable,' said Jean. 'John and I would have been next in line.'

Una nodded. 'Indeed, and today he targeted Ken because he couldn't be sure whether Ken would check.'

Ken gave a giant sigh. 'I've heard enough,' he said. 'I'm fuming. Arthur, you have hurt me beyond words. But I'm going to say something anyway. These people were our friends. Why did you do it? Was it really for the money?'

'Our money,' said Jean.

'I finally had some luck,' said Arthur. 'I felt I deserved it more than you. You lot didn't want me to join your syndicate, and anyhow you can't even prove we were in one. Nothing written down.'

'We've got all our WhatsApp chats,' said Ken.

'Good luck with that,' said Arthur. 'You won't be able to get your hands on the money in any case, as I've hidden it. I've been doing my research on the internet and invested it in alternative assets. A bit of cryptocurrency . . .'

'Yikes,' said Una.

' . . . and a valuable piece of artwork.'

Una started. 'Hang on, it wasn't a vase, was it?'

'No way,' said Arthur. 'I got rid of the only one I had. No, it was a beautiful painting, a landscape. I even had it in my house for a week so I could appreciate it up close – no one would pinch it from there, right? And now it's in storage and you'll never find it. I'm going to be Lucky Arthur from now on.'

'A picture?' said Ken. 'What did it look like?'

'It was a very old picture of a country scene at harvest time.'

Ken's face had turned Alaskan Bridal Suite. 'Would it be a rather murky-looking picture?'

'Indeed so,' said Arthur, brimming with self-satisfaction. 'That's what I paid all that money for.'

Ken looked at Una and Una looked back at Ken. A look that acknowledged that he'd swapped the pictures at Arthur's house. Somewhere in a secret storage unit was a completely worthless but brightly coloured picture of

Eastbourne. The valuable painting had gone to the rubbish tip.

Inspiration struck. 'Just to check,' said Una. 'That painting will be covered by the extensive insurance you took out on it, right?'

Arthur smiled smugly. 'I didn't take any out. Tommo once told me that insurance was a scam and these places never pay out even if things do go wrong.'

Una winced. 'No insurance!'

'So how can we get hold of our money?' said Jean.

'Look, everyone, we're no better or worse off than we were before,' said Ken. 'And at least we know the truth now. Let's worry about the money another time.'

'I just wanted to enjoy being lucky,' said Arthur.

'Are you kidding?' said Una. 'And I forgot, you tried to drop that foot spa on me. You had picked up that I was looking into a set of numbers.'

'Foot spa?' said Anton. 'You never mentioned anything about that. What else haven't you told us?'

'Foot spa?' echoed Jean. 'That had better not be the one from the shop. It was part of my Manager's Monthly Special window display.'

'Yes,' said Una, 'that foot spa, still in its original box.'

'Keep going,' said Mum. 'Don't let him off the hook.'

Unlike the wedding lunch, words were surging towards Una's mouth.

'After that near miss, I was terrified. I wasn't sure I could protect Ken today. But seeing Mum so happy, I knew I had to put my neck on the line, as it were. And as for you, Arthur, you've not once said you're sorry for killing these people, never mind affecting my important research.'

Two police officers were coming along the corridor towards them, with several paramedics behind them.

'Got this all on film,' said Anton, patting the camera. 'It'll be the best wedding video ever.'

Everything after that seemed to happen in fast-forward. Arthur disappeared into the ambulance. The police officers took statements from each of them, and Una showed them the pictures of the numbers she'd taken at each scene and explained her theory about Arthur and the lottery. There was a doubtful look about the WPC as she listened, but Una knew that Anton had the video to back up her account, and it was good to finally have an opportunity to offload all the analysis she'd collected over the last six weeks.

After an hour, the police left and the cloakroom was now down to the core guests.

'Okay, everyone. Let's make the best of things for the rest of the evening,' said Ken, rocking back and forth on his winklepickers. 'I'm still in shock, we're all in shock, but in a time of shock it's best to focus on what's really important.' He looked into the distance, somewhere above the radiator shelf opposite. 'What we should remember,' he continued, 'is that we need to be here for one another. Look out for each other. Jean, you looked after Raj after his fall the other week. We're none of us getting any younger. We are sadly down in numbers, but let's put an end to any tensions in our little group going forward.'

'Hear, hear!' said John.

Ken put his arm around Mum, gave her a squeeze. 'Now then, I've paid for this deluxe room all evening and I'm going to get my money's worth.'

'Would you like this dance?' said Mum, holding out her right hand to him.

'Are you asking?' said Ken.

'I'm asking.'

'I'm dancing,' said Ken, taking her hand. 'Hark, is that the Shamen I can hear?'

It was dusk, and as people drifted back into the main room, where Chrissie was DJ-ing a succession of Ibiza dance hits, Una remembered that she hadn't found her phone. She must have left it in the shed when she was potting Cassie. With the crises of the day over, it didn't seem as dangerous to return there on her own.

Anton approached and put his hand on her shoulder.

'I hope you're okay,' he said. 'You might be in shock.'

'Never felt better,' said Una. Even her shoes weren't hurting that much.

'I'm sorry, I didn't believe what you said when we were in the café.'

She shrugged. 'It was quite an unbelievable story.'

'Are you heading in?' he asked, gesturing towards the disco. 'There's probably a quiet spot somewhere in there.'

'In a bit,' said Una. 'I have to get my phone. I dropped it in the shed somewhere.'

'Do you want me to come with you?'

She shook her head. 'No, after this afternoon, I can walk out there on my own, no worries.'

'Okay, see you in a bit,' he said. 'I'll go and catch up with Rosa and a few of the others. And thanks for protecting Dad. I still don't understand how you worked all of this out.'

'It's all in a day's work for an actuary,' said Una as she stepped outside for her final task.

# 39

## *Back to the Graveyard*

With the light fading, Una wouldn't normally wander about on her own, but there was one more challenge to face. She walked back down the residential road that led from the hotel to the cemetery and headed towards the shed. The gravestones appeared to loom over her as she walked at cloud pace. There were occasional crackling noises and bird sounds that put her on edge. This was ridiculous; it was only just getting dark and the place was empty. Besides, she was within shouting distance of the wedding party and could hear the thud from the disco.

When she reached the shed, she opened the door slowly and stepped inside. It was dark in here, and she could smell the dampness now – there were probably creepy-crawlies all over the place. After a scrabble around, she found the phone and put the torch on.

A moth flew at her as she ventured back outside, and she batted it away. As she came off the path onto the grass, the pointed heels of her shoes sank slightly into the damp soil. Ken's flowers glowed orange in the gloom, drawing her towards them. None of the events today had felt as daunting as walking the twenty feet between the shed and her dad's grave.

The headstone had a black marble effect. Ken had been thorough with his recent cleaning effort; even under the dull sky, the different sparkles in the stone shone out. She looked at *Percy Cheever 1911–1982* next door. His stone had blotches of lichen all over it, and there was nothing in the round metal plant-holder below.

She looked back at Dad's headstone. *Robert McMurray, 1953–2022. Beloved Husband and Father.* Name, dates and close family. It was difficult to reconcile this personal example with the data she used at work. There was so little space to describe someone – it boiled down to the bare essentials etched into the stone.

She crouched down at the foot of the grave and stared at the gravel that covered the plot. She wanted to say something profound, but instead worn phrases came to mind: 'hope you're okay', 'take care'. The sort of sign-offs she got from people glibly ending an email. What she really wanted to say was 'sorry, sorry for not spending more time with you when you were ill and for not coming to visit here until now'. She concentrated hard on that thought and looked upwards for inspiration.

As she stared at the sky, near to but not directly at the setting sun, she shivered as if a shadow was passing over her. There *was* a shadow passing over her. Goosebumps appeared on her arms, as if someone was walking over her grave, a place she'd avoided thinking about. Perhaps this was a sign that her end was nearing. A twig snapped close by.

She took a deep breath. There was a presence behind her. But she only had some aloe vera tissues, a tinted lip balm and her phone.

'Una.' It wasn't a ghoul. It was Mum.

Una turned round. Mum had changed into her black dress from the hen do. Her hair wasn't all scraped on top of her head as it had been earlier, and yes, she was getting frailer and older, but her eyes were full of life.

'I came to find you,' she said. 'Hadn't seen you in the hall for a while. And Anton mentioned you might be out here somewhere.'

'Yes. I dropped my phone in the shed when I . . . Well, I dropped my phone in the shed.'

'I just wanted to check you were okay after all that business with Arthur – your head's okay, no injuries?'

'Didn't get near thanks to Rosa's hairspray techniques,' said Una.

'But you might be in shock, you should take it easy. We can go home if you like.'

'I'm fine.'

'See how you go,' said Mum. 'I loved the photos, by the way. I could tell you and Anton were up to something, but it was a lovely surprise. Ken is going to put it up on his Facebook page.'

'It was quite a challenge to put together, but we got there,' said Una. 'I'm happy the wedding went okay. I'm getting used to Ken.'

Mum gently rested her hand on Una's back. 'Thank you, love.'

The sky had already gone darker in the twenty minutes she'd been outside. They both stared at the gravestone.

'I'm glad you're here,' said Mum. 'Especially today.'

'But what should I do now that I *am* here?'

'You don't need to do anything. I mean, remembering people is enough, right?'

They stood for a few minutes.

'It's getting a bit chilly, Una. I'm going to go back in.'

'I'll come with you,' Una said.

'Quite a few people have left after all the kerfuffle, but let's get you inside. I think a brandy would do you the world of good.'

Mum wrapped her crumpled pashmina around the two of them as they walked back to the hotel.

# 40

## *Make-up and Make-ups*

Una looked in the mirror hanging behind the coat rack in the cloakroom. After all the dirt, dust and tussling, her hair looked like the kind of matted lump that would come out of a full hoover bag. She poked her head around the door into the main hall. Ken was on the dance floor on his own. Anton was talking to Rosa at the bar.

'Who's in the house?' said Chrissie, standing on the raised stage at the front of the hall, shouting into a microphone. 'Grandmother Flash Jean is in the house with LL John. Raise the roof!'

She spotted Una, so Una ducked back out before Chrissie could make any public announcement about her return.

Mum came out of the toilets. 'Shall we go in?' she said.

'Perhaps I should get changed,' said Una. 'My hair's looking a bit worse for wear as well. Where's my bag?'

'No one's going to take any notice after today, but your holdall's just inside by the cheese and crisps if you want to freshen up. I'll speak to Rosa, see if she can do something with your hair if you like.'

'That's okay, I think she's busy.'

They went into the hall and Mum joined Ken on the dance floor.

'Make some noise, Sheila!' Chrissie was jumping up and down on the stage, scrolling on her phone to find more tunes to play.

Una picked up the holdall and was creeping back out when Jean stopped her.

'Hope you're okay,' she said, rubbing Una's arm. 'You had a nasty shock today. I don't know what made Arthur act like that. Why didn't I notice anything was wrong? We have been away quite a bit travelling, and I've been busy at the shop, I suppose.'

'I'm just glad it's all over.'

John and Raj joined them. Raj was holding a paper plate that bore a wedge of Brie and a handful of roasted peanuts.

'Need a little break from dancing,' he said. 'I've been in my aerobic zone for quite some time.'

'Managed to moonwalk with your boot on,' said John, nodding at Raj with encouragement.

'Well indeed, the show must go on,' said Raj. 'But I just wanted to say thank you, Jean, for looking after me while I've been laid up. I mean, I've still been very independent, of course, but it was reassuring to know you were checking on me.'

'Not a problem,' said Jean.

'So I was thinking about what Ken said earlier, and as per, it was a little cheesy and overblown, but you have been kind to me and I wanted to do something in return. I've spent quite a lot of time in my house over the last week and have rounded up some books that I no longer need, and I was thinking of bringing them along to Tread Softly.'

Jean clapped her hands. 'Any donations are much appreciated.'

'And perhaps we could bring back the book club. Put the past in the past,' said Raj.

'I'd love that,' said Jean. 'I really miss our little get-togethers. I could restart the WhatsApp group, put the word out for suggestions for our first book for discussion.'

'Bagsy Franzen,' said Raj.

'Sorry?'

'Bagsy the latest Franzen.'

There was a pause.

'Why not?' said Jean. 'First choice to you. But no more self-help books written by someone in the group without my express permission.'

'Deal.'

They shook hands awkwardly, Raj still clutching his plate of nibbles.

'I'll be back in a bit,' said Una. 'Just going to get changed.'

She headed out of the hall into the toilets and shuffled out of the muddied dress and into her jumper and jeans. She kicked off the sandals, which had etched red lines into her feet, and put on her trainers. Then she looked in the mirror, close up. Her make-up had splurged out from her eyes and mouth.

The entrance door to the toilets opened and Rosa came in.

'Look at you,' she said, standing next to Una so that their faces were side by side in the mirror. Rosa's looked as it had done that morning, meticulously made-up. 'You look like you've been dragged through a hedge backwards.'

'Something like that,' said Una. 'I might just get a cab home.'

'No, I'm not having that. Your mum wants you back out there. I've brought my bag of tricks, we'll have you freshened up in no time.'

Una leant back on the edge of the sink so that the single strip light could illuminate her face while Rosa went about her repair work.

'We've not had a proper chat before,' Rosa said. 'I was just talking about you with Anton, as it happens.'

Una mumbled an answer as Rosa swept mascara onto her lashes. She could smell the spearmint gum that Rosa was chewing.

'He said you'd worked out that Arthur had done in Eileen,' she said.

'It took me longer than it should have done.'

'Don't feel bad. You followed up on it, found out what really happened. You know, I did see Arthur skulking round outside Eileen's doorstep a couple of months ago. I just forgot about it. I mean, of course it was odd, someone hanging around like that. But Arthur's always been quite nosy, so I didn't read too much into it. I should have said something.'

Una hadn't spoken to Rosa. If only she'd done that on the first weekend. Always more data to collect.

'And he was telling me about how you looked out for Ken today,' said Rosa. 'Ken was wonderful to me after Mum died. I was still in sixth form, same year as Anton. Ken's made me feel part of their family.'

'I don't feel I know Ken that well and I'm pretty sure he feels the same about me. It's difficult getting to know people when you're older.'

334

'You just need to put the time in,' said Rosa, attacking Una's hair with a metal comb. 'By the way, did you like Ken's waistcoat? I know you had a peek before.'

'Yes, it was really impressive – I'm no good at stuff like that.'

'Thanks, he commissioned it from me based on a design he came up with. It includes the date he first met your mum, and their favourite song – he said it was to be like a tattoo but on a waistcoat. My first commission. I had to tweak it a bit to make it work, but it's in the spirit of what he was after. We kept it a secret from your mum as a little surprise. She looked made up.'

'I could tell something was going on. Ken was acting in such an unusual way.'

Rosa stopped tugging knots from Una's hair. 'I don't know about Ken,' she said, 'but you're quite unusual yourself in your own way.'

Back on the sixth floor of Katapult Insurance, Una was well within one standard deviation of the average. Her colleagues might even describe her as normal. But normal was only relative to where you were.

'I am a bit different,' she said.

'There you go. All done.'

Una turned round to face the mirror. She looked acceptable. Her hair was knitting-needle-free and drifting somewhere round her shoulders where she expected it to be.

'Thank you, Rosa. I enjoyed talking to you finally.'

'You're very welcome. Now let's get a drink.'

'I'll get you a drink. I owe you.' Una dropped her holdall by the coat rack and followed Rosa inside.

Back in the hall, Chrissie was playing Rihanna's 'Shut Up and Drive' at a conversationally challenging volume. Hips, both natural and replacement, were moving. Ken was making big box, little box shapes. Una sidled over to one of the tables and poured herself a large glass of red wine, then sat down on a chair along the wall.

'May I interrupt,' said Ken, appearing from nowhere. 'I've worked up a bit of a sweat out there. So, I just wanted a quick word. Clear the air.'

'Okay,' said Una.

'I've had time to think now. About Arthur. You stopped that knitting needle getting at me. Although it would have had to be pretty strong to make a dent in this,' he said, rapping his head with his knuckles. 'So, I'm sorry if I was annoyed with you earlier and didn't believe you when you were spouting all those theories about what happened. And, well, thank you for looking out for me. There, I'm done.'

'Well, I'm sorry for not making more of an effort to get to know you properly,' Una said. 'I just wanted to make sure that Mum wasn't going to get hurt.'

'That's highly understandable. And you're very welcome to come and stay with us any time. Just say the word.'

'Is it always so lively here?'

'I hope so,' said Ken. 'Can't imagine it's as lively as London, though. Bet you'll be pleased to get back to spending your weekends there instead of with us oldies.'

On Monday, Una would be returning to her desk with dozens of emails to face and the prospect of Neoliberal Tim as her boss, and her future weekends were looking pretty empty at this point. The usual no longer had its usual appeal.

336

'I suppose so.'

Ken leant towards her. 'One more thing. The painting . . .'

'I've been thinking about that,' said Una. 'No one knows we were there. If anyone asks, we could just not mention it. Perhaps Arthur made a mistake.'

'I do feel bad about it. All that money. But would it have made us any happier? And I was trying to do the right thing . . . Let's keep this between ourselves. Appreciated.' He doffed an imaginary trilby at her and shimmied back onto the dance floor.

Una took another glug of wine.

'Mind if I join you?' said Anton, sitting next to her.

'Of course.'

'You look more normal now. I don't think the bridesmaid scene is for you.'

She looked across at him – he was completely scowl-less.

'Bridesmaid attire is not in the least bit suitable for stopping a murder,' she said. 'Whereas you've got a fancy waistcoat out of it.'

'Yes, Rosa has done a grand job. I'm glad you had a chance to speak to her.'

Following her chat with Rosa, she had to press Anton further.

'She thinks I'm unusual. Do *you* think I'm unusual?'

'You are,' he said, without hesitation.

'Oh, right.'

'But look at everyone here in the hall. Who would you actually say was normal?'

She looked at Jean and John dancing a waltz to 'Gangnam Style', Raj moonwalking with a slight clunk of his boot and

337

Ken meticulously re-creating the original choreography. She thought about what she'd learnt about the people she'd met in Eastbourne as part of her research. Aggregated with everyone else, they wouldn't stand out, but now she knew them individually, they all did.

'You're right,' she said. 'They're all a bit weird.'

'I was thinking,' he said, 'perhaps when you're back in London, I could meet you for a coffee? I need to start looking for a flat share that I can afford, and I owe you after everything that's gone on today.'

'I'd like that,' she said. 'We can even share a vegan brownie.'

'Laters, Rave Generators,' said Chrissie, formally closing the evening's festivities. 'Time to go home.'

Una and Anton headed into the entrance hall with the others to wait for their cab.

Ken plucked a bottle of champagne from the pile of wedding presents and started to unwrap the top.

'One more for the road; the cab's another twenty minutes away.'

Una assumed the brace position while Ken popped the cork. He handed out some paper cups and carefully filled each one.

'I wanted this to be the perfect wedding,' he said to his tiny audience. 'Sure, Arthur tried to kill me with a knitting needle, Una stuck a plant pot on Cassie's head, and the police turned up, but putting all that aside, it's been tremendous.'

# 41

## *End of Life Insurance*

Another day, another spreadsheet. But in the six weeks since she'd opened the mail from the internal audit team, Una had been on a journey. To Eastbourne. She'd survived attacks by a pencil, a second-hand foot spa and a knitting needle. She'd apprehended a dangerous yet boring killer. And she'd uncovered the link between the numbers. But what had she learnt? She'd learnt to appreciate the relative safety of being at work. How good it was to see her water bottle sitting so still upon her desk and the ceiling above it so solid.

The office seemed safer because she had put herself in dangerous situations and survived, and as a result, she'd changed. About 5 per cent, rounded up. She didn't have to fall back on the tried-and-trusted methods she'd used in the past; she could adapt to new situations, learn to trust different sorts of people. She could still spot the worst scenario, but not focus on expecting it to happen.

She was ready to make changes. She deserved more than wilting under Tim's management. It was time for her to leave Katapult Insurance and seek pastures new. Be bold. For a start, there was another insurance company only a few doors down the street.

She looked up and saw that Ajay was free. As she strolled over to his office, she briefly considered the static she was generating on the nylon carpet, then put those concerns aside.

'Quick word?' she asked.

'Of course. In fact, there's something I need to tell you, so great timing.'

'Okay,' she said. 'Well, I'll get to the point. I've been thinking this week about my role here and the recent changes in the team. I realise there was an issue that came up about my figures for Eastbourne, but I have some additional data now. In fact, you may have read in the local news about how I acted to save an elderly man from a knitting needle attack. He isn't even one of our customers.'

'Word did get to me about your heroic efforts,' said Ajay. 'I checked with Programme Management and it definitely falls under our corporate social responsibility pillar, so well done.'

'Thanks,' she said. 'After all that, I don't believe my current role will provide enough of a challenge.' She took a deep breath. 'And so now that I've proved to myself that I'm capable of doing more, I need to leave and try something different.'

Ajay nodded and studied her face as if it were a well-constructed pivot table.

'As it happens,' he said, 'another role within the firm that would give you more of a challenge has come to my attention. But it means moving to a different team.'

'What other team? What sort of role?'

'It's to provide cover for a maternity leave,' he said. 'It would only be for that period, but it's a more senior role and you'll manage one of the graduates.'

340

Managing people. In the past, she'd always avoided this, but perhaps she had the skills to take it on after the negotiations she'd undertaken in Eastbourne.

'Okay, well that does sound interesting,' she said. 'What department is it in?'

She crossed her fingers in her head, even though she didn't believe in superstition.

'It's a growing and exciting part of our organisation . . .' began Ajay.

Space tourism insurance? Robot annihilation insurance? Meteor crash insurance?

'Pets.'

'Pets?'

Pet insurance.

'People are spending more and more on their pets,' said Ajay.

She'd never considered the pet world to be that interesting, but her recent experiences with Pedro had opened her eyes to the potential danger and intrigue.

'I don't know anything about pet insurance,' she said.

'There you go,' said Ajay. 'It will be a great learning opportunity for you. You get to become an expert in a whole new area. Plus, you'll gain vital management experience. I really think this could be a good move for your career.'

'Is it possible for me to find out more about the role?'

Ajay nodded. 'I can introduce you to Marta, who'll be going on leave from the end of next month. And you can speak to Gareth, who's the overall manager.'

Every team had their own culture, and she wasn't convinced that the pet team would see her as a good match based on her recent trip to the fifth floor.

'Thanks, yes, I'd like to get more detail on what it involves,' she said. 'And of course, they have to assess me as well.'

'Full transparency,' said Ajay. 'Gareth asked me if I knew of any suitable people who were looking for a transfer, and when I mentioned your name as a possible, he immediately wanted me to let you know about the role. He said you'd been doing some in-person fundraising on behalf of one of your colleagues and that it was just the type of team attitude he was looking for.'

'And about Internal Audit's issue with my seaside research?' she said. 'I'd like my findings recorded so that my reputation is restored.'

'Good point,' said Ajay. 'They're going to take a new cut of data for this month on Monday and rerun your model. I mean, it was a pretty unusual set of circumstances.'

'I know! You've been making all these decisions about the team structure, and it's not fair if I was penalised because of a killing spree by a briefly millionaire pensioner.'

'Look on the bright side,' he said. 'Your work is being actively reassessed and you've got a new job opportunity. Got a call coming up. Hope all goes well with the pet crew.'

Una returned to her desk and requested a meeting with Gareth and Marta. After everything she'd put herself through in Eastbourne, she'd have to let go of the research that had started it and move on. She got an email back from Gareth inviting her to the team indoor crazy golf straight after work. It didn't sound like her sort of thing, so she decided to put off replying to him while she crafted a polite decline message.

Tim arrived at her desk. He was wearing a smart grey suit. 'Heard you're thinking of leaving us,' he said. 'That would be a big mistake. We make such a great team. Look at how I cracked that Eastbourne case.'

Una gritted her teeth. 'I'm looking at a role in Pet Insurance. I'm speaking to Marta about it this afternoon.'

'It's much better for you to stay here,' he said. 'The pet crew are awful. They're always doing team things – team korfball, team ten-pin bowling, team doughnuts. I don't think you'd enjoy it there.'

'As a matter of fact, I'm going to crazy golf this evening with Gareth and his team.'

Tim's face dropped like a foot spa from a set of railway platform railings. Clearly Gareth was still a sensitive subject.

'Fair enough,' he said. 'Well, good luck with that. I'll let you get on.'

'Thanks,' she said. 'Hold on. You haven't asked me anything about a charity event. Surely there's something I haven't sponsored that you're doing this weekend?'

'I'm taking a break, having some Tim time,' said Tim. 'This new role is great, but it means longer hours and it's made me rethink my work–life balance. What about you, any plans for the weekend?'

Una had spoken to Anton the day before. He was staying on in Eastbourne until Ken's house sale went through, but was coming to London that weekend to stay on a friend's sofa and start looking for a flat share. She'd suggested a visit to the Natural History Museum, including a stop-off at the coffee shop. A safe choice. Unless one of the dinosaurs rean-imated. And she could pick up a present for Ela from the gift shop, to take to Leeds the following weekend when she'd catch up with Amara.

'I'm going to a museum on Sunday,' she said, 'with a friend.'

Tim's face crumpled. 'Sounds good. I should get out and about more.'

'Why not come along?'

His face crumpled further. 'Thanks, but I already have my hour-by-hour schedule planned for this weekend. Better get back now. I have some one-to-ones with my team.'

Una checked her phone and saw that she'd received a new message. Her screen saver was now the old photo of her with Mum and Dad at the caravan site that she'd added to the wedding video. She opened the message. It was a picture of Ken and Mum on their honeymoon in the South of France. Ken was wearing sports sunglasses and holding a bright cocktail, and Mum was wearing a glittering sarong and also holding up a cocktail. Una tried not to focus on the flimsy parasol above them or the splinters that could be lurking in the cocktail stick that allowed Ken's glacé cherry to bob in his blue drink. They'd added a short message: *Having a super time. See you soon. Thanks for the lovely wedding present – pleased to say we haven't used it yet and don't intend to! Love, Mum and Ken.*

Yes, honeymoon insurance was the perfect present. Peace of mind; much better than a casserole dish or a fish slice. She gave a quick glance at the ceiling above her, then returned to her spreadsheet, satisfied that all was well. For now.

# Acknowledgements

It's taken many years, novels and people to get to being published. I've tried to include everyone I should thank below – sorry if I've missed anyone out.

First, a big thanks to my wonderful agent, Marina de Pass at the Soho Agency, who plucked my novel off the slush pile and found it the perfect home.

Which leads me to a huge thank you to my editor, Krystyna Green at Constable, for the enthusiasm and support you have shown for this book; to Amanda Keats for editorial input and guidance (and valuable Eastbourne knowledge!); to Jane Selley for insightful copy edits; and to all the team at Little, Brown who've helped champion the book.

Big thanks to all my course mates from the 2015 Curtis Brown Creative course; you've helped push me to complete this novel from its early dodgy drafts: Ahsan Akbar, Becky Hunter, Ben Walker, Bill Macmillan, Catherine Jarvie, Charlotte Northedge, Ella Dove, Georgina Parfitt, Lynsey Urquhart, Paris Christofferson, Robert Holtom, Sarah Shannon, Sean Lusk and Victoria Halliday. Thanks to our tutor, Matt Thorne. And thanks to Erin Kelly for your helpful feedback at the summer school where I started this book.

During the past few years, I've had a lot of encouragement from my LWS Artists Way group. Particular thanks to Andy McAleese for patiently answering my clearly ridiculous actuarial questions; any errors on the actuarial details in the book are solely mine.

Ten years ago, my writing took a big step forward after I completed a *Guardian* novel course, thanks to the incisive teaching from James Scudamore and feedback from my course mates, Aled, Amber, Andrew, Annie, Jason, Kevin, Lesley, Paul and Sasha, who gave comments on this book.

My novel-writing journey began when I went on a course at City University, where I received both encouragement and a brilliant foundation from tutors Emily Pedder and Alison Burns. And thanks to all my classmates who had to endure my early attempts ... in particular, Charlotte, Ed, Marie, Mike and Paul.

Finally, to my mum, for her infinite patience and support, and all my friends, who I've no doubt bored silly whining about how difficult writing a novel is. Thank you!